The doo
peel **...nd it.**

He wanted to take her in his arms and hold her close. He wanted to tell her how awful these months had been without her, how sorry he felt about their argument. But before he could say a word, she stepped from behind the door. He stared at her, his gaze riveted on her midsection.

"What's the matter? Haven't you ever seen a pregnant woman before?" Ciara asked.

"Well, sure I have. It's just that…well…" His voice trailed off.

To learn that he was going to be a daddy in this sudden, unexpected way was by far the biggest shock of his life. Mitch didn't know whether to throw his arms around his wife or beg her forgiveness from bended knees.

But would she ever forgive him after all she'd been through?

LOREE LOUGH

lives in Maryland with her husband and daughters. Loree got her start writing a five-dollar article about tilt-up construction for a local newspaper. More than two thousand published articles and dozens of short stories later, she wrote the award-winning *Pocketful of Love*. Since then, she's produced over two dozen more novels for adults and children.

When she isn't teaching writing, speaking about writing, helping others ready their writing for submission, or writing her own stories, Loree keeps score in the never-ending war between her cats, Mouser and Billy.

Suddenly Daddy
Loree Lough

Published by Steeple Hill Books™

STEEPLE HILL BOOKS

Steeple Hill™

ISBN 0-373-87028-0

SUDDENLY DADDY

Copyright © 1998 by Loree Lough

Printed in U.S.A.

I am my beloved and my beloved is mine.
—*Song of Solomon* 2:16

To Carolyn Greene, Cindy Whitesel, Robin Morris, Mike Sackett and Carla Butler, for their faith in the story, and to Anne Canadeo, whose faith in my "talents" made this *book* possible.

Chapter One

Like gunfighters of the Old West, they faced each other in the middle of their living room, intent, it seemed, on making their first fight a humdinger.

"Don't be so naive," Mitch shouted. "Things like this don't happen every day. Besides," he added, jabbing a forefinger into the air, "you *knew* what I did for a living when we met."

Ciara matched his ire, decibel for decibel. "Isn't *this* a fine way to celebrate our one-month anniversary... hollering and yelling and—"

"Well, pardon me all the way to town and back," he retorted sarcastically, "but nobody ever told me I was an idiot for becoming an FBI agent before." He threw his hands into the air. "I sure didn't expect to hear nonsense like that *from my wife!*"

"I never said you were an idiot. I said if anything like what happened to Abe ever happened to you..."

He crossed both arms over his chest. She'd never seen him this way before, so it surprised her that her soft-spoken young husband's eyes darkened when he was angry.

Ciara held her ground. Narrowing her eyes, she said, "Abe died in the line of duty, and you have a bullet wound in your left side…pretty good evidence, wouldn't you say, that *you* could…"

He sighed heavily. "I've told you and told you—I was in the wrong place at the wrong time. It was a flesh wound. And it happened years ago, when I was a dumb kid, straight out of Quantico."

Her eyes widened. "Is that supposed to *comfort* me?"

Shaking his head, Mitch's shoulders slumped. "I don't know Ciara. I honestly don't know."

"It's just that I thought…I hoped once we were married, you wouldn't want to take risks like that anymore."

He plowed his fingers through his hair. "Oh for the luvva Pete. Now you're being downright silly. I don't *want* to take risks, but…"

The tears of frustration and fear she'd been fighting since their argument began, now threatened to fill her eyes. Life had taught her that crying accomplished little more than to make her nose stuffy. If she won this debate, it would be because she had *right* on her side, not because Mitch couldn't stand to see a woman cry. She covered her face with both hands and prayed for control of her emotions.

Mitch's hard stare immediately softened, and he crossed the room in three long strides. "Ciara, sweetie," he said, his voice thick and sweet as syrup, "don't look at me that way." He bracketed her face with both hands. "Aw, honey, I don't want to fight with you."

She looked deep into his brown eyes. *This* was the man she'd fallen in love with…warm, caring, understanding. Ciara was about to tell him she didn't want to fight, either, when he said, "Except for that little mishap, I was always careful—" he wiggled his brows suggestively "—even before I had a beautiful wife waiting for me at home."

He stood a head taller than she, outweighed her by seventy pounds, yet she'd bowled him over with one misplaced pout. *Lord, we both know he's nothing but a big softie. Please don't ever let me take advantage of that.*

She laid her hands atop his. "I *love* you, but I don't know if I can..." Her hands slid to his shoulders, and she shrugged, a helpless little gesture. "I'm not like your mother or your grandmother or your brothers' wives." Unable to meet his penetrating gaze, she glanced at the packing boxes still stacked all around the room. "We haven't even finished unpacking yet, and already we're making plans to attend an FBI funeral."

"I know it's hard, sweetie, but—"

Ciara wagged a finger under his nose. "Don't you *dare* tell me that his wife knew what she was getting into."

He grabbed her finger, kissed it. "Ciara..."

Her voice grew raspy, and she bit her lower lip in an attempt to stanch a sob. "I don't know what I'd do in her place. If anything ever happened to you..."

He held her tighter. "I love you, too. And nothing is going to happen to me, I promise. In a year or two, you'll be so bored with my nine-to-five routine, you'll wonder what all this fuss and bother was about." He kissed the tip of her nose. "In the meantime, you've got to remember that I know how to take care of myself. I don't take unnecessary chances."

She looked directly into his thick-lashed eyes. "I'm asking you not to take *any* chances."

The brown of his eyes went black again as he deciphered her meaning. "You're a cop's daughter, Ciara. You of all people should understand. It isn't just a job—being a special agent is my life."

She jerked free of his embrace. "According to the vows you took four weeks ago, *I'm* supposed to be your life!"

Lifting her chin, Ciara added, "You're the center of mine...."

Mitch knuckled his eyes. "Look," he groaned, arms extended beseechingly, "can't we discuss this like grown-ups? Why does it have to be 'either/or'?"

"It doesn't get any more 'grown-up' than this, Mitch. If you keep doing what you're doing, it's just a matter of time until—"

Ciara perched on the arm of the sofa. "If only you could find a safer line of work..."

"Like *what?*"

She ignored his sullen pout. "I don't know. But there must be something...something that doesn't put you in the line of fire quite so often."

His frown intensified. "Well, I could always be a receptionist. Or a secretary, even!"

She ignored his scorn. "Save the sarcasm, Mitch. That's not what I meant and you know it. But at least you're on the right track." Ciara tapped a fingertip against her chin. "My dad left the department," she said thoughtfully, more to herself than to Mitch, "started teaching Law Enforcement at the University of Maryland when—"

"I'd go nuts," he blurted out, "staring at the same four walls all day, every day."

Was he being deliberately mule-headed? Or had this been part of his character all along? Ciara completed her sentence through clenched teeth. "When he realized his job was worrying my mother to death. Dad left the department...because *he cared* about her."

The frown became a scowl. "I care plenty. Why else would I be standing here, trying to justify why I need to bring home a paycheck to support my family!" He paused, looked at her long and hard. "Go ahead, flash those big blue eyes all you want. Getting mad at me doesn't change the facts—your dad quit...because your mom henpecked him into it.''

Ciara gasped. ''My father is *not* henpecked. And he isn't a quitter, either!''

Mitch clapped his palm over his eyes. ''I'm sorry. I shouldn't have said that. But cut me a little slack, will you? I'm still trying to figure out what pushes your buttons.''

She had to admit, they *had* gone through the normal courtship process faster than most folks. A *lot* faster. Ciara wondered how many other couples found themselves at the altar three months after their first meeting.

Gently, Mitch gripped her upper arms, gave her a little shake. ''I don't know what to say, Ciara, except I love you.''

''And I love you. But I want to grow old with you. How can I do that if you end up like Abe?''

He stomped over to the window, leaned both palms on its sill. ''You might be just a little slip of a thing, but you've got a stubborn streak wide enough for an NFL linebacker.'' He faced her, tucked in one corner of his mouth. ''I'd never ask you to give up *your* job.''

Ciara harrumphed. ''I'm not in any danger from my fourth-graders.''

He poked his chin out in stubborn defiance. ''Give me a break. Those kids are crawling with germs.''

She couldn't suppress a giggle. ''Nothing that would kill me—'' her smile faded ''—and make a widower of you.''

He pocketed his hands, stared at the toes of his shoes. ''Frankly,'' Mitch said softly, ''I'm disappointed. I expected better from you. You seemed so different from other women I'd known. That's why I fell forehead over feet in love. You were more than the most beautiful thing I'd ever laid eyes on, you had a heart as big as your head, and—'' Mitch shook his head ''—I never expected you to make me choose between the two most important things in my life.''

He was a gun-toting, badge-carrying FBI agent, for goodness' sake; couldn't he see the evidence that was right under his nose! *I'm so afraid, Mitch,* Ciara wanted to shout, *I'm terrified of losing you!*

Exasperated, she rolled her eyes. ''And here's a 'button' you can avoid in the future, Mahoney—I wouldn't have married a man who could be henpecked. I am not 'making' you do anything.''

''Listen, Ciara,'' he said, massaging his temples, ''I can't talk about this right now. I need to find a neutral corner, where I can think, and—''

''Fine,'' she said, heading for the stairs.

'' 'Fine' yourself!'' he countered at twice the volume. ''I'm going to the office for a couple of hours.''

Simultaneously the bedroom door and the front door slammed.

It would be the last sound either of them would hear from the other for a very long time.

Ciara ran back down the stairs. He'd locked the bolt from outside, and her hands were shaking so hard it took three tries to get the door opened. ''Mitch! Wait!''

But he hadn't heard her, for he was already backing down the drive. He must have been furious, she admitted, to make it that far in so little time. Standing in the open doorway, shivering in the wintry wind, she prayed he would look up and see her there on the porch, pull back into the drive....

Her pleas did not reach God's ear. If they had, the shiny red convertible wouldn't have peeled away from the curb like a speedster in the Indy 500. Probably, when she retrieved the morning edition of the *Baltimore Sun,* she would likely find skid marks from his '66 Mustang stuck to the asphalt, pointing like an accusing finger in the direction he'd gone.

Ciara retreated into the house they'd owned for one whole week and locked the door behind her. Her heart tightened as the bolt slid into position with a metallic *thunk;* it seemed such an ominous, final gesture.

She passed the first half hour pacing back and forth in front of the picture window, elbows cupped in her palms, heart lurching every time a pair of headlights rounded the corner, heart aching when they didn't aim up the drive.

There in the corner, amid to-be-hung pictures and stacks of books, stood their foot-high Christmas tree. Since they hadn't unpacked the ornaments yet, Ciara and Mitch had made do with several pairs of her earrings, a couple of his cuff links, curly ribbon, and a big red bow on top. It had looked adorable when they'd finished it last week—Christmas Eve. It just looked sad now, and Ciara resisted the urge to cry. She should be dry-eyed when he came back, not teary and sniffling, like a spoiled little girl....

It wasn't until she'd chewed a cuticle and drawn blood that Ciara decided to do some more unpacking. The activity, she hoped, would keep her from doing further damage to her fingernails. More important, it would draw her focus from the ever-ticking clock.

She arranged the good dishes and silverware in the glass-doored china closet, stood brass candlesticks on the mahogany sideboard, put a centerpiece of burgundy silk peonies on the table. Ciara had promised that on Sunday she would serve Mitch his favorite meal at this table— lasagna and Caesar salad. Surely things between them would be right by then.

Ciara tossed the empty boxes marked "dining room" into the attached garage, then got started on the family room. On either side of the flagstone fireplace she hung the carved wooden plaques and framed parchment awards he'd earned during his years at the Bureau, stood his guitar and banjo on one side of the hearth, his collection of walking sticks on the other. She filled the bookshelves with hard-bound adventure stories by his favorite authors, Dean Koontz and Jack London, and arranged his assortment of ceramic wolves.

Taking a break, she dropped into his brown leather recliner, which sat in its special place, facing the TV. It was an ancient, cavernous thing that had seen better days, but Mitch loved it, and the deep impressions, permanently hollowed into its cushions, were proof of that. Though it didn't match anything in the room—not the pale oak tables or linen-shaded lamps, not the blue-checked sofa or the white tab-topped draperies—the ugly old chair *belonged.*

She pictured him in it, size eleven feet on the footrest, one hand behind his dark-haired head, the other aiming the remote as channels flicked by at breakneck speed. How many times had she looked at him in this chair, and felt her heart throb with love, her mind reel with amazement that an exciting, adventuresome man like Mitch Mahoney had actually chosen her as his own?

Could she make a man like that happy…for the rest of his life?

Not if tonight was any indicator.

Why did you ask him to choose between you and the agency? she asked herself. Didn't you learn anything from Mom and Dad's mistakes?

They'd been three days into the two-week church-sponsored cruise when her mother found out how much time Ciara had been spending with Mitch. "He's a cop," her mother had said. "You want to live the way I have for thirty years? You want to be miserable all the time, worrying every minute that—"

"He's FBI, Mom," Ciara had gently corrected. "And

besides, we're just *seeing* one another. It doesn't mean we're going to get mar—''

"He's a flatfoot, just like your father. You want to know how he got that name? By stepping all over *me*, that's how!''

Eyes narrowed by fury, her mother had concluded the tirade through clenched teeth. "Why waste your time, *seeing* him at all...unless you're hoping to end up at the altar?''

Ciara glanced at his big, empty chair. He should be sitting there now, she told herself, rather than in some stuffy office...alone and angry and—

She could only hope that when he came home they could resolve the problem, ensure nothing like it ever happened again. Otherwise, scenes like that would become a habit, as it had with her mom and dad.

She remembered her college roommate, whose parents seemed more in love after twenty-five years of marriage than Ciara's parents had likely ever been. Surely Kelly's mom and dad weren't lovey-dovey *all* the time; in quiet private moments, their *real* feelings for each other surfaced. "They fell head-over-heels in love,'' Kelly had said dreamily, "just like in the movies.'' Love at first sight? Ciara had thought. *No way!*

And she'd kept right on thinking that way, until she first caught sight of Mitchell Riley Mahoney....

He'd been in the pool with a half dozen rambunctious youngsters. Judging by his height, his broad shoulders, his muscular arms and legs, she'd decided he must be a professional football player. And when he'd answered "Polo!'' to a little boy's "Marco!'' Ciara felt certain he was probably a loud, clumsy fellow. "Hey,'' she'd heard him shout, "play fair. It isn't your turn...it's *mine!*'' *Self-centered,* she'd added to her list, and maybe even a bit of a bully.

No one was more surprised than Ciara, when Pastor Boone introduced them at dinner that night. His soft-spokenness, his sense of humor, his intelligence, surprised her as much as the polished manners and thoughtfulness that had him pulling out chairs, opening doors and fetching a refill of punch before she'd emptied her cup.

Like Cinderella, she'd fallen in love before the clock struck twelve.

Smiling, she snuggled deep into his recliner and inhaled its faint leathery scent. Running her fingers over well-worn arms, she closed her eyes and remembered the little boy who'd clung to the pool's ladder that first day. She'd thought it unfair at the time, a bit mean, even, the way he'd ignored the child. But when the game ended and the older kids headed off to catch a movie in the theater, she understood *why* he hadn't interfered...the child was terrified of the water.

Somehow, Mitch convinced him to let go of the ladder. Holding the boy close, he'd walked back and forth in the pool's shallow end, letting the youngster's toes drag the water's surface. The kid hadn't seem to notice, as he giggled in response to whatever Mitch was whispering into his ears, that he was being taken deeper, deeper...

Two hours later the kid was doing an awkward breast stroke...on his own.

Mitch had taught her about lovemaking in that same gentle, patient way. The size of a man, she learned that day, was not a barometer of his capacity for tenderness. Even now she only needed to remember their wedding night, when she had trembled, like a child afraid of the water, for proof.

Ciara had always taken pride in her strength, physical and emotional. What she lacked in height and weight, she believed, she more than made up for with something her grandpa had called *gumption*. But surrounded by Mitch's muscular arms, she had felt precious, treasured, like a piece of priceless porcelain.

Inwardly she gave a halfhearted smile. It's your own fault, Mitch Mahoney, that I've become the kind of woman I've always despised...weak, whining, clingy....

Sighing deeply, she rehashed their argument. If I had it to do over, she thought, I would never have brought up the subject of his job.

Mitch had always been forthright about everything, especially his work. He'd told her how long and hard he'd worked to earn his current status within the Bureau. And she had thought she was being honest with him. "I'm a cop's daughter," she'd told him when he'd pointed out that being married to an FBI guy wouldn't be easy. "If *I* don't know what to expect from marriage to an officer of the law, who does?" She'd gone into the relationship with her eyes wide open, thinking her strength—her gumption—would see her through those trying, worrisome times when he was late and didn't call. She would not whimper and nag, not even in the name of love, as her mother had done....

The trouble was Ciara had not counted on loving him *this* much. Everything changed when she realized that without him life would be empty, meaningless, terrifying. It would be easier now for her to be more understanding of her Mom, she knew.

So what had she done, the very first time she was put to the test? She'd acted like a spoiled brat, that's what. Ashamed—and a little embarrassed—Ciara hid behind her hands. You asked him to give it all up, because—

Because she'd turned on the tiny TV in the kitchen, hoping to catch the evening news as she'd loaded supper dishes into the dishwasher. It hadn't mattered that she'd never heard of Special Agent Abe Carlson before. The story affected her as much as it would have if the stranger

had been Mitch's best man, or if he'd lived next door. The
live footage of him, young and handsome...and dying in
the arms of a fellow agent...had sent a tremor through her
that had made her drop the saucepan she'd been holding.
"What are those reporters thinking?" she'd asked Mitch.
"What if his wife sees this film clip? Or one of his kids?
They'd have that picture in their memories, forever...."

Mitch's gaze had been glued to the screen, too, and
she'd watched his expression of horror turn to grief as he
put his plate in the sink and silently left the room. She
hadn't asked if he'd ever met Abe. Instead, she'd followed
him into the living room, and like a pampered little girl,
told him to give it all up, just like that.

"You knew what I did for a living when we met," he'd
said. And he'd been right. As a good Christian wife, didn't
she owe it to him to at least try to be supportive and understanding?

The question gave her new resolve. When he returned—
soon she hoped, peeking at the clock—Ciara would show
him that she'd married him for better or for worse. You
never complained about the "better"—the thoughtful little
things he did, the constant praise, the sweet lovemaking—
so stop whining about the "worse."

"I've always been careful," he'd told her, "even before
I had a beautiful wife to come home to." Being loving
and understanding, even when it was tough, couldn't help
but improve his chances out there in the mean streets. She
would give her handsome young husband plenty of reasons
to survive the day-to-day dangers that were a routine part
of his job, because underneath it all—beneath the fear that
he'd be hurt—or worse—*she loved him.*

Lord, she prayed, *please give me the strength to prove
it—help me become the wife he deserves.*

Lieutenant Chet Bradley knew better than to question
the Colombian. He'd ordered men killed for slamming

doors, for interrupting telephone conversations, for talking out of turn. No one dared cross him; to complain was tantamount to suicide.

He'd been paid well for doctoring files and losing the evidence that would have sent the gangster back to his homeland, not in cash, but in pure, uncut cocaine, whenever and in any amount he requested, no questions asked.

Since the recent deaths of several mules, the Colombian and the U.S. governments had increased the pressure on transport of the white gold. "It's no longer worth the risk," Pericolo explained, ushering Bradley to the door. "Don't be a glutton," he added, handing the agent a small pouch, "for you'll get no more from me."

He'd had to be careful to keep his "fast lane" life in the shadows, so his top-of-the-line stereo equipment, designer clothes, and upscale vacations were things he'd had to hide from fellow agents. If he allowed even one of them to see the way he lived, they'd know in a minute he was on the take, because his life-style was impossible on an agent's salary alone.

No one knew that better than Bradley.

He supposed he could get used to living within his means again, as he had when he'd joined the agency. But he didn't *want* to.

And now, his money supply was dead.

"You look like you just lost your best friend," said Pericolo's next-in-command.

"Not yet," Bradley said, "but it could be terminal...."

"Naw," Chambro said, dropping an arm around Bradley's shoulders. "There are things we can do to, shall we say, save you."

Hope gleamed in Bradley's green eyes. "Yeah? What?"

"Let me walk with you to your automobile, Mr. Agent," the younger Colombian said, "let us talk."

In a hushed voice, Chambro spelled it out: He wanted control of the Pericolo empire, and he could get it...if he got rid of the boss. A few "favors" for Chambro—information leaked, files misplaced, evidence that would get Pericolo out of Chambro's way permanently—and Bradley would be guaranteed a continued supply of ready, untraceable cash. The would-be ruler leaned on Bradley's car door. "I'll leave the details to you, Mr. Agent. I am sure you can come up with a way we can—how do you Americans put it?—kill two birds with one stone." He gave Bradley a jaunty salute, and left him to consider his options.

Three days, Bradley said to himself. You've got three days to figure out how to get rid of Pericolo....

And then he knew.

Something Chambro had said reverberated in his head: "Two birds with one stone," he said, grinning. "Two birds with one stone...."

Mitch never left his office desk lamp on, so the dim light glowing from his cubicle puzzled him.

Lieutenant Chet Bradley hunched over Mitch's desk, riffling through his Rolodex. "Hey," Bradley said, holding up a card that read "Mahoney, Mitch." "I was just about to call you."

Mitch slid his briefcase onto the desktop, glanced at his wristwatch. "Good thing I'm here, then, 'cause it's nearly ten. Kinda late to be calling me at home, isn't it?" he asked, relieving Bradley of the card and returning it to the Rolodex.

He didn't know why, but being around this guy always gave Mitch an uneasy feeling. Maybe it's that weird grin, he told himself; shows every tooth in his head, but it never quite reaches his eyes....

But his mistrust of Bradley went deeper than any grin

and farther back than he cared to remember. He'd hoped that once Bradley assumed his role as boss, the resentment would fade.

It had not.

The proof? He'd gone a long way in his years with the Bureau, but since being assigned to Bradley, Mitch had been given only the dullest, most routine cases, instead of the "newsmakers" he'd grown accustomed to working on. It seemed Bradley was trying to bore him to death...or kill his career.

Bradley made himself comfortable in Mitch's chair and pointed to a thick manila file folder. "Have a seat, Mahoney."

Mitch sat in the chair across from his own desk.

"It's like this," Bradley began, thumb and forefinger an inch apart, "we're this close to nabbing Giovanni Pericolo."

Mitch knew that for years the agency had been trying to put the Colombian away—or, at the very least, have him kicked back to his homeland at the end of a steel-toed boot—but like a greased pig, Pericolo had always managed to slide through the system before they could even issue a warrant that would stick. "What's the charge this time?"

Bradley adjusted the knot of his navy tie. "Tax evasion."

"Like Capone?" Mitch chuckled quietly, despite the fact that his head still ached from having argued with Ciara. "You've gotta be kidding."

"It'll stick, provided we can get copies of certain, ah, financial documents."

Understanding dawned on Mitch. "Ahhh, so that's why you're here. You want me 'inside.'"

Like a rear-window doggy, Bradley nodded. "Philadelphia, to be specific."

If this don't beat all, Mitch grumbled to himself. I'm

lookin' down the barrel of the best case he ever offered me, but— But how could he accept it, after what had just happened at home? Ciara had been harping on the dangers of his job ever since their wedding night, when she'd noticed his bullet wound. Maybe if this case wasn't going to be dangerous...

Mitch scrubbed a weary hand over his face. It had all happened so fast. How would he explain to his boss that during his two-week vacation to the islands, he'd seen Ciara onboard ship and gone completely nuts. Except for the hours between midnight and 6:00 a.m., they'd spent every minute of the cruise together, and it had been pretty much the same story once they'd gone home. Two months to the day after he'd met her, he'd put a ring on her finger. One month later they'd been married, quietly, because that's the way they'd wanted it. And what with shopping for a house and packing and moving, he hadn't been able to find the time to tell his boss about it.

"I don't know if you heard, but I just got married...."

He couldn't tell if Bradley was very surprised or very angry. Mitch sensed an imaginary noose hovering over his head.

"I've been meaning to tell you," he added, "but—"

"Is this the little woman?" Bradley asked, picking up the photograph on Mitch's desk.

He nodded, and the loop dropped onto his shoulders.

The lieutenant's wolf whistle pierced the silence. "How'd you get a beauty like that?" he asked, putting the photo back.

Mitch's heart lurched as he glanced at her sweet, smiling face framed in silver. She was everything he'd ever wanted in a woman and more. *I wonder how she'd answer that question, if it was put to her right now?* he asked himself. "Just lucky, I guess," he said, and meant it.

"I guess you know this puts us in a bind, Mahoney. We

don't like sending married men under...not for stuff like this.''

He swallowed as the rope tightened.

''But you're the best man on my team.''

Mitch shot the lieutenant a look that said ''What?''

''You were handpicked for this one, Mahoney.'' He tapped his forefingers together.

Mitch sat up straighter. ''To be frank...''

''But I have to warn you, this won't be an easy one.''

He'd been around long enough to know what *that* meant; it was FBI code for ''high risk.'' Which was exactly what had bothered Ciara about his job. And, too, he couldn't get Bradley's threat, made years ago on the obstacle course at Quantico, out of his mind: ''One of these days, *I'll* have the upper hand, and *you'll* know how it feels to be bested.'' Mitch had ''bested'' other guys on the gun range, in footraces, on exams, and *they* hadn't taken it personally....

Now I'm supposed to believe he thinks I'm the ''best man'' to haul in a guy at the top of the FBI's Most Wanted list? Maybe he isn't trying to kill my *career,* maybe he wants to kill *me*....

Mitch ran a finger around the inside of his collar. ''How long would I be, ah, in Philadelphia?''

''You know that's impossible to predict. But if I had to guess, I'd say a week, maybe two.''

He couldn't leave Ciara that long. Not after what had just happened between them. Besides, he'd told her he would be back in a couple of hours. ''Sorry, boss. No can do,'' he said emphatically. ''Get yourself another man, because—''

''Let me make something perfectly clear, Mahoney— we don't have time to get another man. You're goin' in, and I'm gonna be your point man or else. Get the point?''

Mitch bristled. He wouldn't have trusted Bradley to get

a black-coffee order straight, let alone act as his only means of communication with his wife and the people who could pull him out if things got rough. He nodded at the file folder. "How much time will I have to prepare if—"

The lieutenant pulled back the cuff of his left shirtsleeve and glanced at his watch. "Not *if...when*. And you're already a day late and a dollar short," he growled.

Instinct—and intense curiosity—compelled him to pick up the folder. Paging through its contents, Mitch found himself biting back the urge to wretch. He'd seen plenty of ugly sights in his years with the agency, but *this...*

He scanned the black-and-white pictures, hand-penned notes, fading faxes and speckled photocopies that depicted Giovanni Pericolo's life of crime. He would have a hard time forgetting any of it, particularly the photo he held. Pretty, petite, blond, the young girl reminded him of Ciara.

Mitch's eyes glazed as he stared at the file, unconsciously clicking his thumbnail against his top teeth. The file was full of reasons to put this guy away, but the government didn't have a shred of evidence to connect Pericolo with these heinous crimes. Like a giant squid, the Colombian's tentacles had reached across oceans, sucking the life from thousands of innocents. He seemed to have no particular method by which he chose his victims. Did he throw darts? Toss a coin? The girl who looked like Ciara...what if Pericolo's random selection pattern had zeroed in on *her* instead?

This was no ordinary thug. Pericolo was bad to the bone. If Mitch *did* manage to get in close, he'd have to keep his back to the wall at all times, because Pericolo wouldn't hesitate for a heartbeat when deciding whether or not to kill him. The material in the file was proof of that.

For the second time in as many minutes, he realized he'd named Ciara's greatest fears.

Mitch knew this case was a career maker. Truth was, if

he'd been offered this carrot six months earlier, he'd have snapped it up so fast there'd have been an orange streak down the boss's palm.

But a lot could happen in six months. Heck, a lot could happen in half that time—he'd met, fallen in love with and married Ciara in three. Before that he'd been responsible for himself and no one else. Now he had a wife who depended on him, and soon, he hoped, they'd have a family. What better inspiration did an officer of the law need for putting guys like Pericolo away for good?

Mitch turned the question over in his mind. Was protecting his family the reason he wanted this assignment, or merely an excuse to do what he would have done in an instant...if he hadn't let himself be swept off his feet by love for a five-foot, two-inch spitfire?

He wanted to do the right thing, for the Bureau, for Ciara, for himself. But what was the right thing? Mitch drove a hand through his hair. *Lord God in heaven, show me the way....*

"Maybe you could give me a little advice, here. See, my wife—"

"Don't look to me for marital advice," Bradley interrupted, hands up in mock surrender. "My old lady took off for parts unknown years ago."

"Ciara saw the Abe Carlson thing on the evening news."

Bradley snorted his commiseration. "Leave it to the media to make a bad situation worse."

"And she knows I got myself winged back in '90." He shrugged. "She put two and two together, and—"

"—came up with one dead hubby." Bradley shook his head. "It's tough, finding a woman who understands. When my wife left, she said right out that she didn't have the backbone for the undercover stuff."

''Well, let's face it. Hazardous duty isn't an easy thing for a wife to live with.''

''Don't get me wrong, Mahoney, I'm really enjoying our little heart-to-heart, but we've got a narrow window of opportunity, here, and we need you in Philly, like, *yesterday*.'' Grinning crookedly, he tried to lighten the mood by adding, ''You're a CPA, with an impeccable record, and you speak fluent Spanish. You're perfect for the job.''

Mitch forced a thin smile. *''Gracias, ser muy mandamas,''* he said guardedly.

''I can't *force* you to take the case, but look at it this way—we both know there's no love lost between us. Go to Philly and consider the hatchet buried.''

Mitch shifted uneasily in the chair. He'd faced leather-jacketed thugs in dark alleys. He'd been shot, beaten, kidnapped…had looked Death straight in the eye more times than he cared to remember. But none of it had stressed him as much as the pressure being put to bear on him now.

''You bring Pericolo in, and you're sure to get another medal.'' Smirking, he added, ''And I'll get a feather in *my* cap, too, for being the guy who handpicked you.''

He gave his words a moment to sink in. Mitch's mouth had gone dry, and he licked his lips. A big mistake, as it turned out, because the lieutenant read it as hunger to go under.

''First order of business…get rid of those sideburns. No more collarless shirts, no pleated trousers. Wingtips, not Italian loafers. You've got to look the part of a pencil-necked geek.'' He hesitated. ''Let's face it, you're the Clark Kent of accountants. Just do the best you can, stay away from kryptonite, will ya?''

Mitch did not join in Bradley's merry laughter. ''The wife and I, we ah, left things in a bit of a muddle tonight. I only came down here to clear my head.''

"You had a fight?" Bradley asked. "After just three weeks of marriage?"

"Four," Mitch corrected.

The lieutenant shook his head. "Tough break, pal. You'll be lucky if you even *have* a wife if you get back from this one."

Mitch stared hard at him. *If?* Thanks for the vote of confidence, pal.

Standing, the boss handed Mitch a five-by-seven manila envelope. "Your new identity," he said, then pointed at Pericolo's file. "You know what to do with that."

It was a copy, of course, and once he'd memorized pertinent information, Mitch would burn it.

Bradley's matter-of-factness did little to blot Ciara's image from Mitch's mind. Every time he blinked, it seemed, he saw the way she'd looked just before she'd rushed up the stairs. He remembered thinking about that as he'd headed for headquarters. Just last week he'd been forced to cock back his arm and punch a thug to get him under control. In those first, tense seconds after fist connected with cheek, the perp's eyes had widened with shock and pain. Ciara had worn the same expression....

He didn't want to leave her, not for a moment, especially not this way. He knew he could get out of going "in." But Bradley had said this case would put a feather in his own cap. He ain't gonna be tickled if you take that feather away, Mitch thought. He'll bump your rank back so far, you'll *never* catch up.

But what if Bradley was right? What if Ciara *wasn't* waiting for him when this was over? What difference did it make if he reached the top if she wasn't there to share it with him?

He needed to be part of this mission, but he needed to know she'd be there, waiting for him, loving him still, when it was all over...because he couldn't afford to be

distracted, not this time. And what could be more distracting than wondering whether or not the job might cost him
Ciara?

He posed the question lightly, as if it were a mere afterthought. "I won't breach security, of course, but if I
could give my wife a quick call, feed her some innocuous
details, so she won't worry...."

Laying a hand on Mitch's shoulder, the boss shook his
head. "Sorry, Mahoney," he said, almost gently. "You
know the rules—the less she knows, the safer you'll both
be in the event that..." His mouth and brows formed a
"you know what" expression.

Mitch fingered through the contents of the envelope.
Passport, driver's license, credit cards, a library card. "It's
just...we didn't part on a very pleasant note," he said
without looking up.

He gave Mitch's back a brotherly thump. "Now, don't
you worry, 'cause ole Uncle Chet is gonna take good care
of your little lady."

The thought of it wrapped around him like a cold, wet
blanket. Mitch shook off the feeling. He had to keep a
clear head.

Every man in his family was or had been a cop. Ciara's
father, too. They'd understand. They'd explain it to her,
they'd be there for her. She'd be fine....

Still, it was a strange, foreign thing, this feeling of resentment bubbling in the pit of his stomach. He'd never
before felt torn between duty and—

"There's a blue Ford Taurus downstairs," he said, grabbing Mitch's wrist, plunking a set of keys into his palm,
"and a reservation at the D.C. Sheraton in your, ah, new
name." Almost as an afterthought, he asked, "Did you go
to church today?"

He nodded.

"Good."

Mitch heard the implication loud and clear. *You'll need all the Divine intervention you can get.*

"Now head on over to your hotel and get a good night's sleep. First thing in the morning get yourself to the nearest mall."

Mitch nodded again. Outfitting himself for undercover assignments had filled his closet to overflowing. Too bad his aliases never had his taste in clothes.

"Pericolo's expecting you, one o'clock sharp," Bradley added, "so when you get your new laptop, have the sales clerk load it up with all the latest accounting software...general ledger, spreadsheet, the works."

"I'm a CPA," Mitch snarled, "I think I know what I need."

"We're gonna get him this time, Mahoney," he continued, ignoring Mitch's pique. He aimed both thumbs at the ceiling. "I can *feel* it!"

Mitch shuffled woodenly back to his desk, plopped the file and envelope near the phone, picked up the receiver. If Bradley hadn't been standing there, watching and waiting, he might have called Ciara, to explain...or try to, anyway. He took a deep breath, shook his head. It's better this way, he reminded himself. She's safer, and so are you....

He dialed nine for an outside line, then banged the receiver into its cradle. "What am I thinking? I can't call a florist—it's nearly eleven, and they'll all be closed."

"So? Write her a note instead."

Mitch met the man's steely gaze, and despite himself, decided there was truth in his words; a note would be better than a handful of cut flowers and a terse message penned by some unknown saleswoman.

He pulled a yellow legal pad and black felt-tip from his desk. "Dearest Ciara," he wrote, "I'm sorry for upsetting you tonight. First chance I get, I'll explain *everything,* I promise." He underlined *everything* three times, hoping she'd read the message between the lines. "Trust me, sweetie—I need that now. Don't ever forget that I love you more than life itself, and I always will." He signed it "Your grateful husband."

He folded the letter, sealed it in a plain white envelope and wrote her name across its front. With a deep sigh, he handed it to the lieutenant.

A chill coiled around Mitch's spine as Bradley tucked it into the breast pocket of his suit coat. It was like watching it go down a rat hole. He shook off the disheartening thought as Bradley said, "You're my responsibility, and I take that very seriously. I won't let you down. You have my word."

He wanted to spell out exactly what he thought Bradley's "word" was worth, but thought better of it. *He's not much, but he's all you've got. You can't afford to rile him now....*

He grabbed the file and the envelope containing his new "self", and they rode the elevator down to the lobby. The silence between them continued as they stood on the sidewalk outside headquarters.

Mitch turned up his collar to fend off the wintry December wind. For a moment he stood on the corner of Ninth and Pennsylvania, oblivious to the screaming sirens and honking horns around him. Far in the distance, pinpricks of light winked from the windows of houses in the D.C. suburbs, reminding him that forty-some miles away, a light glowed in a window in Ellicott City, too. And if he knew Ciara, she was standing in that window right now, watching for him....

Mitch straightened his back. Cleared his throat. Bradley had said two weeks. *Two weeks,* he reminded himself. *Maybe less. Not so long, really....* "Well, I'd better get a move on," he said, and headed for the car.

phone. But that had been a weekday afternoon, not six o'clock in the morning. "Is Mitch Mahoney there?"

"Hold on, I'll check," said the gruff, unrecognizable voice. And a moment later he said, "I don't see him. Want I should take a message?"

Ciara sighed. "No, thanks. I'll try back later."

"Okey-dokey," he chimed merrily, and hung up.

She showered and dressed and called again. And again an hour after that. "Parker, here," said the agent who answered this time.

Briefly Ciara introduced herself. She didn't want the guys at the office knowing their private business, and so she said, "He left a folder on the table. I just wanted to let him know it's here."

"If I see him," Parker said, "I'll tell him."

"Is there any way I could find out where he is?" Ciara tried not to sound anxious. "I really need to speak with him."

"You could ask his lieutenant. Lemme see if he's in his office."

She put on a pot of coffee while she waited on Hold, made it extrastrong, the way Mitch liked it, in case he came in before she got answers to her questions.

"Lieutenant Bradley doesn't usually get in till nine. I left a message on his desk to call you, Mrs. Mahoney."

A minute later she found herself standing with receiver in hand, staring into space. Ciara hung up, hoping she'd had the presence of mind to thank the man for all his trouble.

"Where could he be?" she whispered.

Chester, who'd been staring out the low-slung bow window in the breakfast nook, trotted over to his mistress. She'd more or less been aware that, as she paced back and forth with the phone pressed to her ear, the dog had been pacing, too...from window to window. He sat back on his haunches and whimpered for some attention.

Distractedly she patted his honey-colored head, then opened the back door. "No digging under the fence, now," she warned, wagging a finger. Chester sat in the open doorway, cinnamon brows twitching, caramel brown eyes pleading for a moment of affection.

On her knees, Ciara wrapped her arms around his fuzzy neck. "You're worried about him, too, aren't you?" she asked, smoothing back his shaggy ears. He'd taken an immediate liking to Mitch—something not one of her former boyfriends could claim—so much so that she'd felt a pang or two of jealousy as the dog followed him from room to room. "Don't you worry. I'm sure he's fine."

Chester responded with a breathy bark, then bounded out the door.

Ciara stood on the small porch and watched him, scampering after a squirrel. "If only I could stop worrying that quickly," she said to herself.

Something told her it wasn't just the late-December weather that sent a shiver up her back.

"Come in, Mr. Lewis, please, come in." The swarthy man grabbed Mitch's hand, shook it heartily. "My friend and your cousin, Buddy Kovatch, recommends you highly."

Your friend, Mitch thought grimly, is a stooge. But at least he's earning the big bucks the government pays him to be a stooge. Buddy Kovatch had been a trusted Pericolo employee for nearly two decades. His last bust would have sent him up to Jessup for ten-to-fifteen if he hadn't agreed to help put his boss away for good. The government buried the charges against Buddy, and in exchange, he put in a good word for the agency's "plant." And now Mitch, posing as Buddy's cousin Sam, would "keep" Pericolo's books until he gathered enough evidence to arrest him for tax evasion.

Smiling, Mitch bobbed his head good-naturedly. "Please. Call me Sam."

Though he wore a wide, friendly smile, Giovanni Pericolo's dark eyes glinted with icy warning. "Very well, then, Sam it is." He gave Mitch's hand a tight squeeze and added, "I hope for your sake, Sam, that you can live up to your stellar reputation...."

He took a new deck of cards from his jacket's inside pocket, unwrapped it, and handed the cellophane to a white-gloved manservant. "Pick a card, any card," Pericolo said. Except for a hint of a South American accent, he reminded Mitch of every sleight-of-hand expert he'd seen on "The Ed Sullivan Show." Without looking at the card he'd chosen, he handed it back to Pericolo. The Colombian gave it a cursory glance, replaced it in the deck and, silent smile still frozen on his face, led Mitch into the dining room, repocketing the deck as they walked.

"Darling," he crooned, "I'd like you to meet Sam Lewis, our new accountant. He'll be spending a lot of time around here from now on." He pulled her to him in a sideways hug. "Sam, this is Anna, my lovely wife."

The shapely blonde patted her husband's ample belly, her wide smile barely disturbing her overly made up face. "It's a pleasure to meet you," she said. "Won't you have a seat? Dinner will be served momentarily."

Pericolo's chest puffed out like a proud peacock's as he moved to stand behind a teenaged boy. "My son, David," he said, gently squeezing his look-alike's shoulders. "He's a big boy for fourteen, don't you think? David, say hello to Mr. Lewis."

"Hello, Mr. Lewis."

The boy would not meet his eyes, a fact that made Mitch

tense. "Good to meet you, David. You on the football team at school?"

David shook his head.

"Basketball?"

He glared openly at Mitch. "Don't like team sports," he snapped.

"Don't have the grades to make the team, you mean," said his sister.

David cut her a murderous stare that not only immediately silenced her...it chilled Mitch's blood as well.

"And this," Pericolo interrupted, concluding the introductions, "is my beautiful daughter, Dena."

Mitch guessed her to be sixteen, if that. Her bright red fingernails exactly matched her highly glossed lips, her hair dyed two shades lighter than her mother's. The minidress and mascara-thick lashes told Mitch she had not been taught to dress for dinner by a church-going mother.

She tilted her head flirtatiously to say, "Good evening, Mr. Lewis. It's a pleasure to meet you."

"Same here," he said carefully.

Mitch followed Pericolo's move and took a seat, resisting the urge to excuse himself, find a powder room and wash his hands. Pericolo looked like he'd just stepped out of the shower, so why had the brief handshake made Mitch's palm itch, as if he'd smashed a spider barehanded? He reminded himself that Pericolo had a reputation, too. Not just *any* spider, Mitch told himself, wiping his palm on his pants leg, a Black Widower.

Bradley and the director had spelled it all out during the meeting last evening. Tax evasion would be the *charge* they'd hang Pericolo with, but it wasn't the reason he'd made the FBI's Most Wanted list. Mitch didn't know of an instance when anyone had violated the law...man's or God's...the way Pericolo had.

His crimes were far more sinister, more evil than any

Mitch had seen to date. And he'd seen some grisly things in his years with the Bureau—drug kingpins, hit men, bank robbers, kidnappers, hijackers—tame as pussycats, in Mitch's opinion, compared to Pericolo. Once he'd heard the details of the Colombian's ghastly crimes, how could he turn his back on the assignment?

Like many young men who dedicate their lives to fighting crime, Mitch, too, had started out with typically high-and-mighty ideals. Maturity, and the things he'd witnessed firsthand, had made him leave most of those lofty sentiments by the wayside. But so far, thankfully, he had managed to hold on to one objective: to do his small part in creating a safer, healthier life for kids. Those he and Ciara would have one day, even Pericolo's kids, deserved that kind of protection.

Rumor had it that Pericolo had no shame about what he did for a living, seeing himself as an "entrepreneur" who provided a certain group of "consumers" with a much desired product. Never mind that Pericolo had become one of the wealthiest men in the world by exploiting the weakest, most pitiful side of human nature.

Mitch had to take this assignment. If he didn't, he wouldn't have been able to live with himself if someday, one of Pericolo's "hollow bodies" turned out to be that of a friend, the child of a friend, one of his own loved ones....

"A toast," Pericolo was saying, "to the newest addition to my business family." Shimmering light, raining down from the Tiffany chandelier like thousands of miniature stars, glinted from the facets of his Waterford goblet and the bold gold-and-diamond rings on his long, thick fingers.

Mitch lifted his glass, glanced at Mrs. Pericolo. Was it a carefully disguised warning...or smug satisfaction...that chilled her smile? How much did she know about Pericolo Enterprises? Did she understand *how* her husband acquired the wealth that put her in this thirty-six-room mansion? He'd seen two Rolls Royces when he parked the rented Ford in the circular drive...was Anna's the silver or the gold one? Surely she suspected *something,* and if so, how had she taught herself to look the other way?

Mitch measured the atmosphere, chatting amiably when he thought it appropriate, nodding somberly when he felt he should. At the conclusion of the long, leisurely dinner in the elegant dining room, Pericolo's wife and children excused themselves, and Giovanni invited Mitch to join him for coffee in his study.

"Please, make yourself comfortable," he said, gesturing expansively toward twin bloodred leather chairs that flanked the massive mahogany desk.

Mitch chose the chair on the right, where he could keep an eye on the door...and keep his back to the wall. Pericolo lifted the lid of a teak humidor. "Cubans," he whispered harshly, tilting the box so Mitch could peek inside.

"Never touch the stuff," Mitch said, holding up a hand, "but thanks."

As Pericolo removed a long, fat cigar, Mitch said, "Mind if I ask you a question?"

Pericolo sat beside him, gold lighter in one hand, hundred-dollar cigar in the other. "You can ask," he said smoothly, his accent a bit thicker now that he'd downed a bottle and a half of Chateau Mouton-Rothschild. Swirling the cigar's mouthpiece between his lips, he ignited the lighter. "But I cannot promise to answer."

Mitch nodded and sipped his coffee. "What was the card game all about, Mr. Pericolo?"

"We needn't stand on ceremony, Sam," he mumbled around a mouthful of cigar. "Starting tomorrow, you will have your nose in the pages of my most personal, ah, shall we say 'affairs'? Please, call me Giovanni." His lips popped as he drew air through the cigar's tip. "Now, back to your question. You were referring to the card I asked you to pick, no?''

Another nod.

He lounged in the chair, broad shoulders nearly touching each curving wingback, shining black hair matting against the buttery leather. ''Ah, yes,'' came his satisfied sigh. ''You're sure you wouldn't like to light one up?''

Smiling thinly, Mitch shook his head.

Pericolo blew a perfect smoke ring, poked the cigar's glowing tip into its floating center. ''I have asked many men to choose. Not one has asked me why.'' His dark gaze bored into Mitch's eyes. And then he laughed, a short staccato burst of snorts and grating snickers. ''Perhaps that's because so few *could*.''

Crossing his knees, he took another thoughtful drag from the cigar. ''You drew a red card. Queen of Hearts, to be exact.'' Through cold-as-death, narrowed eyes, he studied Mitch's face for a moment. Grinning, he slurred, ''You are not satisfied with this answer?''

Mitch shifted carefully in the chair, so as not to spill his coffee. ''Ever since I was a boy, I've had this incurable need to know why.''

''I understand completely. I have the same…shall we say…affliction.'' He shrugged. ''I have accepted it as a trait of intelligent, ambitious men.'' He raised one eyebrow as his upper lip curled in a menacing snarl. ''Still…it's sometimes smarter…and safer…not to know the answer.'' The well-practiced smile was gone, and his voice, which had been smoothly polite until now, dropped an octave, growled out as if his throat had been roughened by coarse sandpaper.

To this point Pericolo had been the perfect host, generous, humorous, magnanimous. But this, Mitch knew, was the *real* Giovanni. He felt a bit like he'd walked unarmed into a lion's cage, and found himself face-to-face with a recently captured, seasoned killer that the zookeeper hadn't bothered to feed in a week. To meet the old beast's golden irises meant certain death, for it could read fear in a man's eyes just as certainly as it could smell it emanating from his body. The difference? The lion killed to satisfy his hunger; Pericolo killed *because he enjoyed it.* The similarity? Once their bellies were full, neither gave another thought to their prey.

Mitch pretended to study the delicate rose pattern decorating his Wedgwood teacup. "Perhaps it's because I'm an accountant," Mitch continued, trying to appear nonplussed by Pericolo's not-so-veiled threat, "that I've always believed the devil's in the details. I like to dot all the *i*s and cross all the *t*s." He drained the coffee. "So if you'll indulge me…why ask me to pick a card? And what's the significance of the red queen?" Only then did he meet the beast's eyes.

Pericolo sniffed, gave a nonchalant wave with his cigar hand. "No significance of any importance, really. A man in my position must be careful…I'm sure you understand…."

"I'm afraid I don't."

Another chuckle. "Well," he said, reclaiming his former suave, distinguished persona, "then allow me to explain. One inaccurate assessment of a man could mean—" He drew a finger across his throat. "It has been my experience that people seldom are what they appear to be."

Pericolo, he knew, had taken this roundabout tack to make him nervous. This wasn't the first time he'd been eye to eye with a cold-blooded killer, but it was the first time he believed he might be killed just for sport. Mitch took a slow, quiet breath to ease his fast-beating heart.

"I do as much checking of the backgrounds as I can when bringing a new man aboard," Pericolo continued, shrugging one shoulder. "At best, it's a fifty-fifty propo-

sition. Some will be who they say they are, and others..."
He shook his head, hands extended in a pleading gesture.
"Despite my Oxford education—or perhaps because of
it," he said, laughing softly, "I'm a very superstitious
man. The cards, if you'll pardon the pun, are my ace in
the hole."

"I'm a thick-headed Irishman, Giovanni," Mitch said,
feigning a jolly laugh at his own expense. "I'm afraid I
don't have a clue what you're talking about."

Straight-faced, Pericolo reached out slowly, deposited
the smoking Cuban into the foot-square ivory ashtray on
the corner of his desk. Mitch found it interesting that, despite what this man did for a living, the hand did not tremble, not in the least.

"Allow me to clarify it for you, then," he began. Set-
tling against the chair's tufted backrest, he calmly folded
his hands in his lap.

"If you had picked a black card, you would be dead
right now."

Pericolo spoke so matter-of-factly, he may as well have
been reading yesterday's baseball scores, or repeating the
weatherman's prediction. Mitch leaned forward to put his
cup and saucer on the desk, more to have a moment to
compose himself than because he'd finished the coffee. He
had never been fooled—not about men like this. Every last
one of them were capable of look-you-in-the-eye, drop-
you-where-you-stand murder, but...

"You are a lucky man, Sam."

His best bet, he decided, was to go for broke. "You
would have killed me...for picking the wrong color?"

Pericolo's feral stare was all the answer Mitch needed.
Yet the man felt inclined to add, "I have nothing more to
say, Sam, except that life is fleeting."

Sitting back, Mitch leaned both palms on the chair, careful not to squeeze the armrests too tight, lest this proficient

beast of prey sense his fear. "I've never been much of a card player," Mitch said, grinning sardonically, "but I've suddenly developed a strange fondness for them. Red queens, in particular."

The sound of Pericolo's boisterous laughter echoed in his ears long after Mitch went to bed.

It was 9:05 when Bradley read the pink "While You Were Out" message on his desk. "Call Mitch's wife," Parker had scribbled. Frowning, Bradley wadded the slip of paper into a tight ball, tossed it neatly into the metal wastebasket beside his desk. He'd done the very same thing last night with the letter Mahoney had written to his wife.

If Mahoney hadn't put in for the same promotion, none of this would be necessary. As it was, he'd made himself the unwilling pawn in Bradley's dangerous game against Giovanni Pericolo.

Two for the price of one, he thought, slouching in his chair.

Except for Buddy Kovatch, no one but Bradley knew where Special Agent Mitch Mahoney was right now. And Kovatch wouldn't be doing any talking. Not if he wanted to stay out of prison. He clasped his hands behind his head and smiled. "Sure is nice, bein' boss," he said to himself.

He didn't like admitting that if his uncle hadn't risen through the ranks to a position where he could pull strings, down in personnel, he wouldn't *be* boss.

His uncle's hands had been tied by that very same string—too many promotions would alert the rest of the brass to what was going on downstairs. Mahoney was Bradley's only competition for the upcoming administrative job slot, and there wasn't much doubt in Bradley's mind who'd get the job. Especially if the big dumb guy pulls off this case the way he's pulled off others in the past....

Well, Lady Luck had kissed Mitch Mahoney for the last time, Bradley thought, sneering. And if the fickle gal felt inclined to pucker up for him again, Bradley would be there to see that her lips never made contact.

Bradley had gone undercover once himself, and knew from personal experience that an agent had better not let anything distract him from the task at hand. And nothing, he'd discovered, was more distracting than a rift with a spouse.

His grin grew. Two for the price of one....

He had no intention of being Mahoney's message boy. Or his wife's delivery man, for that matter. He wants to make fast tracks to the top, let him do it without my help!

Mahoney would nab Pericolo, all right. Bradley would be surprised if he lasted three days after bringing in the evidence the U.S. Attorney needed to convict the Colombian. If Pericolo didn't give the order—from his prison cell—to make a door knocker out of Mahoney's head, Bradley had plans of his own for the Irishman....

Two for the price of one....

He snapped the mini-blinds shut, effectively closing himself into his ten-by-ten office. He propped the heels of his wingtips on his desktop and leaned back in his high-back chair.

His thin lips curled into a malicious grin.

Two for the price of one....

Chapter Three

When he got the call and heard the agent say he was on his way home, Bradley knew he'd better act fast. As he made the forty-minute drive from D.C. to Ellicott City, he slammed a fist into the steering wheel. You should have done this weeks ago, he reprimanded himself. It isn't like you didn't have plenty of opportunity....

Grinning crookedly, he recalled the many times he'd visited pretty little Mrs. Mahoney. That first time in particular stood out in his mind. It had been a week to the day after Mahoney went undercover. She'd looked like a high school kid in her faded jeans and oversize Baltimore Orioles T-shirt, long blond hair tied in a ponytail on top of her head. The whites of her big blue eyes were pink from crying, and there had been a box of tissues tucked under her arm when she opened the door. When he flashed his badge, she would have slumped to the floor for sure...if he hadn't reached out to steady her.

"I thought...I thought you were here to tell me he'd been...killed," she'd stammered once she'd regained her balance.

He'd given her a moment to calm down before

explaining how things worked. "Mitch has left town, on…well, let's just say…company business."

"Left town? But…but we were just married." Several silent seconds passed before she said, "I suppose you sent Mitch because you had to. I mean, there wasn't anyone else avail—"

"Actually, Mitch volunteered. Seemed quite eager to go, in fact." Shaking his head, he'd added, "I think he's out of his ever-lovin' mind, 'cause *nothing* could have made *me* leave a pretty little thing like you at home."

She had paid absolutely no attention to his blatant flirtation. Ciara's bright eyes had brimmed with tears as she stood wringing her hands, trying hard not to cry.

"Now, just to make sure everybody stays safe," he'd continued, "there can be no direct communication between you two." He had to sound convincing, because one thing Bradley didn't need was a hysterical wife phoning the director, asking when her husband would be home.

She could write letters to her husband, he instructed, as many and as often as she wanted, and Mahoney could answer, when and if his situation permitted. In any case, all messages would be written in Bradley's presence…and immediately destroyed by him once they'd been read.

Her eyes filled with tears again, and she'd looked so much in need of a comforting hug that Bradley gave her one. "I have a feeling you have what it takes to be patient," he'd added, stroking her back.

Even now, seven months later, he remembered how she felt in his arms. She'd trembled, like a baby bird that had fallen from its nest, felt so small, so delicate, that he had to force himself to hold her gently, taking care not to press her too close. *Too bad she has to be part of the plan,* he'd thought. But the reality of it was that without her, he couldn't pull it off. It was as though she'd read his mind, because no more than a second, perhaps two, ticked by before she'd stiffened, wriggled free of his embrace. The look on her face reminded him of the time when, at sixteen, he'd been caught, red mouthed, kissing Mr. Cunningham's daughter. Hands pressed to her tear-streaked cheeks, Ciara had seemed ashamed to have allowed another man to touch her, even in a gesture of comfort.

Now, as he peered at his reflection in the window beside her front door, Bradley admitted that he'd told one truth that day. "If I had a woman like her waiting for me at home…" The memory of her pretty, sad-smiling face flashed in his mind. If she was *your* wife, he told himself, a lot of things would be different today….

The hostility he'd harbored toward Mahoney intensified as he acknowledged that, yet again, he'd been bested. The grudge went way back, to the days when Mahoney outshot, outran, outscored him at Quantico. These months of watching his wife's devout fidelity only served to sharpen his prickly envy. Would a woman ever love *him* that much? Bradley wondered. Never a woman like Ciara…beautiful, warm, intelligent, endlessly devoted to her man.

He blinked, shook his head. You can't afford to feel anything for her, he admonished. Not admiration, not respect, certainly not concern! It would mean letting down his guard, and to do that around a guy like Pericolo…well, he may as well put a gun to his own head.

Two for the price of one, he reminded himself. Two for the price of one.

Bradley straightened his tie, ran a hand through his reddish blond curls, nervously tugged the cuffs of his sports coat and rang her doorbell. As he waited for Ciara to answer, he rehearsed the plan…one more time.

"Lieutenant Bradley," Ciara said, smiling when she opened the door. "Please, come in." Once he was inside, she asked softly, expectantly, "Is there a letter this time?"

He could have said no and let it go at that. Could have

shaken his head sadly, feigning commiseration. "I told you, this is just the way Mitch *is* when he's on assignment." Winking, Bradley lowered his voice. "He says if his babes worry enough, he's guaranteed a memory-making homecoming!"

Sometimes he got the impression that once he'd told her there was no word from Mahoney, she simply tuned out everything else he said. This time, Ciara's silence—and the heat emanating from her blue eyes—told him she'd heard every word.

"I'm sorry. Guess I shouldn't have said that."

As always she shrugged it off. "Then...if there's no news..."

If there's no news, why am I here? he finished, gritting his teeth. I was wondering how long it would take you to get around to saying it this time.

The third or fourth time he'd visited her, Bradley had brought a bouquet of flowers. It had surprised him more than a little to discover that neither his corrupt behavior nor the people he'd been hanging around with lately had snuffed out his conscience. If she hadn't been so doggoned *sweet,* maybe he wouldn't have felt so bad about using her. Guilt had nagged him into popping for two dozen long-stemmed white roses. She'd thanked him. Said he shouldn't have. And stuck the box on the foyer table. May as well have tossed that hundred bucks in the trash, he reprimanded himself, because he had a feeling the prickly green stems would never see water. Not because she was an ungrateful sort. Quite the opposite, in fact. Ciara Mahoney would consider it improper to display flowers given by a man who was not her husband...particularly when that husband had vanished from her life like chimney smoke.

A couple of months back, he'd brought donuts and coffee, hoping this less extravagant, more friendly gift would help her warm to him, even slightly. Ciara had arranged the treats on a blue-flowered plate, poured his coffee from the paper cup into a matching mug and placed a white cloth napkin beside it. Two bites of a cruller and a sip of coffee later, he realized she had no intention of joining him. She sat stiffly across from him, smiling politely, her gaze darting to the kitchen clock every few seconds, as if counting the minutes until he'd leave. She was too polite, too kindhearted to say it straight out, but Ciara Mahoney wanted no part of Chet Bradley.

"Just stopped by to see how you were doing," he said, forcing the bitter memories from his mind. He sighed resignedly as if his message wouldn't be an easy one to deliver. "And to tell you that I saw Mitch again yesterday."

Well, you don't have to look so all-fired pleased about it, he thought when her eyes lit up. You haven't heard a word from that bum in seven months, but *I've* been here every week, like clockwork!

"He looked great," Bradley continued, "happy, healthy, well rested. Seems our boy is having a grand old time on this assignment, so don't you worry your pretty little head about him, you hear?"

He watched a myriad of emotions play across her delicate features before worry lines creased her smooth brow. "When will this nightmare ever end?" she whispered, and he suspected she hadn't intended to ask the question aloud. Her shoulders rose on a deep breath. "Can I get you something? Coffee? Lemonade?"

He plastered a practiced look of concern on his face. "Can't stay. I only came by to make sure you were okay. Is there anything I can do? Something I can get you?"

"No, but thank you, Lieutenant."

Grinning, he took her hand, gave it an affectionate pat. "'Lieutenant?' Ciara, you're breakin' my heart!" He chose his words carefully. "I've spent more time with you than your husband has these past seven long months. It wouldn't be improper for you to call me Chet, would it?''

She gave it a moment's thought. ''You're right, of course...Chet.''

He placed a mental check mark beside Part One of his plan. And now for Part Two:

''Did you hear something?''

His tense, slightly crouched posture had the desired effect. Ciara hovered near the wall, cringing, hands clasped under her chin, eyes wide with fright. ''No, I—''

A forefinger over his lips, he warned her to be quiet. ''Now, don't you worry,'' he whispered. ''Chances are practically nil that Mitch has tipped his hand...and that's the *only* way those goons would know how to find you.''

Assuming the 'ready, fire' position, he unholstered his weapon, and as though he really believed a gun-toting bad guy had invaded the second floor, Bradley slowly made his way upstairs, darting into doorways, aiming the Glock at imaginary felons skulking along the hall, as if he truly expected an assassin to pop out and draw a bead on him.

The moment he ducked into Ciara's room, he straightened, calmly reholstered his service revolver. Smirking, he reached into his pocket and withdrew a small vial of Homme Jusqu'au Dernier. ''Now for Part Three,'' he said, his voice echoing quietly in the white-tiled master bathroom. '''Man to the Last,''' he translated the cologne's gold foil label. Opening the medicine cabinet, he placed the decanter on a glass shelf and gently closed the door.

Swaggering toward the hall, he pocketed both hands. It was all he could do to keep from whistling a happy tune. Pericolo was safe behind bars. ''One down, one to go,'' he singsonged.

First chance he got, Bradley would pay the newlyweds a little visit. If he knew Mahoney, he wouldn't be in the house five minutes before the subject of the cologne came up. They'd have words over whose fingerprints were all over pretty Mrs. Mahoney.

It wouldn't take much to convince Internal Affairs that the man of the hour had snapped after all those months in Pericolo's headquarters. Bradley's story that he'd killed the enraged husband in self-defense would go uncontested.

"One down, one to go," he repeated, grinning. "One down, one to go...."

Mitch spent the first day and a half of his freedom down at headquarters, typing up the detailed report that outlined the case. He'd turned down the chance to be there when they picked Pericolo up; he'd seen enough of the Colombian to last several lifetimes. He glanced at the clock. They'd have him in custody by now.

He's probably already complaining about the way his orange jumpsuit clashes with his complexion. His Italian mother had been a fashion designer in Milan; maybe that explained why Pericolo was so focused on outward appearances. Ill-fitting prison garb was Giovanni's problem, and Giovanni was the U.S. Attorney's problem from here on out.

Mitch had troubles of his own, starting with the fact that he'd been away from home a long, long time. He'd known from the start that Bradley had underestimated the amount of time he'd be gone. *But seven months?*

The lieutenant had not been in touch once, a fact that had deeply concerned Mitch at first. But he'd been in situations like that before, and knew how to handle himself. It turned out to be a blessing, really, that he hadn't been able to make a single contact with the outside world once arriving in Philly; he may well have picked a red card from the Pericolo's slick deck, but the Queen of Hearts hadn't squelched the man's suspicions....

The phone in Mitch's room had been bugged, and he

couldn't drive to McDonald's for a burger and fries without spotting a "tail." Whether brushing his teeth or watching TV or adding up columns in Pericolo's ledger books, he got the sneaking suspicion that he was being watched. Two-way mirrors…or paranoia?

Mitch discounted anxiety when, on a warmer-than-usual January day—the kind that gets folks hoping for an earlier-than-usual spring—he made it to a secure phone. He'd dialed FBI Headquarters in Washington, D.C., but Bradley hadn't been in, so he'd talked to Parker instead. "What's the weather like down there?"

"Same as there, I reckon…ice, snow, freezing…."

Mitch hadn't wanted to break the connection. He'd been in Philly for over a month by then, and the stress of being on Pericolo's payroll was beginning to take its toll. He hadn't been sleeping. Had lost ten pounds. And Ciara was never far from his mind….

He was about to leave a message for Bradley, when he spotted a black Cadillac rounding the corner. He'd seen that car in the rearview mirror nearly every time he'd climbed behind the wheel of his Ford. Mitch banged the phone into its cradle and quickly blended in with the crowd of people milling around the hot dog vender's cart. It had been a close call. Too close. And Giovanni must have agreed, because his men pressed in closer still after that.

Like a babe in the woods, Mitch had no protection in Philadelphia. He had no way to ask for help if he needed it. Didn't even have a weapon. He couldn't risk another phone call…until last week, when he finally got hold of Bradley to say he was in the Philadelphia Metro station. "Had to leave the car, the clothes, the laptop behind," he'd explained, "but I've got photocopies like you wouldn't believe. There's enough in my wallet to get me back to D.C. on the Amtrak. I'll call you when I get in."

Prayer had helped get him that far. Mitch hoped it would be enough to get him through this phone call.

"Hello?"

It felt so good to hear her voice that Mitch found himself swallowing a sob. "Hi, Ciara."

He heard her gasp. "Mitch? Is that...is it really you?"

Thank you, God, he thought, because she sounded genuinely pleased to hear his voice. He hadn't expected that. Not after the way they'd parted. Not after seven whole months apart. You don't deserve a woman this understanding, he admitted.

"I—I thought," she stammered, "it's been...you were...I just—" After a slight pause, her voice tightened. "Where have you been?"

He said it softly, gently, because that's exactly how he felt. "Sweetie, I wrote you...." At least he'd managed to get that one message through before Philadelphia had swallowed him up. Mitch thanked God again.

"Give me credit for having *some* intelligence, Mitch. I admit my behavior that last night was a little out of line, but to punish me this long..."

"Punish you?" He sat forward in his chair. What on earth is she talking about? He took a calming breath. "I know the letter was vague, but I couldn't give you any details. It would have been too dan—"

"What letter, Mitch? I never saw any letter. The only explanation I got about your disappearance was from your father and your brothers. 'All in the line of duty,'" she singsonged, the quote thick with sarcasm.

"But..." Now he understood why that sense of dread had loomed over him when he'd handed the envelope to Bradley.

"But *nothing*. All I can say is, thank God for Lieutenant Bradley. He stopped by every week to see if I needed anything...and tell me you'd missed another rendezvous.

Which told me one of two things—either you were in too much danger to keep the appointments, or you didn't *want* to keep them.'' There was a long pause before she added, "He never said it outright, but I got the impression he believed it was the latter.''

"Bradley's a bald-faced liar,'' he blurted out. "I can't believe he never gave you that letter!''

Until the pencil he was holding snapped, Mitch hadn't realized how tense he'd grown. He dropped the pencil halves and ran his hand through his hair. Bradley had put him out there alone, and he'd left Ciara the same way. Burning anger roiled in his gut. He didn't know what Bradley had to gain by his blatant lies—and he'd obviously told Ciara a pack of them—but he knew this much, he thought, balling up a fist, he had better not run into him, because what he would do to him would cost him his badge.

Mitch gulped down a mouthful of cold black coffee. He would deal with Bradley later. "I can be home by noon.''

Home. The word reverberated in his mind like gentle rain, defusing his fury.

"Don't hurry on my account,'' she snapped. "You've been away from *home*,'' she said, putting an entirely different emphasis on the word, "for seven long months. What's another couple of hours?''

He stared at the buzzing receiver for a moment before hanging up. She had a perfect right to be upset. He only hoped when the time was ripe, God would feed him the words that would make things right.

He never would have agreed to take the case if he'd known he would be gone so long, but once he'd gone in, one week became two, and before he knew it, months had passed. There had been no turning back then. Not if he'd wanted to survive.

An icy sense of dread inched up his spine as he recalled

the last thing Pericolo had said to him. "I'm fairly certain that the last words of men who dared to betray me were 'I'm sorry.'" His near black eyes had glittered when he made his hateful promise. "I have a long memory, Mr. Sam Lewis, and an even longer reach. Don't *you* become one of the 'sorry' ones."

Did the Colombian pack enough power to extend that "reach" beyond the walls of his prison cell? The U.S. Attorney didn't think so. "He's a has-been," the man assured Mitch. "Eduardo Chambro has been chomping at the bit to get control. Kovatch told me he said he owes you a debt of gratitude for getting Pericolo out of his way."

Mitch could only hope the lawyer had been right…and pray that all of Pericolo's soldiers were now loyal Chambro followers.

A moment ago he'd wanted nothing more than to get his hands on Chet Bradley. Now he only wanted to cuddle up with Ciara, close his eyes and let her kiss his worries and fears away, as she'd done on their wedding night, when the horrible dream woke him. Tiny as she was, she'd wrapped him in her arms and made him feel safe and secure and *loved*.

He refused to focus on her angry words, chose instead to remember the relief he'd heard when she'd said, "Mitch? Is that you?" The melody of her voice had been enough to raise goose bumps on his flesh. If it had been that good to *hear* her, Mitch could only imagine how much better would it be to *see* her. And once they were face-to-face, the misunderstanding would fade away.

After rushing through the final paragraphs of his report, he filed it, then drove like a madman around the D.C. beltway toward their home in the Baltimore suburbs. He'd spent a total of four nights in their new Cape Cod-style home on Sweet Hours Way before their argument…before going undercover. It would be good, so *good,* to sleep beside her tonight in their low-ceilinged room at the top of the stairs.

It wasn't quite 10:00 a.m. when he pulled into the drive. She wasn't expecting him till noon. Mitch glanced at the window on the second floor. Their bedroom. Was she up there, getting ready for him, applying mascara, spritzing herself with perfume, brushing her long, lush hair?

He ached to see her, hold her, kiss her sweet lips.

Mitch slid the wallet from his back pocket and withdrew the photograph he'd been carrying for nearly a year now, the one his brother Ian had taken during the church-sponsored cruise. Mitch's big fingertips gently caressed her glossy image—as they'd done thousands of times since he'd left her that cold, bleak night—and smiled tenderly.

There had been other pictures he might have chosen to carry with him—Ciara, looking like a fairy princess in her wedding gown; Ciara in the pink suit she'd worn after the reception; Ciara in sweats and a baseball cap on the day they'd moved into this house. But this, by far, was his favorite.

Weeks after his family and hers had walked away from the cruise ship, long after the film was developed, Ian would look at this picture and remark, "Y'know, you two look good together. You're a perfect fit."

Mitch couldn't deny it then. He couldn't deny it now.

Everything about them was different—size and weight and coloring, and the contrasts were good. She was femininity personified, he, man to the bone, and the balance was right.

He recalled the events leading up to the taking of this picture. They'd been too busy swimming, sight-seeing, playing shuffleboard, to watch the sun set. Once, she'd been sitting in a deck chair, so caught up in her book that she didn't hear the gaggle of kids headed her way. If he hadn't scooped her up, they'd have run right into her. "My hero," she'd said, grinning and fluttering those long, dark lashes of hers.

That night they scheduled a time to watch the sun set. Arm in arm, they'd positioned themselves at the boat's bow, waiting to see the blazing fireball slip behind the horizon and disappear. When it finally disappeared, like a coin in slow motion, sliding into a slot, she'd faced him, and in a womanly, wifely way, tucked his windblown necktie back into his jacket. She hadn't removed her hands once she'd finished. Instead, Ciara had looked up at him and smiled. From the dreamy, wide-eyed expression on her face, he had expected her to say, "It's such a lovely evening," or "Isn't the view spectacular?" Instead she'd grinned mischievously. "My stomach's growling like an angry bear. What say we hunt ourselves up a snack?"

"You're a little nut," he'd said, gently chucking her chin.

She'd bobbed her head and launched into her own musical rendition of the once-popular candy bar commercial: "Sometimes I feel like a nut—" her silliness slipped away, like the sun's fading light "—sometimes I don't...."

That quickly the mood shifted, from lighthearted merriment to something he hadn't been able to identify. He only knew that his heart was thumping and his pulse was pounding as she looked into his eyes.

They skipped dinner that night, preferring instead to stand at the prow until the earth darkened and the black sky above the cruise ship was haloed by the glow of the midnight moon. The boat rocked gently as it slogged through the inky island waves. She'd pointed toward the horizon. "The water is so bright, so clear blue during the day. Amazing, isn't it, that now it looks like black velvet."

He'd grasped her shoulders, turned her to face him. It was as he gazed into her eyes...eyes as bright and clear blue as the daytime Caribbean, that he knew how to define that look—love. And he'd kissed her, long and hard, as if to seal it between them for all eternity.

He'd walked her to her cabin, kissed her again in the narrow hall outside the door. "Let's do this again tomorrow," he'd whispered.

"Which," she'd asked, wiggling her brows suggestively, "the walk around the deck or the kiss?"

"Both."

And so they had. The very next evening, Mitch missed the sunset altogether, because he hadn't been able to make himself focus on anything but Ciara. After an hour or so of gazing into her eyes, listening as she talked about the kids in her fourth-grade class at Centennial Elementary, as she told him about her golden retriever, Chester, he wrapped her in his arms, pulled her close.

"Oh, my," she'd gasped, fanning her face with a delicate hand when the kiss ended. "You're getting pretty good at that."

Grinning like a love-sick schoolboy, he'd placed a hand upon her cheek, and she'd copied his movement.

That's when Ian snapped the picture.

Looking at this photo of them, outlined by the amber-orange sky, had brought him countless hours of comfort, had given him immeasurable peace in Philly, as he crossed the days, the weeks, the months off the calendar pages.

She was a vision, brighter and more beautiful than any sunset ever photographed. Her hair riffled by the breeze, billowing out behind her like a sunny sail as sun-sparkled waves danced in the background. It was a profile shot, a silhouette almost, with the fire yellow light of evening shimmering around her head like a golden halo.

He'd worn an ordinary summer suit. Nothing ordinary about Ciara's outfit! Even if he didn't have the picture to remind him of it, Mitch knew he'd never forget that dress.

It was pale blue, and made of a flimsy material that floated around her shapely calves on salty air currents. She'd wrapped a matching gauzy shawl around her narrow shoulders, and with every slight draft, it fluttered behind her like angels' wings.

He hadn't seen his bride in seven long months. Their last evening together had been little more than an accumulation of angry words and misunderstanding, and they hadn't communicated, in any way since that night...thanks to Chet Bradley. He wanted their reunion to be so much more...the fulfillment of seven months of yearning and loneliness and dreams.

Would she be his angel still?

Would he be her hero?

When he walked into headquarters, that's exactly what Parker had called him. And so had the TV reporter who'd wanted to interview the man who'd snagged Giovanni Pericolo. Admittedly the case had ended well, with everything falling neatly into place. But Mitch knew he couldn't have done it without Pericolo's help.

Smart as he was, Giovanni had made a stupid mistake: because he'd outwitted the Feds so often, he'd begun to believe himself invincible. Feeling cocky and full of himself, he'd boldly marched down to the Immigration office and applied for U.S. citizenship. And because he'd never been formally charged with any crime, he had as much right to pledge allegiance to the flag as any other immigrant. He greased a few palms, cutting through the usual red tape, and two weeks before Mitch uncovered the final piece of evidence to convict him, Giovanni Pericolo stood among several hundred soon-to-be Americans, raised his right hand and swore to honor his new nation.

The U.S. Attorney's office would have had a long, expensive fight on its hands, had Pericolo still been a full-fledged Colombian when the charges hit the fan. But Giovanni's dream of becoming a U.S. citizen became his nightmare; he would never enjoy the perks of being a free American from his four-by-eight-foot prison cell.

The praise of Mitch's comrades and a few extra dollars on his paycheck were worthless if he couldn't have Ciara. He needed her steady, sure love now more than ever, to help blot the grotesque images of this case from his mind. He remembered how she'd reacted to the scar on his rib cage, to the news of Abe Carlson's death. It wasn't likely he'd ever tell her any of the details of the Pericolo case. If it messed up a hard-nosed Fed like you this much, he told himself, think what it'll do to a sweet little thing like Ciara.

Mitch tucked the photo back into his wallet and checked the time. Ten-thirty. Too early to knock?

He glanced at the front door. It had been painted black when he'd left home. Ciara had given it a coat of rust-red, and it reminded him of the bright, welcoming doors of Ireland's thatched cottages.

A lot had changed around here in the months he'd been gone, Mitch noticed. Spindly tree branches that had been brown and bare on the cold December night when he'd left now combed the clouds with leaves of every verdant hue. And in flower beds that once sat barren and bleak beneath the many-paned windows, white daisies and pink zinnias bobbed their brightly blossomed heads. She'd planted clumps of hosta along the shaded, curving walkway, yellow tea roses beside the privet hedge.

All by herself she'd transformed what had been an ordinary yard into a warm and welcoming retreat. He could only imagine what magic she'd performed inside, what more she might have been able to accomplish...if he'd been here, at her side.

Mitch got out of the car and slammed the door, wondering what to say when they were face-to-face for the first time in so many months. How are you? You're look-ing well. Don't shoot...I'm unarmed, he added with a wry grin.

Hands in his pockets, he debated whether to ring the bell or use his key. She had no doubt grown accustomed to her solitary status; he might frighten her if he barged in as he would have done before their fight.

He shook his head, hoping the hundreds of prayers he'd said while undercover had inspired the Lord to soften Ciara's heart. Taking a deep breath, he straightened to his full height and rang the bell.

Ten seconds, twenty ticked by before impatience made him ring it again.

"Don't get your socks in knots," came her voice from the other side of the door, "I'm movin' fast as I can...."

Mitch grinned. At least that hasn't changed, he thought. She's still the same little spitfire.

The light coming through the peephole darkened. His heart hammered with anticipation; maybe she would de-cide not to open the door when she saw who was standing on her porch.

But the door did open, slowly, and she peeked out from behind it. "Mitch," she whispered, blue eyes wide, "you're early."

He wanted to take her in his arms and hold her close, inhale the fresh clean scent of her soap and shampoo, kiss her as she hadn't been kissed...in seven months. "Didn't take as long as I thought to finish up the report."

Ciara stepped back, smiling a bit as she opened the door wider. "Well, come on in. The electric company already gets enough of my hard-earned money without air-conditioning the front yard, too."

Mitch glanced around the sunny foyer. Last time he'd been in this part of the house, the floor had been piled high with as-yet-unpacked boxes. Now he could almost see his reflection in the highly polished hardwood. "Smells like pine," he remarked, shoving his hands back into his pockets. "Nice...reminds me of my grandma's house."

The way she stood, half hidden by the door, Mitch had barely seen her. He yearned for an eyeful, and faced her now, fully prepared to apologize, eat crow or humble pie, or whatever else it took to get back into her good graces. He wanted to tell her how awful these months without her had been, how sorry he was for having left the way he had, how many thousands of times he'd thought of her. His gaze started at her tiny, white-sneakered feet, climbed to the shapely legs inside the black stretch pants—

And froze on her protruding abdomen.

"What's the matter, haven't you ever seen a pregnant woman before?"

He forced himself to look away from her well-rounded belly. Her eyes seemed bigger, bluer, longer-lashed than he remembered, but there were dark circles beneath them now. And despite her swollen stomach, Ciara appeared to have lost weight. "Well, sure I have. It's just, well..."

"I'm eight months along," she said, answering his unasked question. "You were gone a month when I knew for sure."

He did the math in his head. "So...so you were—"

Ciara nodded. "We didn't know it then, but we were 'in a family way' on the night you left."

To learn that he was going to be a daddy, in this sudden, unexpected way, was by far the biggest shock Mitch had ever experienced. A myriad of emotions flicked through his head. One moment he was overjoyed at the prospect of fatherhood, the next, terror thundered in his heart, because, what did *he* know about being a dad? On the one hand it thrilled him to know that the girl of his dreams was carrying his child, on the other, his stomach churned as it dawned on him that she couldn't have informed him.

She had gone through all this alone.

Mitch didn't know whether to throw his arms around her or get on his knees and beg her forgiveness or continue standing there, gaping with awe at the sight of her.

Ciara headed for the kitchen. "I'm going to have some lemonade. Can I pour you a glass?"

Mitch stood alone in the foyer a moment, staring after her, then followed her down the hall. "Are you all right? Is everything okay? With you and the baby, I mean?" he began, falling into step beside her. "Gee, Ciara, I wish I had known...."

She opened the refrigerator door, wincing as though the slight effort caused her discomfort. "I *tried* to tell you," she said again. Ciara inclined her head and placed a fingertip beside her chin. "Goodness. It seems our devious Lieutenant Bradley has been scheming on *both* sides of the street!"

The sarcasm rang loud, and Mitch knew it was proof she didn't believe he'd written any letter. Mitch clenched his jaw, fully prepared to tell her what he thought of Lieutenant Bradley. But when he noticed her, struggling to lift the half-full pitcher from the fridge, his ire died.

This isn't like her, he told himself. She was always such a sturdy little thing. Instinctively, he relieved her of it. "Sit down, will you, before you fall down," he scolded. Frowning, he added, "You look..."

"Terrible?"

"Yeah." His cheeks reddened as he realized he'd unintentionally insulted her. "No, of course not. Well, gee whiz, Ciara," he fumbled, "haven't you been taking care of yourself at all?"

"Well, golly gee, Mitch," she mocked, hefting her bulk onto a long-legged stool at the snack bar, "you sure are great for a girl's ego."

He grimaced. "I didn't mean to— It's just that you look like you haven't slept in—"

"I *haven't* slept in days."

"In your condition," he continued, "shouldn't you be paying more attention to your health? You know, eating smart, taking vitamins, getting plenty of rest...."

"*You* try sleeping with a watermelon superglued to your body, Mahoney, see how well you rest!"

Ciara pointed to the cabinet above the dishwasher. "Since you're so determined to '*do*' for me," she said, "the glasses are in there. And while you're pouring, give this some thought, Secret Agent Man—you can't just waltz in here after all this time and start bossing me around." She aimed a forefinger at him. "And stop pretending you're so concerned about my well-being. I might have appreciated it...*seven months ago!*"

Anger had put some color back into her pale cheeks, and the flash had returned to her blue eyes. If she didn't look so all-fired beautiful, he might have shouted his response. As it was, Mitch's defense was barely audible. "I'm not pretending anything. I wrote you, the night I left, and I tried—"

She tucked in one corner of her mouth and raised a brow. "Maybe it would have been a good idea to attend a couple of those meetings Chet scheduled, so he could have delivered your concerns." Ciara tucked a wayward lock of hair into her ponytail. "He warned me you'd have a list of lame excuses for not having been in touch."

He'd known the guy more than a decade, and even *he* didn't call him Chet. Mitch rummaged in the freezer for a handful of ice cubes, dropped them noisily into the tumblers. "*Chet?*"

"He asked me to call him by his first name," Ciara explained, "and I agreed because—" she frowned, crossed both arms over her chest "—because at least *he* was here for me, every week of the seven months you were gone."

"Here for you?" he thundered. "If he didn't deliver my letter to you, and he didn't give you any news at all, exactly what was he here *for,* Ciara?" He glared at her for a moment, then poured the lemonade and shoved a glass toward Ciara. He sat the pitcher down with a thud, splattering the countertop with drops.

"So you're saying you wrote a letter," she said, grabbing a napkin to blot up the mess, "personally handed it to Lieutenant Bradley, and he didn't bother to deliver it."

"That's what I'm saying."

"And you expect me to believe that?"

"Yes, I do."

His words hung in the air like a spiderweb, intricately taut, yet fragile enough to disintegrate with the slightest disturbance. The last time he'd spoken the words, he'd stood in front of the altar at the Church of the Resurrection. "Do you, Mitchell Riley Mahoney, take this woman to be your lawfully wedded wife?" Pastor Rafferty had asked. Heart pounding with anticipation, and love, and joy, Mitch had gazed deep into Ciara's eyes, taken her small hand in his and breathed, "Yes, I do."

Her voice brought him back to the present. "I'm surprised you're having so much trouble with the numbers...considering you have an accounting degree and all. When you left me seven months ago, you said you'd be back in a few hours." She wasn't smiling when she tacked on, "Were you lying to me then, or are you lying to me now?"

"I've never told you a lie, Ciara. And I don't see how you can say I—"

"There's a lot you don't see, Mahoney, because you've got your blinders on again, just like...just like the lieutenant said."

Mitch snorted, knowing she'd hesitated because she'd wanted to say "Chet" instead of "lieutenant." "Your buddy *Chet* doesn't know diddly about me, Ciara, but it's beginning to look like even *he* knows me better than you do."

She shrugged. "Can't get to know a man who isn't around."

He planted both palms flat on the counter, leaned forward until they were nearly nose to nose. "Listen, I don't know what he told you—or why—but I know this—I had a tail on me every minute. If I had tried getting in touch with you, we'd both be—"

He clamped his jaws together, knowing he'd just put himself between the proverbial rock and the hard place. By admitting he couldn't contact her, he was supporting her claim that his job was too dangerous.

Just tell her you love her, Mahoney. That's what she needs to hear right now; you can work out the rest of this mess later. He opened his mouth to do just that when the tight, skeptical look on her face stopped him cold. His lips formed a thin straight line. "Seven months ago you asked me to choose. Sounds to me like *you've* chosen to believe that slimeball Bradley over me." He ground his molars together. "Believe whatever you want," he snarled. "Everything I've said is true."

Her eyes misted, and she swallowed. "While you were gone, I saw a movie about an agent who went undercover. *He* managed to call his wife. Even managed to sneak off and *visit* a few times!"

"This isn't Hollywood, Ciara. In the real world we do things by the book...or *die.*"

"It was based on fact."

"Did your buddy *Chet* tell you that story, too?"

Ciara only stared at him, eyes blazing and lips trembling. "You know what, Mitch?" she said after a moment.

"I was an independent woman before we met, and believe it or not, I managed quite well after you left...once I got used to the idea. I'll admit, those first couple of weeks were pretty rough, but look around you," she added, up-turned palms drawing his attention to their surroundings, "I got a lot accomplished, *all by myself.* This house is a home now, thanks to the endless hours I've spent working on it...*alone.*"

Suddenly she was on her feet, pacing back and forth across the black-and-white linoleum tiles, arms swinging, eyes flashing. "What was I to think, when you vanished like something from a magic show...and never came back?" she demanded, coming to a halt in front of him.

"I've given it a lot of thought and prayer since you stormed out of here that night." Hands on her hips, she raised her chin slightly. "I think it would be best if you just packed your things and moved out."

In response to his grim expression, she tossed in, "I can afford the mortgage on this place, thanks to my teacher's salary, so don't you worry about how I'll manage. In fact, every time one of your checks arrived from the Bureau, I put it into *my* bureau, uncashed. I didn't need your help turning the house into a home, and I don't need your money to stay in it. And I *am* staying, because it's a nice, safe neighborhood, with plenty of children, and good schools, and..."

She has every right to be angry, he told himself. She's been alone for a long time, not in the best of health, listening to Bradley's lies. Maybe if he sat quietly and let her vent, the anger and resentment would fade, and she'd look at him the way she had on the cruise ship, as she had at the altar, on their wedding night....

The cruise ship, the marriage, the separation, the pregnancy. All these things had happened in less than a year, yet it seemed like an eternity to him now.

Mitch leaned against his stool's backrest, wondering what she'd do if he just gathered her up in his arms and silenced her with a big kiss. But before he had a chance to put his plan into action, she plunged on, fingers drawing quotation marks in the air, reminding him of something he'd said the night he left:

"So don't feel 'duty-bound' to take care of me. I know your old-fashioned need to meet your responsibilities is supposedly the reason you work as hard…and as *long* as you do, but…"

Was it his imagination, or had her face paled even more in the last few minutes? All this ranting and raving couldn't be good for her *or* the baby. Suddenly it didn't matter who was right and who was wrong. Calming her down, that was all that mattered.

"Ciara, I know I said those things," he began, his voice softly apologetic, "but I never meant it to sound as though taking care of you is a burden. Bottom line—I love you. Have since the day we met, will for the rest of my life. Providing for you will always be an honor, a privilege." He grinned slightly. "Believe me, I've had plenty of time to think about that while…"

Oh, how she *wanted* to believe him! But Ciara had convinced herself that she must focus on the pain his absence had caused in those early days, when she'd been forced to admit the ugly truth: the oath he'd taken for the Bureau meant more to him than the vows he'd made to her. She loved him with everything in her, but if she was going to survive, if her heart was ever to heal, she must stand firm on this issue. She could *not* give in simply because he was standing there, looking at her with those sad brown eyes of his, imploring her to be something she believed she could not be.

She forced a cold, careless tone into her voice that she did not feel. "I'm sure you *did* have lots of time to think while you were away. Well, guess what, James Bond? While you were off living your life of adventure, I had a little time to think, too, and…''

He held up a hand to silence her. "I want to show you something," he said quietly, pulling out his wallet. Slapping her photograph on the counter, he said, "You see that? *That's* what kept me going for seven months. *That's* what gave me the incentive to think smart, to do whatever it took to drag my sorry self home.

"I won't deny that before I met you, I liked the danger and excitement of undercover work, but back then, getting the job done was the only focus." Mitch shrugged, then emphasized his point. "That's why I took unnecessary chances. That's how I accomplished in nine years what it takes most agents twenty. Because who was I, that my passing would make such a difference?"

She picked up the photograph. He must have held it in his big, strong hands hundreds of times, and the proof was that the paper it had been printed on now felt soft and supple as cotton. Her aching heart pounded. All right, so maybe he loves you a little bit after all, she thought.

But wait…something he'd said pinged in her memory. He couldn't possibly believe his life had no value, that his existence wasn't important to anyone. He mattered plenty—to his parents, his siblings and their children—to *her*.

Ciara handed back the photograph, tensing when their fingers touched, for she yearned to hold him, to be held by him. "Everyone would miss you if you were—" Ciara hesitated, unable to make herself say "killed in the line of duty." She began again. "A lot of people would be very upset if anything happened to you."

He dismissed her comment with a flick of his fingers.

Ciara straightened her back, reminded herself that she'd decided she couldn't, *wouldn't* go through that agony again. Even if she had the strength to survive the next case—and the next, and the one after that—their children deserved a full-time dad.

"I saved some of the boxes from our move," she began, looking anywhere but into his haunted eyes. "They're in the garage. If you like, I could pack for you. I wouldn't mind...." She was rambling and she knew it, but seemed powerless to stanch the flow of words. "Your brother, Ian, has an extra room, now that Patrick is off at college. Did you know he was accepted at Stanford? Of course you didn't.... Well, I'm sure Ian wouldn't mind if you stayed there until you found a place to—"

"Shut up, Ciara. Just *shut up*."

He'd never spoken to her in such a vulgar, vicious way before, and she felt a sharp pain, deep in the pit of her stomach.

"I realize I've messed things up pretty well," he said, "but I think we can work this out." He took her hand in his. "Give me a chance to make all this up to you." Mitch stroked her fingertips. "Please?"

Hang tough! she reminded herself. Be strong, or these seven months that are behind you now will be a road map of the rest of your life. "Maybe you'd rather do the packing yourself," she continued, as if he hadn't spoken at all. "Or, we could do it together, to make the job go easier and faster."

"I don't believe this!" he bellowed, dropping her hand. "I know we didn't have much time together before—" He stopped. Took a deep breath. And, hands on her shoulders, he started again. "We had something special once. At least, I thought we did. I think it's worth fighting for. Let me prove that to you."

Ciara couldn't believe how much intense physical pain a moment like this could cause. Though she'd rehearsed it and rehearsed it, she'd never imagined it would ache this much.

In response to her strained silence, he walked away from her, stood his empty glass in the sink. "All right. I'll leave, if it's what you want. But…"

She doubled over and gripped her stomach with both hands. "Mitch," she groaned, slumping to the floor, "it hurts. Hurts bad."

Ciara had always been the type who poked fun at people who whined and complained about everyday aches and pains. He knew she must be in considerable agony to have admitted it straight-out like that. Kneeling, he wrapped his arms around her. "It's way too early for the baby, isn't it?"

She nodded. "Call 911."

"No time for that—could take the ambulance an hour to get here." He spoke in a calm, reassuring voice that belied the terror he felt…raw, surging fear like he'd never experienced on the job.

Mitch grabbed the telephone, seeing that she'd jotted her obstetrician's number on the tablet beside it. He dialed, explained that they were on their way to the hospital and hung up. "The nurse says Dr. Peterson will meet us there," he said, gently helping her to her feet. And as if she weighed no more than a baby herself, lifted her in his powerful arms and carried her to the front door.

She melted against him like butter on a hot biscuit. Unconsciously he pressed a kiss to her temple. "Have you been taking childbirth classes?" he asked, kicking the door shut behind them. He wanted to kick *himself*, because he should have been beside her at those classes.

She burrowed her face into the crook of his neck. "Yes," came her hoarse reply.

"Who's your coach?"

"Mom."

"What would she be doing," he asked opening the car door, "if she were here right now?"

Ciara began to sob uncontrollably. "I don't want to lose the baby, Mitch. I love it so," she said, one arm hugging her tummy. "I don't think I've ever been more afraid...."

He'd never seen her cry before. He wanted to hold her this way forever. Comfort her. Tell her whatever she needed to hear. But there wasn't time for that now. Gently he put her into the car. "You're not going to lose the baby, sweetie." He ran a hand through her hair. "The best thing you can do is stay calm. Right?"

Nodding, she wiped her eyes as he pulled the seat belt around her. Ciara grabbed his hand as he clicked the buckle into place. "I don't know how well I'd be handling this if I were alone."

Without even thinking, he placed a quick kiss on her cheek. "You're never gonna be alone again, sweetie, not if I have anything to say about it."

As he ran around to his side of the car, she couldn't help but admit how much she wanted to believe him. *Oh, Mitch, please don't give me false hope, especially not now....*

It was as he shifted into Reverse that Ciara noticed her blood on his hands. He followed the direction of her gaze and gasped involuntarily.

"'It's nothing,'" she rasped, quoting word for word what he'd said when she'd first noticed his bullet wound, "'a flesh wound. No big deal.'"

Mitch turned on the flashers and the headlights, and prayed for all he was worth: *No traffic, no potholes, no red lights,* he begged God as he pealed away from the curb. He glanced over at her, held his breath when he saw how much blood had already soaked the seat. *Get us to the hospital, Lord, and us get there fast!*

Chapter Four

"What do you mean, I can't go with her?" Mitch demanded.

The nurse was nearly his height and likely outweighed him by fifty pounds. She tilted back her red-haired head and held up one hand like a traffic cop. "You'll only be in the way. Now have a seat," she ordered, pointing to the chairs against the wall.

Mitch didn't want a confrontation with this woman. He just wanted to be with his wife. He'd promised never to leave her alone again. He couldn't let her down. Not now.

Ciara had looked so frail and fragile when the orderlies put her on the gurney, so pale and drawn it was hard to tell where she ended and the starched white sheets began. She'd reached out her hand as they wheeled her past, but in the flurry of activity, he couldn't get close enough to take hold of it. The last thing he saw were her teary eyes, wide with fear and pain.

"Listen, lady," he ground out, "that's my *wife* in there, and she needs me. No amount of your self-important hoo-ha can stop me from going in there."

He took a step, and she blocked it. Crossing both arms over her ample chest and tapping a white-shoed foot on the shining linoleum, her eyes narrowed. "I'm calling Security," she snapped.

"You do what you have to do," he shot back, shrugging, "and I'll do what I have to do." With that he barged into the emergency room. Almost immediately he felt guilty for having behaved like a caveman, but he'd have done whatever it took to be near Ciara.

"Did you see where they took my wife?" he asked the first nurse he saw.

"Little blonde, pregnant out to here?" she asked, making a big circle of her arms.

He nodded.

"Second bed on the right. Now, stop lookin' so worried, hon. Women have babies every day…I've had seven, myself. Trust me," she said with a wave of her hand. "It's a cakewalk."

He didn't bother to point out how elaborate and difficult cakewalks had been for the slaves who'd competed for slices of dessert…. "Thanks," he said, and headed for his wife's cubicle.

"Mitch," she sighed when she saw him. "I heard all the ruckus. I didn't think you'd ever get past her…."

He kissed her cheek, then flexed his bicep to lighten the tense atmosphere. "Hey, it's gonna take more than one coldhearted nurse to keep me away from you, especially now."

She smiled feebly, gave his hand a grateful little squeeze.

"So how're you feelin', sweetie?" he asked, pulling a chair closer to the bed.

"I'm okay," she whispered.

But she wasn't, and he knew it. Smoothing wispy blond bangs from her forehead, he looked into her blue eyes. It was hard to tell the agony from the fear. He felt incredibly powerless, because she was bleeding and in pain, and there wasn't a thing he could to help her. Where were the doctors? And the nurses? Did they intend to let her lie here and bleed to death? Did they...

Well, there was *something* he could do!

Mitch leaped up and stomped toward the pastel-striped curtains. "Hey," he hollered, half of him in the cubicle, the other half leaning into the hall, "can we get some help in here? My wife is—"

A blue-smocked man blew past Mitch. "Mrs. Mahoney?"

Ciara nodded weakly.

"It's about time you got here," Mitch snarled, letting the curtain fall back into place.

Ignoring the husband's grumbling, the doctor stepped up beside Ciara. "First baby?" he asked, a knowing smile on his face.

Another nod, and a small smile, too.

"Well, don't you worry, little lady. We're gonna take real good care of you, I promise." He pulled the blood pressure cuff from a hard plastic pocket on the headboard. "You see, there was a six-car pileup on Route 95 about a half hour ago," he explained, his voice calm and reassuring as he fit it to her upper arm. "The paramedics brought in the last of the injured just minutes before you arrived." A half shrug. "Contusions and abrasions for the most part, but the nurses are hot-footing it, just the same."

He stood silent for a moment, reading the gauge, then put everything back where he'd found it. "You don't mind a lowly resident working on you, do you?" he asked, scribbling a note on the file attached to the clipboard he held.

"It takes a lot of hard work to become a resident," Ciara

said, smiling. "There's nothing 'lowly' about your position."

She's lying there getting weaker by the minute, Mitch thought, and he's making small-talk! Frustration got the better of him. "It's been my experience," Mitch interrupted, "that chitchat can't stop hemorrhaging...."

"Mitch," Ciara protested, a restraining hand on his forearm, "it's all right, I'm—"

"First of all, Mr. Mahoney," the young doctor said, writing another note in Ciara's file, "your wife is losing some blood, but she's not in immediate danger. Secondly, I have a wife, and a kid, myself. If either of them were here now, I'd be breathing fire, just like you are." He clicked off his ballpoint and slid it into his shirt pocket. "Trust me," he said, meeting Mitch's eyes squarely. "We're going to do everything in our power for your wife and baby."

He didn't wait for Mitch's agreement or approval. Instead, he plowed through the curtains and began barking orders, commanding attention, demanding assistance. When he returned a moment later, shoving a tool-laden cart, he looked at Mitch. "How well do you handle the sight of blood?"

"He's an FBI agent," Ciara answered on his behalf. She sent Mitch a crooked little smile. "My husband has seen more than his share of blood."

The doctor snapped a pair of surgical gloves over his hands. One corner of his mouth lifted in a grin. "Stand over there, then, near the wall. If you don't get in the way, maybe I'll let you stay."

Mitch crossed both arms over his chest, fully prepared to follow the doctor's orders to the letter. He'd been away from her long enough. No way he would leave her now, especially not now. He pressed a knuckle against his lower lip, and watched.

He'd been on the scene when emergency medical technicians tended the victims of shootings, stabbings, near drownings. Once, he'd been the only one available to help a woman give birth to twins. Always before though, as his adrenaline had pumped and his heart raced, he'd managed to keep a professional distance from the lifesaving—or life-giving—experiences. Keeping an emotional arm's length from them had been easy, because the people involved had all been strangers.

Admittedly, he hadn't known the beautiful young woman on the gurney very long, but she was his wife, and the great bulge beneath the sheet that covered her was his unborn child. Unconsciously he began to gnaw his thumbnail.

As a small kid his mom was forever admonishing him to keep his fingers out of his mouth. By the age of seven, he'd left the habit behind, along with his nightlight and Peppy, the stuffed bear. And no matter how stress- or pressure-filled the situation, he hadn't chewed his fingernails since, not when he took his SATs, not when he sat for the CPA exam, not before the final test at Quantico.

A tiny stab of pain told him he was back at it again. Mitch searched for a napkin, a paper towel…anything that would blot the bloodstain from his thumb. He spotted some tissues on the small counter against the wall and plucked one from the box. Wrapping it around his thumb, he squeezed.

He tried to see Ciara. She was all but hidden from his sight as doctors, nurses, interns and residents gathered round. He felt like that seven-year-old nail-biter again. He'd been through terrifying situations. He'd faced death at point-blank range. Through it all, he hadn't shed a tear for himself, or anyone else involved. So why was he on the verge of tears now?

Because you could *lose* her, he admitted.

For the first time, Mitch understood how the bad guys must feel once they'd been snagged, frisked and cuffed, because *he* felt caught—smack between his career-focused, solitary life-style and the reality that without Ciara life would be meaningless.

Snap out of it, Mahoney! he berated himself, gritting his teeth. Pull yourself together, for Ciara's sake.

Mitch chanced a glance over his shoulder, caught a glimpse of her between the broad shoulders of the young resident and the shower-capped head of a nurse. He'd seen blood—his own, fellow agents', criminals'—hundreds of times. So why did the sight of Ciara's make him feel as if a tight band had been wrapped round his chest?

Mitch swiped at the sweat that had popped out on his forehead, discovered that his palms were damp, too. His ears started to ring, the room started to spin, and he realized if he didn't get out of there fast, he'd keel over.

He took another look at her: eyes closed, jaw clenched, fists bunched at her sides. She hadn't uttered a word of complaint since he'd cradled her, there on their kitchen floor, when she'd admitted how badly it hurt. You weak-kneed wimp, he chided himself. She's the one going through this, so why are you swooning like an old woman?

Mitch closed his eyes again, took a deep breath and prayed the extra oxygen would clear his head.

It didn't.

Pressing his forehead to the wall, he prayed the dizziness would pass, at least long enough for him to make it into the hall. He turned and headed for the curtain.

''Mitch,'' came her exhausted voice, ''you're pale as a ghost. What's wrong?''

Humiliation washed over him like a tidal wave. Even in her weakened condition, and surrounded by half a dozen medical professionals, her thoughts were of him, not herself. He didn't know what minor miracle had prompted her to say yes when he'd asked her to marry him, but he knew he'd never done a thing in his life to deserve a woman like Ciara.

Too ashamed to meet her eyes, Mitch looked at the young doctor instead. "I, ah, I..."

"Get out of here, Mr. Mahoney," he said, frowning over his round-lensed glasses. "The room's too crowded as it is. I'll come for you when we're finished here, bring you up to speed."

With a nod of gratitude, and another of relief, Mitch hurried out of the cubicle. He slumped into the first chair he came to, a ghastly orange thing of molded plastic, being held up by four aluminum legs. What in God's name is the matter with you? he demanded of himself, an elbow resting on each knee. Mitch hung his head, stuck his face in his hands and prayed for all he was worth.

"Let her be all right," he whispered into the warm dark space between his face and his palms. "Give me a chance to show her how much she means to me...."

"You're doing fine," Dr. Peterson said, patting her hand.

"I'm so glad the hospital was able to get hold of you," she admitted.

"Relax, now. Everything's under control."

But was it?

The baby hadn't moved, not once, since—since right after Mitch had come home. She remembered the exact moment because, when she'd felt the baby stir, she had wanted to interrupt him, in the middle of explaining that he *had* written, to say, "Mitch...our baby is moving...give me your hand...."

Instead she'd stared into the handsome face of the man in her kitchen...her husband, yet a virtual stranger. Had she refrained from sharing that warm "baby" moment with him because he'd left her alone for seven long, lonely months? Or had she kept it to herself...to *punish* him for those months?

A little of both, she admitted, a twinge of guilt knotting in her heart.

"You doin' all right?" Peterson asked.

Ciara nodded.

"Then why the big sigh?"

"Oh, just talking to myself. I do it all the time."

He grinned. "Well, keep it down, will ya? We're tryin' to concentrate here."

His teammates snickered. "Yeah. You're noisier than a gaggle of geese," a nurse said.

"What's the matter," said another, "aren't you gettin' enough attention?"

Ciara smiled weakly. She knew the purpose of their lighthearted banter was to keep her calm, and while she appreciated their attempts to reassure her, she could have saved them the bother. Nothing could calm her as long as she was worried....

She was terrified, right down to the marrow of her bones, that the baby had stopped moving because something terrible had happened.

And what if Mitch didn't want the baby?

Possible, she thought, but not likely. He'd been so sweet and understanding during the drive from the house to the hospital, saying all the right things, patting her hand lovingly, concern flashing in his big brown eyes. But had it all been a joke, like those the doctors and nurses had been telling, to keep her quiet and still? If not, why had he dashed out of the room just now, looking like a deer with a hunter hot on its trail? And why had his usually ruddy complexion gone ashen? Perhaps because the sudden news had overwhelmed him....

She'd known from the moment he'd seen her belly that

he would need time to come to grips with the fact that he'd be a father soon. She'd had *months* to get used to the idea—he'd had half an hour before the bleeding started.

Since they'd arrived at the hospital, she'd been lying there telling herself that, in time, Mitch would be as overjoyed and exuberant about the prospect of parenthood as she was.

But what if he wasn't?

Ciara's lower lip began to quiver, and she bit down to still it. Her eyes welled with tears, and she squeezed them to keep new ones from forming. Stay calm, she scolded herself, for the baby's sake.... But the lip continued to tremble, and the tears fell steadily.

"We're almost finished here, Ciara," Dr. Peterson said.

Sniffling, she summoned enough to control to say, "Um...the baby...hasn't moved, not once in all this time...."

"Perfectly normal under the circumstances. You've gotta give the little tyke credit...he's already smart enough to know when to lay low."

He?

Ciara's heart lurched as she pictured a miniature Mitch, running around the house on chubby bare feet. "So...the baby's all right?"

"We've had him monitored the whole time. If there was a problem, I'd have brought in a neo-natal specialist, stat. Trust me."

His words calmed her, soothed her. She thanked God and all the saints and angels. Thanked God again.

So why on earth are you making a spectacle of yourself, she thought, embarrassed by the tears, the hiccuping sobs. Ciara crooked an arm over her eyes, like the child who thinks because he can't see his mama, mama can't see him, either.

"Get her husband back in here," the resident said to

the nurse beside him. "He was lookin' a little green around the gills when I kicked him out. You'll probably find him in the men's room...."

"You know," the nurse said, cocking an eyebrow, "you're gonna be a fine surgeon someday."

He gave her a grateful grin. "You think so?"

"Uh-huh." Smiling, she shoved through the curtain. "You're a natural...already a master at barking out orders and making nurses feel like peons."

He met Peterson's eyes, then Ciara's. "Nurses," he huffed good-naturedly, "can't live with 'em, can't live without 'em."

Ciara giggled nervously, and she didn't stop until Mitch wrapped his big warm hand around her small, cold one.

Once things were under control, Mitch stayed with Ciara while she slept, and Peterson left to make a few phone calls. When he returned, seeing that Ciara had fallen asleep, Dr. Peterson said, "I have a few questions, but I don't want to wake her." He stood at the foot of her bed, reading her chart. "Tell me, Mr. Mahoney, has she been staying off her feet, like I told her to?" he asked without looking up.

Mitch's heart pounded. She'd been told to stay off her feet? How long ago? And why? If she'd been told to rest, how did he explain the flower gardens, the spotless house, the—

Peterson was looking at him now, a puzzled frown furrowing his brow. Mitch knew it was a simple enough question. Knew, too, that the doctor was probably wondering why Ciara's husband didn't have a ready answer for it.

"It's my understanding that you've been out of town," the doctor said, peering over his half glasses at Mitch. "Maybe she hadn't had a chance to tell you everything...yet."

Mitch swallowed. The man thinks you're a no-good husband...because that's what you are.

"We've been carefully monitoring the baby for several
weeks now, ever since Ciara started spotting." Narrowing
his eyes, he said, "She didn't tell you *any* of this?"

He hung his head. "I'm afraid not." She hadn't told
him anything about the pregnancy, because he hadn't been
around. The thought of her going through this alone caused
a nagging ache inside him.

"Well, she does tend to be a secretive little thing,
doesn't she?"

It was Mitch's turn to frown. "How do you mean?"

"Most young mothers—particularly first-time mothers—love to talk about their plans. You know," he said,
shrugging, "the nursery, baby names, whether or not to
breast feed...." He looked at Ciara. "Not your wife." After a long pause, Peterson met Mitch's eyes. The doctor
cleared his throat. "What happened today is proof she
hasn't been taking proper care of herself."

"What *did* happen, exactly?"

"Placenta previa. The baby gets its nourishment and
eliminates its waste by way of the placenta, you see," he
explained. "In Ciara's case, the placenta began separating
a bit. That's what caused the bleeding."

His gaze fused to Mitch's. "She'll have to stay off her
feet for the duration of the pregnancy. That means she'll
need someone with her at all times." He glanced at his
patient again. "From here on out, she cannot be left alone.
Not even for short periods of time."

"That's impossible," Ciara said, her voice thick with
drowsiness. "My parents are touring Europe. I couldn't
get in touch with them, even if I wanted to."

Why can't *you* take care of her, Mr. Mahoney? was the
question written on the doctor's face. He turned to Ciara.

"Do you have a sister? An aunt? A grandma, maybe?" he asked instead.

"I'm the only child of only children," she stated, "and my only living grandmother is in a nursing home."

"Hmm. Well, that pretty well covers it, doesn't it." He thought for a moment, then said to Mitch, "You could hire a live-in nurse."

Ciara sighed. "They're bound to cost a small fortune." Passing a trembling hand over her worried brow, she added, "I know my teachers' insurance won't cover that. I doubt the agency's will, either."

Mitch was still bristling over the fact that the resident had also zeroed in on what he construed to be a problem between man and wife. Who does that little twerp think he is, sticking his nose in where it doesn't belong? "Doesn't matter if the insurance covers it or not," Mitch all but snarled. "We won't need any live-in nurse. I'm perfectly capable of taking care of my wife."

The doctor removed his glasses and gave Mitch a hard, appraising stare. "Day in, day out...."

What does he expect from me? Mitch asked himself. I come back from seven months undercover—life on the line every day of it—see my wife for the first time, and she's eight months pregnant! And during our first hour together, she collapses. "I have some R and R coming. I'll be there round the clock."

"I'll be back after I finish my rounds," he said, and headed for the door. He left nothing behind but the memory of his smug, know-it-all smirk. Harrumphing under his breath, Mitch remembered his dad's quote: "Give authority to a fool, and create a monster."

But in all fairness, the entire medical team had done a fine job. Mitch couldn't hold any of them accountable for the guilt roiling in his own gut...or for the shame boiling in his head.

You're the fool, he told himself. And if anybody's a monster, it's you. Because, hard as it was to admit, if he hadn't left Ciara alone all those months, she wouldn't have felt obliged to turn their house into a home all by herself. All that work, no doubt, put a terrible strain on her, mentally, physically....

He leaned his forearms over the bed's side rail, clasped his hands together and watched her sleep. He'd watched her sleep on their wedding night, too. Then, as now, she'd breathed so lightly, he'd had to strain to hear her inhale and exhale, the whisper softness of her sighs, he imagined, were what angels' wings might sound like. What had he ever done in his life to deserve an angel for a wife?

Just before she'd collapsed, Ciara had asked him to pack his things and leave. He hadn't wanted to do anything of the kind at the time, and he certainly had no intention of doing that now.

Well, they'd be spending a lot of time alone together in the few weeks to come. With God's help, Mitch hoped, he could earn Ciara's forgiveness, could make up for the many months he'd left her alone. He would take better care of her than her mother would. Mitch fancied himself a fair-to-middlin' cook, and his stint in the navy had taught him a thing or two about keeping his quarters shipshape.

He tucked the covers under her chin, smoothed the bangs from her forehead. Lord, but she's lovely, he thought. Her gracefully arched brows set off the long, lush lashes that dusted her lightly freckled cheeks, and her perfectly shaped full lips drew back in the barest hint of a smile.

What are you smiling about, pretty lady? he wondered, tucking a tendril of honey-blond hair behind her ear. You married the village idiot, and now you're stuck with him...at least till our baby is born.

Our baby....

Gently, so as not to wake her, he laid a hand on her stomach. "Hey, little fella," he whispered. "How's it goin' in there? You don't know me yet, but I'm your—"

The baby kicked, and Mitch's heartbeat doubled. He'd never experienced anything quite like it in his life...the sudden, insistent motion of his child, squirming beneath his palm. Ducking his head, Mitch leaned in closer and lifted his hand, like a boy who'd captured a butterfly might steal a peek at his prize.

The breath caught in his throat when he saw something—a tiny knee? a little heel?—shift beneath Ciara's pebbly white blanket. The egg-sized lump reminded him of the way Scooter the hamster looked, scurrying beneath Mitch's little-boy bedcovers. Grinning like the Cheshire Cat, his hand covered the mound yet again, following its passage, until the baby finally settled down.

If he knew he had an audience, would he continue to smile? Would he keep his hand pressed to his wife's stomach? Would his gaze remain glued to the stirring of the child—*his* child—alive inside her?

Ciara didn't think so. And so she continued to watch him through the narrow opening between her eyelids. *Thank you, Lord,* she prayed, *for showing me that Mitch does want this baby as much as I do.*

They were going to be spending a lot of time together in the next few weeks. Perhaps in that time, with the Lord's guidance, they could find a way to repair the damage they'd done to their marriage. A girl can hope and pray, she told herself.

Chapter Five

Peterson insisted that Ciara spend the night in the hospital, where she and the baby could be constantly monitored. At midnight, as the floor nurse was busy taking Ciara's vital signs, the doctor ushered Mitch into the hall.

"If you're smart," he said under his breath, "you'll go home, right now, and get a good night's sleep, because starting tomorrow, she's going to need you for everything." There in the dim hallway light, he'd lowered his voice to a near whisper. "I don't want her on her feet *at all*."

Mitch nodded.

"I know it's none of my business, Mr. Mahoney," the doctor added, "but it's obvious that *something* isn't right between you two." His voice took on a tone that reminded Mitch of his dad, scolding the four Mahoney boys when they allowed anything to interfere with school. The doctor continued, "Whatever your problems are, set them aside. Doesn't matter who's at fault or what it's all about. The only important thing right now is that we keep Ciara healthy so we can to take that baby to term."

Mitch remembered the thirty-six-week explanation: it's the critical time, the doctor had said, after which the baby's vital organs are mature enough for survival outside the womb without requiring mechanical assistance.

Peterson's voice had come to him as from a long, hollow tube. He shook his head to clear the cobwebs and focused on the man's words. "You realize she's lost a lot of blood...."

Another nod.

"And she may lose more...."

He met Peterson's eyes. Suddenly Mitch understood why, despite the belly, it seemed she'd lost weight. "I thought the bleeding had stopped."

"It has, for now. But placenta previa is a progressive condition," he said matter-of-factly. "She'll have good days and bad days."

"Until the baby's born?"

The doctor nodded somberly. "I'm afraid so."

"Not as much as today...." Four more weeks of that, and she would waste away to nothing....

"I want you to understand the gravity of Ciara's condition, Mr. Mahoney."

As he waited for the doctor to explain it Mitch's stomach twisted into a tight knot. He gritted his teeth so hard, his jaws ached. And deep in his pockets, his nails were digging gouges in his palms.

"If the placenta should tear, even slightly more, Ciara could hemorrhage." He paused, giving Mitch time to wrap his mind around the seriousness of his words. "If it should separate completely, it will mean instant death for your child."

Mitch's head began to pound. "Wouldn't...wouldn't she be better off here, in the hospital, where you guys could keep an eye on her? I mean, if something like that happened at home..." He ran a hand through his hair, scrubbed it over his face. "At least here, she'd have everything she'd need——"

Shaking his head, Peterson said, "I disagree. Placenta previa is a very stressful disorder. The mother is constantly aware that one wrong move could be fatal, for the baby, and possibly for her as well. It's been my experience that mothers-to-be rest and relax far better in their own homes, surrounded by the things—and the people—they love."

Despite the air-conditioning, Mitch began to perspire. He couldn't get his mind off the possibility that, if he hadn't left her alone, none of this would be happening. "What causes plug...ah——"

"Placenta previa," Peterson said, helping him along. Shrugging, the doctor shook his head. "There's no cause or reason for it that we can determine. We only know that it's there, to one degree or another, from the beginning of the pregnancy."

"Should we...should we take precautions so she won't have this problem in the future?"

"Are you asking whether or not the condition will repeat itself in future pregnancies?"

Mitch nodded.

"Despite the way things look now, Ciara is a healthy young woman. There's no reason to believe her next pregnancy will be anything but perfectly normal, with absolutely no complications."

Mitch breathed a sigh of relief. *So if you can pull her through this one, Mahoney...* "I don't mind tellin' you, doc, I'm scared to death. What if I mess up? I mean, there are two lives on the line, here...my wife's and my child's. I can't afford to make a mistake. Not even a small one." He met Peterson's eyes. "You're sure she's better off at home? Because I want to do whatever is best for Ciara."

Peterson smiled for the first time since he'd met the

man. "What you said just now is all the assurance I need that she'll be in the best of hands at home."

"But…but what if something goes wrong? What if the spotting turns into something more? What if—"

"I'm going to put in a call right now, so the equipment will be ready for delivery when you get home tomorrow."

"Equipment? What equipment?"

"The home monitor. Hooks up to the telephone and the TV, so we can get a look at what's going on without Ciara having to endure the trauma of driving back and forth for tests. Plus, every other day or so, a visiting nurse will stop by to see how things look, do a blood count. It's costly, but…"

"I don't give a whit about that. I only want what's best for Ciara and the baby." He hesitated. "How reliable is this equipment?"

Peterson's smile widened. "It'll do its job. You do yours, and everything will turn out just fine."

Mitch had undergone years of extensive training to become an FBI agent. Had never felt anything but capable and competent, even in the most dangerous of situations.

So why did he feel totally inept and inadequate now?

For the first half hour, Mitch walked through the house, turning on lights and investigating the contents of every room. Even his staff sergeant would have been hard-pressed to find a speck of dust anywhere. Everything gleamed, from the old-fashioned brass light fixtures hanging in the center of every ceiling to the hardwood and linoleum floors beneath his loafered feet.

He flopped, exhausted, into his recliner—a treat he hadn't enjoyed in seven long months—and put up his feet. From where he sat, he could see every award and citation he'd ever earned, hanging on the flagstone wall surrounding the fireplace. His guitar and banjo stood to one side of the woodstove insert, his collection of canes and walking sticks on the other. The ceramic wolves he'd acquired from yard sales and flea markets held up his hard-cover volumes of Koontz, King, Clancy and London.

The knowledge that, despite the way they'd parted, despite their many months apart, she'd turned this into "his" room swelled his heart with love for her...love and gratitude that she hadn't given up hope...no thanks to Bradley.

He grabbed the chair arms so tightly his fingertips turned white at the thought of his lieutenant's part in their separation. But one glance at their wedding portrait, framed in crystal beside the photo of Mitch taken as he trained at Quantico, cooled his ire. You can deal with Bradley later, he thought, grinding his molars together. Right now, you have to concentrate on Ciara.

Mitch closed his eyes and pictured her as he'd seen her last.

After thanking Peterson, he'd headed back to her hospital room, to tell her good-night and let her know he was heading home. Her eyes were closed, and thinking she was asleep, he'd started for the door.

"I'm glad to see you have *some* sense in your head," she'd said, her voice whisper-soft and drowsy. "It's about time you went home and got some rest."

He'd pulled the chair beside her bed closer, balanced on the edge of its seat. "How're you doin'? Feeling any better?"

"A little tired, but otherwise I'm fine." With a wave of her hand she had tried to shoo him away. "Go on, now. Get some sleep."

"I will," he'd said, taking her hand, "in a minute." He held her gaze for a long, silent moment. "You had me pretty scared there for a while." He kissed her knuckles. "It's good to see a little color back in your cheeks."

She'd smiled, sighed. "I'm sorry to be such a bother."

He kissed her knuckles again. "You must be delirious, because you're not making a bit of sense."

"I'm just trying to see things from your point of view. You come home from seven months of terrifying, dangerous, undercover work, and what do you find? Your wife, eight months pregnant and grouchy as a grizzly bear. And then—"

Gently, he'd pressed a finger over her lips. "Shhhh. You should be sleeping."

"True. At home. In my own bed. I know it's irrational, but I've always hated hospitals!"

"Dr. Peterson says you can come home tomorrow."

"But I feel fine. Why can't I—"

She'd looked so small, so vulnerable, lying there in that tilted-up hospital bed, that he couldn't help himself. Mitch leaned forward and silenced her with a tender kiss. A quiet little murmur had escaped her lips as she pressed a palm against his cheek. "You could use a shave, mister," she'd said, grinning mischievously as she rubbed his sandpapery whiskers, "unless you're going for that Don-Johnson-Miami-Vice look."

He'd assured her he wasn't, and promised to be clean shaven when he came to pick her up, first thing in the morning. Smiling now, Mitch opened his eyes and glanced at the carriage clock on the mantel. Two-thirty-five. And he still hadn't done anything to prepare for her homecoming....

Mitch dropped the recliner's footrest and got to his feet. Was the linen closet in the upstairs hall? Or was it the extra door in the main bathroom? He didn't have a clue, because they'd spent the first two weeks of their marriage traipsing back and forth between his condo in the city and her apartment in the suburbs as they'd waited for the former owners of the house to move out. And even after settlement, they'd spent alternate nights in his place or hers, too exhausted after putting in a full day at work, then packing all evening, to make the trip to their new home in Ellicott City.

They'd only been in the house, full-time, a few days when Mitch had left on assignment. And what with pictures leaning against every wall waiting to be hung, and stacks of books cluttering the floors, he'd spent most of that time picking his way through the mess.

Taking the stairs two at a time, he went in search of linens for Ciara's daytime bed.

The extra door in the bathroom, as it turned out, was where Ciara stored bathroom linens. Beneath neatly folded towels and washcloths, the shelves had been lined with muted green and blue plaid paper that matched the shower curtain. There had been a hideous black and silver wallpaper in here when they'd bought the place, and a putrid gray rug on the floor. Now, the walls were seafoam green, the door and window frames dusty blue. Like the family room, she'd chosen patterns and colors that were neither overly feminine nor masculine. "A man's home is his castle," she'd said when they'd discussed the changes they would make in the house. "When he comes home from a hard day's work, a man shouldn't be made to feel like he's about to be smothered by ruffles and chintz."

Mitch grinned and headed for the hall. He was beginning to understand why she'd been able to sweep him off his feet.... The things she'd said during their three-month courtship had dazzled him. No woman he'd known had ever talked of being there for him, of doing for him, of taking care of him. As he looked around at square-edged shams that topped off tailored comforters, at fabrics and carpeting and bold-framed prints—each that had been carefully selected and positioned—he realized Ciara had meant every word.

A pang of regret clutched his heart. You could have

been enjoying this all these months. And where were you instead? Playing cops and robbers.

He opened the linen closet door, where sheets and pillowcases, blankets and comforters had been tidily folded and stacked. He'd seen department store displays that didn't look half as orderly. On a high shelf he saw that she'd stowed away a delicate-looking pink-and-lavender-flowered sheet set. Beside it, a set with a bright blue background and big bold sunflowers. She'd put a lot of thought into making this house a home he'd be comfortable in. The least he could do was give equal care to which sheets he'd put on the bed where she'd be spending endless hours. The soft-toned floral pattern reminded him of Ciara…feminine, dainty, utterly womanly. But the sunflowers were like her, too, in that they were spritely, happy, youthful.

You could play it safe…put plain white sheets on the bed…. He bounced the idea around in his mind for a moment. In college, he'd learned a thing or two about the psychology of color. White symbolized purity, cleanliness, and often served as a pallet, an enhancer for other colors. It enlivened, energized, expanded spaces. Shades of purple offered comfort and assurance, while yellow created an atmosphere of energy and cheerfulness….

He grabbed the sunflowers and headed downstairs.

During his three-year stint in the navy, he'd learned a thing or two about making up a bed. Those lessons were for naught, since the sofa bed's mattress was too thin to turn sharp hospital corners, or tuck the ends under, ensuring a snug, smooth fit. But it would do for resting during the day.

During the drive home, he'd worked it all out in his head: at bedtime, he'd carry her upstairs and tuck her into bed, and in the morning, he'd carry her back down to the sofa bed. Because if he'd been the one who'd been confined to quarters for an entire month, he would go stir-crazy, alone in an upstairs room. Besides, she'd spent enough time all by herself already, thanks to him.

Mitch turned back the bedcovers in a triangle, as the maids on the cruise ship had done, smoothed them flat, then stood back to admire his handiwork. Nodding with approval, he headed for the kitchen. As he filled a tumbler with the lemonade she'd made that morning, Mitch noticed a red circle around today's date. It's three-fifteen in the morning; yesterday's date, he corrected, yawning, that's *yesterday's* date.... He squinted, read the reminder she'd printed in the date box. "Pick up Chester at Dr. Kingsley's."

He hadn't given a thought to the dog, and wondered what malady had put the retriever into the vet's office. Fleas? Ingrown toenails? Mange? He'd never been overly fond of canines, and Chester could be a miserable pest, sitting beside the bed at five in the morning, whining until Mitch or Ciara got up to let him out. Just one more of the compromises he'd made in order to get Ciara to agree to marry him.

She hated big-city life, so he'd sold his condo in the singles building near Baltimore's Inner Harbor and agreed to live in the suburbs. He didn't want a dog, but she'd had Chester for five years and couldn't part with him. He'd wanted to honeymoon in a johnboat on the Patapsco River, where he could spend a lazy week casting for trout; she'd wanted to luxuriate in the islands, where they'd met. And so they'd gone to Martha's Vineyard, spent two days fishing and two days walking on the windy beaches. Mitch had a feeling that in the weeks to come, he would experience *compromise* on an entirely new level.

He swallowed the last of his lemonade and headed upstairs, set the alarm for seven. Four hours' sleep would do; he'd gotten by, plenty of times, on less. After a quick shower and shave, he would look up Kingsley's address in Ciara's personal phone book. Wouldn't she be surprised when she got into the car, to find her shaggy pup hanging over the front seat to greet her!

Mitch stepped into the closet with the intention of grabbing the jeans and a short-sleeved pullover to wear the next day. But when he flipped on the light, he could only stare in wonderment at Ciara's handiwork. She'd given him the entire left side of the walk-in, and had hung his suits and sports coats on the rack above his shirts and jeans. Casual and dress shirts had been grouped by color and sleeve length. His neatly folded jeans had been stacked on an eye-level shelf, sweaters on the next, shoes in a precise row on the bottom. Ties and belts had been given their own sliding racks, to make one-at-a-time choosing easier.

How long ago had she organized this? he wondered, moving to the dresser in search of socks and briefs. There, too, her homemaking skills were evidenced by the systematic placement of tennis shorts, T-shirts and pajamas. She couldn't have been serious when she'd said he should pack up and leave. If she *had* been, would she have aligned his possessions in such a creative way?

Mitch didn't think so. She loves you—whether you deserve it or not—and the proof is all over this house! Sighing, he dropped the clothes he'd been wearing into the clothes hamper, pulled back the dark green quilt and maroon blanket and climbed between crisp white sheets. The minute his head hit the pillow, the scent of her—baby-powder light, yet utterly womanly—wafted into his nostrils. He fell asleep, a half grin slanting his mouth, hugging that pillow tight.

"Me and you, and you and me, no matter how they tossed the dice, it had to be," the Turtles crooned, "happy together, so happy together...." Mitch slapped the alarm's Off button and, rolling onto his back, yawned heartily. After a moment of noisy stretching, he climbed out of bed and padded into the bathroom to adjust the spray for his morning shower, humming the melody of the oldies but goodies song that had awakened him. "...and you're the only one for me," he sang off-key. If you've got to have a song stuck in your head, at least this one is appropriate, he told himself, belting it out, then grinning as the sound of his own voice echoed in the master bathroom's tiled stall.

Here, too, Ciara had seen to it there would never be a doubt whose house this was. The walls were white and the trim the same dusty blue she'd used in the hall bath. Like a professional interior designer, she'd carried the color scheme throughout the house, creating a feeling of organized unity that was both warm and welcoming. How'd you get a woman like that? he wondered as he toweled off.

Bradley had paid him a similar compliment that night in his office when Mitch had been given the undercover assignment. The lieutenant had taken one look at the picture of Ciara on his desk and said, "How'd you get a beauty like that?"

Mitch felt his blood boil just thinking about Bradley.

One thing was certain, Mitch knew, as he swiped steam from the mirror, not even nepotism was going to net Bradley the job they'd both been drooling over for over a year. The lieutenant's uncle may have wielded enough power to garner him a grade hike in the past, may have packed enough punch, even, to get him the job that put him in charge of a dozen field agents, but—

"Enjoy it while it lasts, *Chet*," Mitch said, smiling to himself, "'cause when the director hears what you did to me, you'll be history."

It had been Bradley's job...no...his *duty* to act as the

go-between for husbands under his command and the wives they'd left behind. He had lied, repeatedly and deliberately, about the letters that should have gone from Mitch to Ciara and back again, and he'd done it to set Mitch up.

At first Mitch blamed the chill snaking up his back on cold air from the floor vent. But he knew better. The creepy "somebody's watching" feeling had nothing to do with air-conditioning. Bradley hated him...enough to see him dead. That's what caused the sensation.

He was hoping that not hearing from Ciara would screw up my head, distract me, make me mess up. Didn't much matter whether those mistakes would cost the government its case...or Mitch his life. Either way, Bradley's competition for that job...and any other down the road...would be forever eliminated.

If he could do it to Mitch, Bradley was just as capable of putting other agents in harm's way...if he saw them as a threat of any kind. Mitch owed it to the agency to see to it Bradley never got the chance to repeat his crime. He was aching to get the old ball rolling...right over Bradley, if possible. But filing reports, verbalizing complaints, setting things in motion would take countless hours down at headquarters. And his place was beside Ciara now, not avenging a wrong.

There'll be plenty of time to see that Bradley pays, Mitch thought, opening the medicine cabinet. "Good gravy," he said aloud, "she's alphabetized this, too." Grinning, he recalled the pantry, where canned goods and cracker boxes had been lined up in *A, B, C* order. Same for the spices. "So my Escada would be..." His forefinger drew a spiral in the air as he tried to guess which of the bottles held his favorite aftershave.

The first, Armando, then Comandante, and beside it, a travel-size flask of Homme Jusqu'au Dernier. "What's this?'' he asked aloud. "Hamma Jooo Aw...?'' But try as he might, Mitch could not pronounce the fancy French name. "So, Mrs. Mahoney,'' he said, rearranging the bottles, "you're not perfect after all...*E* comes before *H*....''

Curiosity compelled him to unscrew the foreign bottle's cap and take a whiff of the cologne she'd added to his regular stock. "Bleh-yuck,'' he complained, coughing as he peered into the tiny opening.

Half-empty? That's odd....

Even if Ciara had bought it the day after he left, it wouldn't have evaporated this much in seven months. Eyes and lips narrowing, he asked himself why the aroma seemed so familiar. The rage began slowly, then escalated, like an introductory drumroll: It was that no-good Bradley's brand. What's *his* aftershave doing in my—

With trembling hands, Mitch recapped the container and pitched it into the wicker wastebasket beside the vanity. Heart pounding and pulse racing, his mouth went dry, and despite many gulps of water, it stayed that way. He had a hard time swallowing, because his throat and tongue seemed to have swelled to three times their normal size. A vein began throbbing in his temple, and his ears were ringing. His hands became suddenly clumsy, knocking over the toothbrush holder and the soap dish as he attempted to hold a paper cup under running water.

Unable to stand still, he began pacing in the small space, his big feet tangling in the scatter rug on the floor. Mitch steadied himself, one hand on the counter, the other pressed tight to the wall. "What's Bradley's aftershave doing in my medicine cabinet?'' he demanded, his hoarse whisper bouncing off all four walls.

Ciara's face came to mind, all sweet and smiling and big-eyed innocence. She'd been a devout Christian girl when he'd left her. Had loneliness and despair driven her into another man's arms? Had she turned to Bradley for comfort, and—

"No!" he bellowed, bringing his fist down hard on the sink. "That's *my* kid she's carrying, *not* Bradley's!" The mere thought of her in another man's arms started his stomach turning. Because she'd asked him to pack his things and leave, even after he explained everything....

But it had been *his* hand she'd reached for in the emergency room, and *his* gaze she'd locked on to for encouragement and support. He thought of their goodbye kiss in her hospital room the night before and the way she'd so tenderly touched his cheek, looking into his eyes as if she believed he'd hung the moon.

She *had* believed that once, before he'd gone to Philadelphia. Did she believe it still? Or had her love for him been strangled by the choking loneliness of endless days and nights without a word from him?

No...she'd genuinely seemed to need him, there at the hospital. But then, she'd been scared to death, for herself *and* the baby. If Bradley had been there instead, would she have clung to *his* hand? Would she have looking lovingly into *his* eyes?

Everything around him, every towel and curtain, every knickknack and picture, every stick of furniture, screamed out that she loved him. What more proof did he need than the way she'd turned this place into a haven for him in his absence?

He ran both hands through his damp hair, held them there. A strange grating sound caught his attention, and he attuned his ears, trying to identify it. He exhaled a great huff of air when he determined that what he'd heard had been the rasps of his own ragged breathing.

He remembered that moment in the foyer, when she'd announced in her calm, matter-of-fact way that she'd been carrying his baby on the night he left. His baby. Of *course* it was his baby! She'd been so proud to be his wife that in those first weeks of their marriage he'd found things all over the house—envelopes, lunch bags, the TV listings—covered with her fanciful script: "Mrs. Mitchell Riley Mahoney. Ciara Neila Mahoney. Ciara Mahoney. Mrs. Ciara Mahoney."

And what about the way she'd trembled virginally in his arms on their wedding night, when he'd made her his wife in every sense of the word? It had taken time, but his soft-spoken words and gentle touches and tender kisses soothed her fears. "I'll never hurt you," he'd vowed. "Trust me, sweetie...."

Their eyes had met—hers glistening with unshed tears of hope and joy and anticipation, his blazing with intensity—and she'd sent him a trembly little smile.

He'd absorbed the tremors of fear that had pulsed from her, returned them to her as soothing waves of love and comfort. "It's all right, sweetie," he'd crooned, stroking her back. "We'll take our time...."

He'd kissed her eyelids, her cheeks, her throat, his fingers combing through her lovely silken hair. "I love you, Mitch," she'd breathed. "I love you so much!"

And then her touches, her kisses, her words of love rained upon him, as if she sought a way to show him that she'd meant it when she'd said that she trusted him, that she loved him with all her heart.

And for the first time in his life, Mitch understood why God had decreed that marriage was a sacred and blessed thing. The Lord intended this kind of loving warmth as a gift...a physical illustration of His own intense love for His children.

In the morning, he had awakened first, rolled onto his side to watch his sleeping bride. Her cheeks were still rosy from the night's ardor, and he'd reached out to draw a finger lightly down the bridge of her lightly-freckled nose.

Her long-lashed eyes had fluttered, opened. "I love you, Mitchell Riley Mahoney," she'd whispered. Then she'd snuggled close.

Later, as she lay cuddled against him, Ciara had said, "Remember what you said last night...?"

He'd met her eyes. "You mean that verse from Ecclesiastes, 'Enjoy life with the wife whom you love.'"

"Yes," she'd whispered. "Marriage to you is going to be very romantic, I think...."

Now, in the distance Mitch heard the dim notes of the carriage clock on the family-room mantel and counted eight chimes. He couldn't have stood there, lost in memories, for nearly an hour! But he hadn't dawdled when the alarm sounded at seven; he'd leaped out of bed and stepped straight into the shower.

Taking a deep breath, he faced the sink. "She loves you. Of *course* she loves you," he told the wild-eyed man in the mirror. Either that, or she's the best actress ever born.

One bottle of aftershave was no proof of any wrongdoing. It might not even be Bradley's...perhaps her father had spent a night or two in the house, to help out, keep an eye on his daughter's failing health. Maybe—

Lord Jesus, he prayed, *I don't want to believe the worst, but*— "You're a special agent with the Federal Bureau of Investigation," he said to himself, squirting an egg-sized dollop of shaving cream into the palm of his left hand. With the right, he painted it over the lower half of his face. "If you can't get to the bottom of this," he added, touching the razor to his cheek, "you don't deserve to carry the badge."

One bright splotch of red bled through the white foam, then another, as his quaking hand dragged the blade over his skin. Mitch barely noticed. The stinging, biting sensation of the tiny razor cuts was nothing compared to the ache in his heart.

Chapter Six

The golden-haired retriever scooted back and forth across the linoleum like a pendulum counting the happy seconds until Mitch managed to attach the leash to the dog's collar. "C'mon, fella," he said, ruffling Chester's thick coat, "let's go get Mom."

Chester whimpered.

"I know, I know," Mitch said, unlocking the car door, "I miss her, too."

And he did. He'd decided on the way to the veterinary clinic that it must have been a horrible coincidence that Chet Bradley's brand of aftershave had ended up in his medicine cabinet. Maybe Ciara got a free sample in the mail, he thought. Wrinkling his nose, he thought of its odor, which reminded him of rearview-mirror air freshener and horseradish. He could only hope if the freebie had come with a coupon for a bigger bottle, Ciara hadn't saved it.

By the time he had parked in the hospital parking lot and passed through the main entrance, Mitch believed his head was in the right place. At least he hoped it was. It had better be, he warned himself, or this next month is going to be miserable, for both of you.

As he strolled down the hall toward her room, he heard the melodic notes of Ciara's girlish laughter. The lilting sound of it thrilled him…until the grating tones of a man's chortle joined it, sending waves of heated jealousy coursing through him. "If your husband ever gets bored with you," the young man was saying when Mitch entered the room, "give me a call, 'cause women like you don't grow on trees." He spotted Mitch, leaning on the door frame, one foot crossed over the other, hands in his pockets. "You Mr. Mahoney?"

A tight-lipped grin on his face, Mitch nodded.

The blood technician scribbled Ciara's name on two white labels. "Lucky man," he said. "Where's a woman like this when *I'm* in the market for a relationship?" He stuck the labels to the vials containing her blood samples, lifted his case and walked toward the door. "The lady I'm dating now thinks *man* and *diamonds* are synonymous," he said from the hallway. And with a quick glance back at Ciara, he repeated, "Lucky man," and headed for his next patient.

Not once in the months he'd been gone had Mitch considered the possibility that she'd violate their marriage vows. *One lousy bottle of stinking cologne,* he told himself, *is no cause for mistrust now.* He had no reason to be jealous of Ciara, because she'd given him no reason to be.

The image of that cologne, standing on the glass shelf in the medicine cabinet as if it belonged, flashed in his mind. And right on its heels, the blatantly flirtatious comments of the good-looking young man who'd just left her room. So he told himself: you'd better get used to guys flirting with your wife; it's what you did, first time you saw her. Besides, what did you expect when you married a knockout? Mitch grinned despite himself, and looked at his wife. Yeah, she sure was a knockout.

Despite a night's sleep, Ciara still looked pale and drawn, but she was smiling and seemed happy to see him. "Good morning," she said brightly, her eyes still puffy, her voice early-morning raspy. "Did you sleep well?"

"Like a baby," he answered, the memory of her scent, clinging to the pillowcase, hovering in his mind.

Ciara raised a brow. "Are you aware that babies wake up every two hours?"

Mitch chuckled. "You trying to scare me? 'Cause if you are, you'll have to try harder."

She sent him a knowing grin that was both motherly and wifely. "I'm glad you slept well." The grin became a soft, sweet smile as she leaned back against her pillows. "I remember the way you always prepared for bed. I used to think if it wouldn't mar the woodwork, you'd have cross-barred every opening with two-by-fours and ten-penny nails. It's a wonder you get any sleep at all, worrying the way you do."

Some might call his before-bed ritual eccentric to the point of psychotic. Not Ciara. Even the first time she'd witnessed it, she had treated his fussiness matter-of-factly, as if all the men in America bolted every door, locked each window, pulled the blinds...and checked twice to make sure he hadn't overlooked anything. He'd never explained it, and Ciara had never asked him to. But Mitch had been out there, had seen the vile and vicious things human beings could do to one another. He wasn't about to take any chances. Not with his wife's safety.

She'd viewed it as routine, like showering and shaving. Which amazed him, considering his recurrent nightmare.

It had disturbed his sleep almost hourly those first months after he'd been kidnapped. Gradually it plagued him less often. By the time he met Ciara, the horrid images only came to him when he'd skipped a night's sleep or went to bed more tired than usual.

They'd been married exactly two days, and he'd gone to bed that second night of their honeymoon. The excitement of the wedding, all that dancing at the reception, the long drive to Martha's Vineyard…Mitch should have expected it, should have warned her. But he'd been so happy, so content with his new life that he hadn't even thought to bring it up.

When she'd roused him, he'd almost slugged her, because in that instant between sleeping and waking, he'd mistaken her for the unseen enemy of his nightmare.

He'd felt a deep, burning shame when she'd seen him that way, trembling, breathing like he'd just run a mile, on the verge of tears like a small helpless boy. The man of the family was supposed to protect his wife, he'd chided himself as the tremors racked his perspiration-slicked limbs; the husband was supposed to comfort and reassure the wife after a nightmare, not the other way around.

But her strong yet delicate hand, gently shaking his shoulder, had brought him to, and her soft, sweet voice, had pulled him from the nightmarish haze. Ciara had snuggled close, her cool fingertips smoothing the sweat-dampened hair back from his forehead. "You were having a bad dream," she'd whispered, "but it's all right now. Everything is all right."

Amazingly, it had been. Relieved to be in her arms, he clutched her to him and moaned into the crook of her neck. "Thank God," he'd rasped. "Praise Almighty God."

And she'd rocked him, kissing his tightly-shut eyes. "Shhh. It's all right," she'd crooned. "It's all right."

He remembered thinking at the time that she'd be a terrific mother someday, because she was certainly good at this comforting stuff.

Until she'd begun kissing away his tears, he hadn't been

aware he'd started to sob. Her soft touches, her tender kisses, her soothing words of love rained upon him and slowly washed the agony away. The festering sore of his fear healed that night; he hadn't had the dream since. *God in Heaven,* he prayed, *I love her...love her like crazy.*

It had been on the morning after she'd witnessed the aftereffects of his nightmare, as she drew lazy circles in his chest hair, that Ciara had discovered the gunshot wound on his rib cage and he'd told her the story of how it had happened. She'd been shocked, horrified. "It's such a *dangerous* job, Mitch," she'd said, on the verge of tears. Between that and what had happened to Abe Carlson, the idea of his leaving the Bureau was never far from her mind after that.

The sound of her voice reached his ears, bringing him back to the present, and Mitch wondered how long she'd been happily chattering there in the hospital bed, while his mind had been wandering.

"And I don't suppose you got one decent night's sleep the whole time you were gone," she was saying in that affectionate, scolding way that made him feel loved and protected and wanted, all rolled into one. She shrugged, then aimed the finger at him again. "How could you, when the job required that you sleep with one ear perked and one eye open the whole time?"

Mitch chuckled. "You make it sound like I was fighting a war."

She wasn't smiling when she said, "You *were.*"

This was the Ciara he had thought about day and night, the Ciara he'd dreamed of while he'd been away. *This* was the Ciara he'd fallen in love with...caring about his every need, even in her very delicate condition. How could you have even suspected her of being unfaithful? he asked himself.

She's as innocent as that baby she's carrying; either that or she missed her calling as an actress.

The dark thought hovered there in his mind for a moment, blotting out the joy the bright one had given him. Her innocence, her sweetness...could it be nothing but an act?

"I've taken care of the paperwork," he heard her say, "so you wouldn't have to bother when you got here." Ciara sighed, and smiling, a hand on her big tummy.

"Thanks," he said, forcing a grin. "You're too good to me."

"I hate to admit it," she said, her eyes alight with mischief, "but I didn't do it for you." She patted her tummy. "I just can't *wait* to get us home!"

"I have a surprise for you...in the car," Mitch said, and pictured Chester, who was no doubt slathering the rear windows of the Mustang with what Ciara lovingly referred to as "joy juice."

"I don't know if I can handle any more surprises," she said, a half smile on her face.

He sat beside her on the edge of the bed, a hand atop her stomach. "I did this while you were sleeping last night," he said, "and this kid of ours did quite a dance for me. Any chance I'll get a repeat performance?"

She patted his hand. "The little imp wakes me up every morning between five and six. Sorry, but you missed the first show."

Unable to hide his disappointment, Mitch screwed up one corner of his mouth.

"Don't pout, Mahoney. There's usually a matinee right around lunchtime." She tilted her head, studied his face for a quiet moment. "Free admission for dads only," she added, winking.

"I'll be there, front row center," he said, looking into

her beautiful, exhausted face. "Now what say we get you dressed and go home?"

Ciara nodded and threw back the covers.

"You were dressed under there?"

"I've been ready since dawn." Then, sending a glance toward the door, she whispered, "They must set the thermostat at ten above freezing. I was shivering in that flimsy T-shirt and stretch pants!"

He tucked a tendril of hair behind her ear. "Then you'll be happy to know it's still a pleasant seventy-five degrees at home," he said. "Now you sit tight, while I scrounge up a wheelchair."

Ciara rolled her eyes and harrumphed. "Wheelchair? I'm going to hate this."

He held up a silencing hand. "I know that lying around for a whole month is going to be tough on a go-get-'em gal like you, but you'll do it...for the baby's sake." He drew her to him in a sideways hug. "Why not look at these 'lady of leisure' weeks as a gift from heaven?"

Ciara leaned her head on his shoulder and nodded. "I suppose you're right. I'll be getting all kinds of exercise once the baby is born, won't I?"

Suddenly she bracketed his face with both hands. "No matter what I say, you stick to your guns, you hear? Keep a tight rein on me, even if I give you a hard time...and I think we both know that's possible."

"Possible!" he said, laughing softly, then kissing her temple. "You may as well say 'It's possible the sun will rise in the east. It's possible spring will follow winter, it's possible—'"

"I'll try to be a good patient, Mitch."

He rested his chin on top of her head. "'Course you will. And I'll be the best doctor stand-in you ever saw." He wagged a finger under her nose. "But I feel it's only fair to warn you…I'm going to be a tough taskmaster where your health is concerned.''

She nodded. Sighed. ''So go get the wheelchair, Doctor Killjoy,'' she said, grinning. ''I want to go *home*.''

Mitch carried her into the family room and gently deposited her on the sofa bed, got onto his knees and began untying her white sneakers. Their trip home had been swift and Ciara's reunion with Chester had been well worth the trouble of bringing the big guy along.

She grabbed his wrists. ''Mitch, you don't have to—''

He sent her a silent warning that silenced her.

Ciara rolled her eyes. ''I never thought I'd see the day when I'd be so helpless I couldn't even take off my own shoes,'' she complained.

''Look at it this way—once they're off, you won't be putting them on again, so you were only 'this helpless' once.''

She grinned. ''When did you start seeing the silver lining? I thought you were the type who just saw dark clouds?''

Mitch shrugged. ''Things aren't always what they seem. You know what happens when you judge a book by its cover?'' he smirked good-naturedly. ''You bite the hand that feeds you, that's what.''

''Please—'' she laughed, hands up in surrender ''—one more bad cliché, and I'm liable to explode.''

He patted her tummy and twisted his face into a pleading frown. ''Please, don't. At least not till the equipment arrives.''

''Equipment? What equipment?''

''Didn't Peterson tell you? He put in an order for a home monitor. You're gonna be on TV, pretty lady!''

Ciara frowned. ''What in the world are you talking about? Dr. Peterson didn't say anything to me about—''

"The machinery will be delivered today. Way I understand it, we're to plug you in to the monitor, then plug the monitor into the phone and the TV, so Peterson can read the printout that'll come out at his office."

"A fetal heart monitor?"

He shrugged. "Guess so. I never thought to ask what kind." He plunged on. "Plus a nurse will be stopping by every other day to do a blood count—" he winked "—make sure you're not melting or anything. You'll get used to it. Maybe you'll even grow to like it."

She'd harrumphed. "'Fetal' attraction, huh?"

"There's more than one way to kill a rabbit." He held up a hand to forestall another cliché warning. "Sorry," he said. "But technically, that was a pun, not a cliché."

Ciara rolled her eyes. "It's going to be a long, long month...."

"No way, honey. Time always flies when you're having fun. And I'm going to see to it you have plenty of fun. Now sit still so I can get your shoes off. You're supposed to keep your feet elevated as much as possible." He tugged at the snow-white shoelace. "First chance I get, I'm gonna write a letter and complain about the condition of the roads in this county. There are more potholes between here and the hospital than a zebra has stripes. That trip home is likely to have—"

She laid a hand alongside his cheek. "No need to waste a stamp on my account. I'm fine. Tired, but fine."

She must have read his mind again, and knowing he was about to say she didn't *look* fine, Ciara glanced around her.

"When did you find time to do all this?" she asked. "You must have been up all night. The bed's made up all nice as you please, and you've moved the end table forward so I can reach it, even while I'm lying flat on my back,'' she said. ''You've thought of everything...tissues, books, magazines, the remote.''

She met his eyes, her own wide with surprise. ''Wait just a minute, here...you're giving *me* control of the clicker?'' Ciara tilted her head and propped a fist on a hip. ''Why, Mitchell Riley Mahoney, are you flirting with me?''

The way you flirted with Bradley while I was away?

Mitch shook his head, cleared his throat. Where did *that* come from? he wondered, surprised by the sudden intrusion of the suspicious thought. He forced a smile. ''I was hoping you'd be sleeping a lot, and I could slip it out from under your hand now and then.''

He pointed at the summer-weight gown and matching robe he'd laid out for her. ''Let's get you into your pajamas, and once you're all tucked in, I'll see what I can rustle us up for lunch.''

When Ciara glanced at the nightclothes, Mitch noticed the slight flush that pinked her cheeks. They hadn't had much time together as man and wife, but he'd seen her in a nightie before. Surely she wasn't still feeling timid and shy, as she had on their wedding night. *I'll bet you weren't this modest with—* He stopped himself, wondering where on earth those thoughts were coming from.

''How 'bout I start lunch, let you slip into these...by yourself.''

She bit her lower lip. Rolled her eyes. ''You must think I'm the silliest thing on two feet.'' Hiding behind her hands, she mumbled, ''It's just— I'm...I'm so *huge*, Mitch. Last time you saw me, I had an hourglass figure, and now I look like a—''

''You've never been more beautiful. Don't you say one negative word about my gorgeous, very pregnant wife,'' he scolded, ''or I'll have to arrest you.''

They hadn't been together long, but had managed to

develop a private joke or two. Ciara had always known that despite outward appearances—tough-cop sternness, badge and gun, the sometimes violent things he'd been forced to do in the line of duty—Mitch was nothing but a big softie.

Ciara leaned her cheek against his upheld palm, nuzzled against it, like a house cat in search of a good ear scratching. He'd been sitting on his heels and rose to his knees now. "If you don't stop looking at me with those big, blue eyes..." Those big blue *loving* eyes....

"Can't help myself," she sighed. "I'm just so glad to be home." Ciara hesitated, then added, "I'm glad you're back, Mitch."

His arms went around her, as naturally as if he'd been doing it dozens of times daily for the past seven months, and hers slipped around him just as easily. Their lips met, softly at first, and what began as a gentle kiss intensified.

Oh, but it felt good to be with her this way, as man and wife again. He'd missed her while he'd been away, but until this moment—now that her condition had stabilized and she was out of danger—he hadn't realized exactly how much.

She pulled away, inhaled a great draft of air.

Like a man too long in the desert yearns for water, his lips sought hers again.

"Do you still love me?" she murmured against his open mouth.

A palm on each of her cheeks, he sat back to study her face. Surely she wasn't serious.

The raised brows and pouting lower lip told him she was. Did she really think it was possible for him to *stop?* "Ciara, sweetie, I've always loved you. From the minute I first saw you, looking out to sea at the rail of that beat-up old cruise ship, I loved you...."

"Beat-up? I'll have you know that was once *The Love Boat*."

"Yeah. Right. Like they had such things a century ago. But you can't distract me that easily," he said, an eyebrow cocked. "Every minute that passes, I love you more. I've never stopped. Not for a heartbeat. Couldn't if I tried." *Not even if I find out that you and Bradley—* Mitch swallowed. His ping-ponging emotions were sure to make him crazy…if they didn't give him a heart attack first.

"Thank you," she said, her voice thick and sweet as syrup.

"Thank you?" he echoed, a wry grin tilting his mouth. "You've been to the movies. You know how it's supposed to be done." He held a finger aloft and began the lesson. "I say 'I love you,' and you say 'I love you, too.' Not 'thank you' but 'I love you.'" Mitch chuckled, tenderly grasped her lips with the fingertips of both hands, and gently manipulated her mouth. "'I love you,'" he said, as if he were the ventriloquist and she his dummy. "Go on, now you try it, all by yourself."

She kissed his playful fingers. "I *am* grateful, Mitch. What's wrong with admitting it?"

She branded him with an alluring, hypnotic gaze. His heart ached and his stomach flipped. *There's nothing wrong with admitting that,* he wanted to tell her, *but it isn't what I need to hear right now.*

After a seemingly endless moment, Ciara closed her eyes. "I love you more today than yesterday," she whispered, reciting the old promise with heartfelt feeling, "but not as much as tomorrow."

He held her, and she melted in his arms, her rounded little body feeling warm and reassuring as it pressed tightly against him. "It's good to be home," he admitted, putting aside his worries that she might be carrying another man's child. "I'm sorry I was gone so lo—"

She silenced him with a kiss.

The memory lapse was short-lived.

Did she kiss Bradley? The ugly thought took his breath away, and he ended the intimate moment. Mitch sat on the edge of the sofa bed with his back to her and ran both hands through his hair. *What's wrong with you, Mahoney? One minute you're sure as shootin' she couldn't have cheated on you, the next you're just as sure she did. What's it gonna take to make up your mind!*

He could ask her, straight-out, for starters. If she was innocent, she'd be shocked, hurt, furious, that he hadn't trusted her. But if she was guilty, didn't he have a right to know?

Mitch shook his head. Asking her was out of the question. At least for now. *If you haven't figured it out by the time the baby's born...* He gulped down the last of the coffee he'd brought her. *Until then, she's to rest and stay calm.*

If the child was his, he wanted to ensure a healthy birth. Even if it wasn't, well, the baby hadn't played a part in the duplicity that led to its conception. It deserved nothing but good things, no matter who its father was.

"Fine waiter you are," she teased, "bringing me fresh-brewed coffee, then drinking it yourself."

He looked over his shoulder at her sweet, smiling face. "I'll get you a refill."

Let it be my kid, he prayed as he headed for the kitchen. *Please let it be my kid....*

Ciara listened to Mitch in the kitchen, clattering pots and pans and utensils, and remembered that kiss. Guilt hammered in her heart. She would never have deliberately hurt him, but she had, and the proof had been the abrupt way he'd ended their brief intimacy.

She'd said a lot to hurt him yesterday. Maybe after lunch

they could discuss it a little more quietly than they had the night he'd left, or yesterday morning when he'd phoned from headquarters, or later, before she'd collapsed.

That old spark is still there, strong and bright as ever. Ciara touched her fingertips to her lips, remembering how wonderful it felt to be in his arms again, to be kissing him again. She hadn't realized how much she'd missed him, until the old familiar stirrings of passion erupted within her.

But I need time, she thought, *time to forget all those months alone, time to be sure he won't do it again.*

Every wifely instinct in her had made Ciara want to reach out and comfort him when he'd ended the kiss, turned away from her and held his head in his hands. But what would she have said? What might she have done? Since nothing had come to mind, she'd chosen instead to make light of it, to behave as if she hadn't noticed at all. "Fine waiter you are," she'd teased when he drained her cup in one gulp.

You're not in this alone, you know, she reminded herself. *It's hard for Mitch, too.* She sipped the refill of decaf he'd brought her and sighed. Their love had been as deep and wide as the Montana sky, bright with joy, deep with companionship, hot with passion. *Will we ever get back to that?* Ciara slumped against the cool, pillowy backrest of the sofa bed and closed her eyes. *Please God, help us find our way back.*

Right from the start, she and Mitch, like the boy and girl next door who'd known each other a lifetime, had felt relaxed and at ease in each other's presence. It had been that factor more than any other that told her it would be safe to fall in love so soon after the pastor's cordial introduction.

Ciara missed that serenity, the satisfaction born of the comfort they shared. Not take-you-for-granted comfort, but the old-shoe-dependable kind that she sensed would wrap around them—warming, soothing, nourishing their love—for a lifetime. She'd heard all about the fireworks-and-sparks kind of love, and had never wanted any part of it. *I'll take charcoal over flash paper any day,* she'd thought, because paper burned hot and quick...and died the same way. Coal might not heat up as fast, but it stayed warm a whole lot longer. She likened Mitch to charcoal—steady, sure, lasting. No one had been more surprised than Ciara to discover that her calm, dependable guy turned out to be a hot-blooded, passionate man.

You can't judge a book by its cover, he'd said earlier that day. But Ciara had said it first...on their wedding night.

Once they'd passed that initial test, she and Mitch had not needed the traditional "getting to know you" time her married friends had warned her about. It was a miracle, Ciara believed, that they'd *started out* feeling like life-mates. Their time apart had all but destroyed that comfortable, companionable feeling. But the passion was still there; that kiss proved it. Perhaps that was God's way of telling them the rest could be salvaged, if they were willing to work at it.

Ciara prayed for all she was worth. "Lord," she whispered, "I love him, Lord. Help us." She shook her head. "Help us repair the damage, so that our child will never know the loneliness that comes from living with parents who aren't in love."

Her mom and dad had always claimed to love each other deeply, and from time to time, they'd actually put on a pretty good show of it. She suspected things weren't quite right before she was seven. By the time she turned ten, Ciara had seen through their ruse. She didn't want her child wondering the things that she'd wondered as a girl: had their love for *her* been an act, as well?

"I hope you're cooking up an appetite," Mitch called from the kitchen, breaking into her thoughts, "because I'm cooking up one special lunch out here...."

He'd fixed her a meal once, days before he left. Breakfast, as she recalled, chuckling to herself. She'd been in the front hall, trying to decide whether to store their winter hats and gloves on the shelf in the closet or in the sideboard near the front door. "Sweetie," he'd called from the kitchen, "I hate to bother you, but—"

She'd had to jam a knuckle between her teeth and bite down hard to keep from laughing when she walked into the room. Covered by a red-and-white gingham apron, his jeans-covered legs had poked out from the bottom, and the bulky sleeves of his University of Maryland sweatshirt stuck out from its ruffly shoulders. He held a pancake turner in one hand, hot dog tongs in the other. If he'd worn the outfit to a Halloween party, he'd have won the Silliest Costume Prize, hands-down.

"What?" he'd asked, mischievous dark eyes narrowing in response to her appraisal.

"I just missed you," she'd replied, "because you're the most handsome husband a girl ever had."

He'd grinned. "You think?"

"I do." She wiggled her eyebrows flirtatiously, wrapped her arms around his aproned waist. "In fact," she'd said, winking, "I'm giving a lot of thought to kissing you, right here, right now."

The turner and the tongs had clattered to the floor as he pressed her closer. "And they say aggressive women are no fun...."

After their warm embrace, Mitch started digging in a box marked "Kitchen." "Can't make my home fries till we find the big black skillet."

She'd glanced at the counter, where he'd piled enough peeled-and-sliced potatoes and onions to feed the Third

Regiment. Ciara opened one box as Mitch popped the lid of another. "I've already looked in that one," he said, poking around inside another. "If you find the vegetable oil, salt and pepper, and Old Bay seasoning, let me know."

"Old Bay?" she'd asked, incredulous. "That's for steamed crabs and shrimp, not potatoes and—" At the startled, almost wounded expression on his face, she'd quickly added, "Isn't it?"

"Just wait till you taste 'em, sweetie," he'd said, licking his lips and scrubbing his hands together. "They're gonna spoil you for anybody else's potatoes. From now on, you won't be able to settle for anything but Mitch Mahoney's breakfast spuds."

He'd given her dozens of memories like that one...before that awful night. Memories that had lulled her back to sleep when a bad dream awakened her, memories that gave her the energy to unpack every box in their new house within the first week, so he'd have a proper home-coming...*when* he came home.

Night after night as she'd headed for bed, Ciara had stood at the foot of the stairs, one hand on the mahogany rail, the other over her heart, listening for the sound of his key in the lock. Day after day she woke hoping that when she walked into the kitchen, he'd be sitting at the table, reading the morning edition of the *Baltimore Sun,* lips white from his powdered sugar donut as he grumbled about the one-sidedness of the newspaper's politics.

When the nights and the days turned into weeks, it got harder and harder to find a reason to hope he might be there waiting when she got home from teaching, a big smile on his handsome face. "Where have you been!" she imagined he'd ask. "I've been dying to see you!"

Every time Lieutenant Bradley's car pulled into the drive, her heartbeat doubled...maybe this time he'd have a letter for her. Ciara played her tough-girl routine to the hilt. She would show the seasoned agent that she knew a thing or two about bravery. She'd prove she knew how to handle being married to the Bureau. Because when Mitch *did* come home, she wanted him to be proud of the way she'd conducted herself.

In truth, her bravado had been almost as much for Bradley as for herself. "I'm so sorry, Ciara," he would say every time, taking her hand, "but Mitch missed another meeting." And every time, she'd pull free of his pressing fingers and focus on the look on his face. It could mean one of two things: Bradley was truly distressed to have delivered unpleasant news...again, or his wingtips were two sizes too small.

She'd never given a thought to the possibility that he'd deliberately kept her and Mitch apart. Why had it been so easy to believe him, instead of her husband? Oh, he was a smooth one, all right, starting out in complete defense of his comrade, slipping in a little doubt here, casting a bit of suspicion there, until he had her thoroughly convinced that the only possible reason Mitch hadn't written was because he hadn't wanted to. But she'd *let* him put those mistrustful thoughts in her head.

Those first unhappy weeks, she'd spent so much time on her knees, hands folded, it was a minor miracle she hadn't developed inch-thick calluses. She had gone over it in her mind a hundred times: from those first, thrilling stirrings of love, she had beseeched the Almighty to show her a sign; if Mitch wasn't the man He intended her to spend the rest of her life with, she would take her mother's advice and stop wasting her time.

And then Mitch had taken her in his arms and kissed her, and it had felt so good so right. How else was she to have interpreted the emotions, except as God's answer to her heartfelt prayer!

She'd waited a long time to meet the right man. Had

she jumped into the relationship because she'd been lonely? Had she misread God's response? Maybe it had been nothing but hormones, she'd fretted, dictating her interpretation of the Lord's intent.

The pastor had said, more than once, that prayer alone is not enough to prevent doubt. It takes faith and lots of it, he'd insisted, to forestall suspicion, to keep uncertainty at bay. It was a lesson, Ciara realized, that she'd have to learn the hard way, through time and trial; for try as she might to look for reasons to believe Mitch would contact her—or come home to her—hope faded with each lonely, passing day.

And just about the time she was about ready to give up altogether, Dr. Peterson confirmed what she had suspected for weeks: Ciara was going to have a baby. *Mitch's* baby! The news changed everything. Surely when he heard their baby would be born the following summer, Mitch would do everything in his power to come back. She wrote a long, loving letter, outlining her hopes and dreams for this child growing inside her. When she handed it over to the lieutenant, Ciara had wanted to believe that Mitch would find a way to be with her, to share the joyous news, face-to-face.

But Lieutenant Bradley returned the very next week, wearing that same hang-dog expression she'd come to expect of him, and she set all hope aside. Her mother had been right: he was a cop, first and foremost, and would always put his job ahead of everything—every*one* else—including their unborn baby.

"Mitch missed another meeting," he'd said, hands outstretched, as if imploring her to forgive *him* for her husband's transgressions.

One of the teachers at Ciara's school was married to a divorce attorney, and on the day Dr. Peterson let her hear the baby's heartbeat, she made an appointment to see the lawyer. For the child's sake if not her own, she had to make plans. If Mitch never came back, she had to ensure a stable, secure future for her child. If he did return, it wasn't likely he'd be a dedicated father, and she must protect the baby from such callousness.

She had no one to talk to about the situation. Who would understand such a thing! Certainly not her mother, because from day one, the woman's bitterness against Ciara's father spilled onto Mitch as well.

"He'll never love you as much as he loves his job," she'd said when Ciara showed her the sparkling diamond engagement ring. "The only enjoyment he'll get from life will be related to his work."

Judging by the furrows that lined her father's handsome brow and the way his mouth turned down at the corners when working a case, Ciara found it hard to believe her dad loved his job at all. She'd put the question to him on the night Mitch asked her to marry him.

Her father had answered in his typically soft-spoken way. "All I ever wanted was to see right win out over wrong."

"That doesn't happen very often," she'd countered. "It's in the news all the time...the way criminals get away with murder."

He'd nodded his agreement. "That's true far too often, I'm afraid. But it's so satisfying when the system works as our forefathers intended it to," he'd said, dark-lashed blue eyes gleaming as he plucked an imaginary prize from the air and secured it in a tight fist. "And you forget when the D.A. botched up, or the lab lost evidence, or the arresting officer forgot to read the suspect his rights. You forget that a lot of the time, everything goes wrong, because you're able to focus on what went right."

Her father didn't love his *job,* Ciara understood when the conversation ended, he loved *justice.*

During her first weekend home after finishing up her freshman year in college, Ciara and her mother had been alone in the kitchen, chatting quietly as they'd washed the supper dishes. The contrast had reminded her of the weekend she'd gone home with her roommate, Kelly, to a cozily cluttered house that throbbed with the cheerful sounds of a big family. It hadn't been the first time Ciara had compared other households to her own—somber as a funeral parlor, quiet as a hospital. If her parents were that unhappy, why not get a divorce? she'd often wondered. She hoped they hadn't spent nineteen miserable years together for her sake, because if *she* was the reason they'd endured all that misery...

Perhaps they'd stuck it out because of the "for better or for worse" line in the marriage vows. But was that what God intended? That two individuals—who made a promise while they were too young and too foolish to understand the gravity or longevity of it—spend the rest of their lives locked in an unhappy union?

Ciara had always seen marriage as a loving gift, hand delivered by the Father. Her parents' marriage had been more a jail sentence than a gift of any kind. When *she* married, Ciara had decided, it wouldn't just be for love. No, she'd consider the future, as her parents obviously had not, because she would not, could not inflict a bitter loveless marriage on any children she might have. Ciara knew only too well what that could be like. If only she had siblings, maybe things wouldn't have seemed so bleak....

She dried the plate her mother had just washed. "Mom, why don't I have any brothers or sisters?"

The answer had come so quickly, Ciara figured out much later, because it was something that was often on her mother's mind. "I didn't think it would be fair to bring more children into this world, children who'd feel neglected and slighted by their own father."

"I've never felt anything but loved by Daddy," Ciara had admitted.

It had been the wrong thing to say to her mother.

Following a disgusted snort, she'd said, "Kids are adaptable. Besides, how would *you* know a good father from a bad one? You have nothing to compare him to."

"My friends' fathers spent as much time at work as Daddy did when he was a cop," she'd said, more than a little riled that her own mother had put her in the position of defending her father, "and they weren't policemen."

"Kids are adaptable," she'd repeated, "and they're good at justifying what's wrong in their lives, too. Well, I'm *not* so good at those things." She'd jammed a handful of silverware into the cup in the corner of the dish drainer. "Now you know why you're an only child."

"Why are you so *angry* with Dad?"

Her mother had stared out the window above the sink for a long moment, as if the answer to Ciara's question hung on a shrub or a tree limb. "I'm angry because I asked him to give it up, to do something safer—for my sake— and he refused."

"But he *did* give it up."

"I asked him to quit long before he was shot, Ciara. You weren't even born yet when I told him how hard it was for me, worrying every minute he was on the job, scared out of my mind if he was five minutes late, imagining all the terrible things that might have happened to keep him from coming home on time." She hesitated. "I found a solution to my worrying."

"What?"

"I taught myself not to care."

Now it all made sense. She'd been eleven when her father had been wounded in the line of duty. The injury to his hip would heal, the doctors had said, but he'd walk with a permanent limp…and because that would put him in harm's way on the job, he was forced to retire.

Strange, Ciara had often thought, that though he worked fewer hours at a far less stressful job, teaching at the university seemed to tire him like police work never had. Stranger still, before the second anniversary of his retirement, his dark hair had gone completely gray and his clear blue eyes had lost their youthful spark. And in addition to the gunshot-induced limp, he began to walk slightly bent at the waist, as though the burden of being unable to make his wife happy was a weight too crushing to bear, even for one with shoulders as broad as his.

One line from a poem she'd read in her English Literature class popped into her mind, "Joy is the ingredient that puts life into a man's soul, just as sadness causes its death." Her father, though the doctors claimed his vital organs were strong and healthy, was dying of unhappiness.

In the kitchen making her lunch, Mitch finished singing one Beatles tune and immediately launched into another, his voice echoing in the cavernous room. From her place on the sofa bed, Ciara smiled. He sounded happy, despite their predicament, and she wanted him to stay happy. The only way she knew to accomplish that goal was to set her own needs aside and let him continue the dangerous undercover work he seemed to love so much.

Could she do that? Should she, now that there was a baby to consider?

"I hope you're hungry," he called to her, "'cause I've made enough food for two Boy Scout troops and their leaders."

She closed her eyes. Oh, how I love him! she admitted silently.

But she couldn't allow love to blind her, not when the baby's future, as well as her own, was at stake. She wouldn't spend decades chained to a loveless marriage, as her mother had done. Had her parents stayed together, simply because of the vows they'd exchanged? Ciara and Mitch had spoken those same words. "What God has joined together, let no man put asunder," the preacher had said.

Ciara closed her eyes. "Lord Jesus," she whispered, "I want to do Your Will, but You'll have to show me the way."

"Ciara, sweetie," Mitch said, poking his head into the family room, "you can finish your nap later." He popped back into the kitchen. "Make a space on your lap for the breakfast tray." His face reappeared in the doorway, a confused frown furrowing his brow. "Ah, do we *have* a breakfast tray?"

"Yes," she answered, giggling softly. "It was a wedding gift from your Aunt Leila, remember?"

"Oh, yeah. Right," he said, nodding before he disappeared for the second time. In seconds he was back again. "Um…where do we keep the breakfast tray?"

She was reminded of an episode of "I Love Lucy," when Ricky insisted on making breakfast so his pregnant wife could sleep in…but continued to call Lucy into the kitchen to find this and that. Grinning, Ciara mimicked Lucille Ball. "Oh, Ricky, it's in the cabinet under the wall oven, standing with the cookie sheets and pizza pans."

"What?"

And after a terrible clatter, she heard him say, "Bingo!"

Yes, Mitch seemed happy. But was she wife enough to keep him that way? Was her faith strong enough to stick with it and to find out?

Chapter Seven

He hadn't been deliberately eavesdropping later that day, but the kitchen and the family room shared a common wall with an open vent. He made a little more noise with the ice cubes and lemonade, hoping to drown out Ciara's mother's nagging voice:

"I just don't understand why you couldn't have married someone like that nice Chet Bradley. He's always so—"

"Mom, please," came Ciara's harsh whisper. "Mitch is right in the next room. You want to hurt his feelings?"

Kathryn laughed. "Feelings? Please. He's a cop, and as we both know, cops don't *have* any feelings."

A moment of silence, then, "He left you alone for seven months, Ciara. Alone and carrying your first child. And a difficult pregnancy to boot!"

"It wasn't his fault," countered his wife. "He was just following orders."

"That's not what Chet said...."

He heard the rustle of sheets. "What are you talking about, Mom?"

"Did you know that Chet is single?"

Ciara had told Mitch that her mother was English, through and through. *There must be a wee bit o' the Irish in 'er,* he thought, *'cause she's answerin' a question with a question....*

"Not single, divorced," her daughter corrected. "There's a difference...not that it matters. I'm a married woman, and pretty soon now, I'll be a mommy, too."

His mother-in-law's bitter sigh floated to him. "Don't remind me." She clucked her tongue. "I just hope you're happy, young lady, because now you're stuck in the same leaky boat I was in for two solid decades."

Kathryn had never made a secret of her feelings for Mitch, insulting him at every turn, trying to make him feel small and insignificant every chance she got. *Obviously,* he thought, *my little "vacation" hasn't improved her opinion of me.*

"If you had listened to me and married a man like Chet, you wouldn't be in this predicament now. At least he has some breeding, unlike certain Gaelic immigrants." She snorted disdainfully. "Chet wouldn't have left you high and dry. He—"

"He's a cop, too, don't forget."

"True. But his job doesn't put him on the front lines. His ego isn't all wrapped up in how much attention the 'big cases' give him."

"Lieutenant Bradley is Mitch's superior officer. He's the guy who made Mitch go away."

"That's not the way he tells it."

"You skirted this question earlier, and if you don't mind, I'd like a straight answer to it now. What do you mean, 'That's not the way he tells it'?"

If he stood just to the right of the stove and crouched slightly, Mitch could see their reflections in the oven window. He saw Kathryn narrow her eyes and incline her head. "Where *was* Mitch all those months, anyway? I distinctly got the impression from Chet that—"

"That doesn't answer my question. And besides, when have you had an opportunity to discuss Mitch with him?" Ciara asked, sitting up straighter.

Kathryn waved a hand in front of her face, as though Ciara's question were a housefly or a pesky mosquito. "Last time I stopped by, he was here when I arrived, remember?" She tucked a flyaway strand of dark blond hair behind one ear, inspected her manicured fingernails. "That was the time he brought you roses, to cheer you up." She smiled brightly. "Such a caring, thoughtful, young man!" She straightened the hem of her skirt and added, "We were in the kitchen, fixing coffee, remember? I didn't see any harm in asking him a few questions. You're my daughter, after all. If I don't have a right to know the details about something that affects you so directly, who does?"

Roses? He brought *roses*...to cheer Ciara up? Mitch ground his molars together. It was understandable that his wife would be down in the dumps, considering the way they'd parted and all, but... How often had good old Chet been in his house, anyway? Often enough to feel comfortable upstairs...in the master bathroom?

Ciara's voice interrupted his self-interrogation. "What did he tell you?"

He knew Ciara well enough to recognize annoyance in her voice when he heard it. She was annoyed now.

Kathryn huffed. "All right, Ciara. I guess a child is never too old to be reminded to mind their manners. I'll thank you to keep a civil tongue in your head when you're talking to me, young lady. You may be a married woman now, but I'm still your mother!"

"I'm sorry if I sounded disrespectful, Mom. Blame it on cabin fever."

She has been in the house an awful lot these past

months, Mitch thought. And she always loved to take long walks…must be hard, being cooped up this way….

"You should try your hand at writing mysteries," Ciara added, giggling, "because you're a master at dropping hints and clues. I admit it, you've hooked me. Now *please* tell me what Chet said about Mitch!"

Kathryn joined in on what she believed to be her daughter's merriment. Mitch knew better. Shouldn't a mother be able to recognize when her daughter is getting angry? He'd only known her a few months before leaving for Philly, and even he recognized that Ciara's laughter was rooted in frustration.

"Well," Kathryn said, a hand on Ciara's knee, "it was like this…. It seems Mitch came to Chet late one night with this ego-maniacal idea for capturing a man on the FBI's Most Wanted list. Notorious criminal, Chet said. Mitch had it all worked out, right down to the kind of clothes he would wear. He'd pretend to be a CPA to trick the man.

"Chet didn't want to let him go, once he found out that you two had just been married, but Mitch insisted." Kathryn sighed. "Chet tried and tried to talk him out of it, but in the end, he had no choice but to admit that Mitch *had* come up with a good plan…."

"Interesting," Ciara said.

And Mitch could tell by the way her fingers were steadily tapping against her tummy that she was chomping at the bit to hear the rest of the story. Frankly, I'd like to hear it, too, he admitted.

"Chet didn't hear from Mitch the whole time he was undercover. Did you know that? It's his duty to report to his commanding officer, and he didn't phone in once! If he's that irresponsible about his job, think what a wonderful father he'll be."

Her voice dripped with sarcasm and bitterness. *I love you, too, Kathryn*, was his snide thought.

"I've told you and told you," Ciara said, "Mitch *couldn't* call. They were watching him night and day. One false move, and he might have been—"

Kathryn patted her daughter's hand, turned to face the kitchen. "Mitch! What's keeping you?" she called. She leaned forward and lowered her voice. "Send him to the kitchen for lemonade, and he's gone a half hour. Send him on a week-long assignment, and he's gone seven months."

That low-down lout, Mitch thought. *What was he doing telling her the details of a case that hadn't even gone to court yet?*

Kathryn snickered behind her hand. "Being elusive must be part of his nature. Now, if you had married a man like Chet..."

He'd heard about all of that he could handle. Straightening from his position in front of the oven window, Mitch left the glasses of lemonade on the kitchen counter and barged into the family room. "I don't mean to be rude, Kathryn, but Ciara looks awfully tired."

Ciara shot him a grateful look.

"I promised her doctor that at the first signs of fatigue, I'd make her take a nap." Gently he grabbed Kathryn's elbow and helped her up. "Why don't you come back in a day or so and bring Joe next time. I haven't seen him in—"

"In over *seven months!*" his mother-in-law finished, jerking free of his grasp.

Mitch handed her her purse and walked toward the front door. One hand on the knob, he smiled politely. "Why don't we make it Sunday afternoon. I'll fix a nice dinner. I'm sure Ciara will be rested up by then. Won't you, sweetie?"

Her blue eyes were twinkling when their eyes met, but

when her mother faced her, she slumped weakly against her pillow. "I don't know...maybe you'd better call first, Mom, just to make sure I'm up to having company...."

Kathryn laid a hand on her chest, eyes wide and mouth agape. "Company! Your father and I aren't 'company,' we're *family!*"

"Thanks for stopping by," Mitch said, opening the door. "As always, it's been...an experience."

"'Here's your hat, what's your hurry?'" Kathryn quoted, snatching her purse from his hands. "You'd better not let anything happen to my daughter," she snapped, shaking a finger under his nose. "I intend to hold you personally responsible for—"

"Kathryn," he said, calmly, quietly, "you have my word that I won't let anything happen to your daughter. She happens to be the most important person in my life."

She huffed her disapproval. "You sure have a funny way of showing how you feel."

Smiling thinly, Mitch said, "You know, you're right about that." He opened the door and with a great sweep of his arm, invited her to step through it. "See you Sunday?" he asked once she was on the porch. "How does two o'clock sound?"

"I'll..."

"Drive safely now," he added as the door swung shut, "and be sure to give Joe my best."

Whatever Kathryn said in response was muffled by the closed door.

"Is she gone?" Ciara whispered when he came back into the family room.

Nodding, he sat on the edge of the sofa bed.

"Thank goodness. I love her, but she doesn't make it easy sometimes."

Mitch flexed a thick-muscled biceps. "You want her to stay out, it'll be my pleasure. *Trust me.*"

Ciara giggled. "I couldn't keep her away. She means well, it's just that she has—"

"The personality of vinegar?"

She pursed her lips. "Well, lemons, maybe...."

He stood, picked up the empty cookie plate he'd brought out when her mother had arrived. "I'm going to throw a load of sheets into the washer," he said, bending down to kiss her forehead. "How 'bout catching a catnap while I'm gone. You look like you could use it."

Yawning and stretching, she smiled. "I might just do that."

He started to walk away.

"Mitch?"

He stopped.

"What are we going to do? After the baby is born, I mean?"

Mitch held his breath. His heartbeat doubled, and his pulse pounded in his ears. She'd turned onto her side, making it impossible for him to read her expression. Was the question a throwback to her suggestion that he pack up and leave?

"You're taking such good care of me...of everything...that I'm going to be spoiled rotten by the time this baby gets here."

Relieved, he exhaled. "You've done more than your share, turning this house into a home all by yourself. You deserve to be spoiled rotten."

She lifted her head and grinned.

"At least until the baby is born," he finished, winking.

She snuggled into her pillow and in moments was fast asleep.

I didn't tell you the whole truth, he admitted to his peacefully sleeping wife. *I have no intention of spoiling you rotten just till the baby comes. I'm going to treat you like a queen for the rest of your life.*

* * *

The next few days passed quietly and without incident. The lines of communication between them were beginning to open, as he took her temperature, brought her her vitamins, saw to it she drank plenty of water....

Ciara admired him, for although he had a different way of doing things, he accomplished every task with productive efficiency.

He had a plan for everything—usually written out on a five-by-seven tablet—and made so many checklists, Ciara believed all the ballpoint pens in the house would run out of ink before he had accomplished every task.

Mitch had written up his first list the night before he brought her home from the hospital. Once he helped her get settled the next morning, he whipped out a little notebook and sat on the edge of the sofa bed. "Breakfast at nine, lunch at one, supper at seven, a light snack at ten, lights out by eleven. You can read or watch TV in between, but I want all the power off a couple of hours in the morning, again in the afternoon, so you can catch some shut-eye. What do you think?"

The dog sidled up to him and nudged Mitch's hand with his nose, as if to say Where do I fit into the plan?

"Don't worry, boy, I won't neglect you." Mitch flipped to the second page in his tablet. "See," he said, as if Chester could read what he'd printed in bold black letters, "you'll get yard time while your mommy, here, takes her naps." Patting the top of the dog's head, he'd added, "I'm afraid long walks around the block are going to have to wait till she's up and at 'em, 'cause we can't leave her alone."

Chester's silent bark seemed all the approval Mitch needed. "It's settled, then." To Ciara he added, "I've already put clean sheets on our bed, so…"

"I don't really have to go to bed at eleven," she said, hoping he'd agree because she'd said it so matter-of-factly.

His stern expression told her that she did have to retire at eleven.

"But...but I like to watch the eleven o'clock report on Channel Two before I turn in," she protested. "Besides, it isn't like I'll be doing anything to wear me out. Staying up late won't hurt me."

Unconsciously he ruffled Chester's thick coat, frowning as he turned her words over in his mind. "I hate TV news—nothing but a serving of pap for the feel-good generation, if you ask me. So..."

"I didn't ask you," she interrupted, grinning.

He held up a hand, and she'd giggled.

"How 'bout we make it an every-other-night thing," he had continued. "Tonight, the news. Tomorrow, bed at eleven."

She hadn't heard anything but *bed*. The word echoed in her mind. She hadn't shared anything with him—not conversation or a meal, their home, *certainly* not a bed—in seven long months. Did he really expect her to pick right up where they'd left off, as if he'd been away on some fun-filled, weekend fishing trip with the guys? Didn't he understand that during nearly every moment of their separation, she had reviewed thousands of scenarios that would explain his lengthy absence—shootings, stabbings, beatings, kidnappings—horrible, torturous images.

She blinked those images away. "There's no reason for you to cart me upstairs every night, then back down in the morning." Consciously, deliberately, she phrased it as a statement of fact.

"You can't get a decent night's sleep with a metal bar diggin' into the small of your back," Mitch pointed out. "You'll sleep upstairs on a real mattress or—"

"I'll be fine, right here on the couch."

He crossed his arms over his chest, lifted his chin a notch. Mitch was not smiling when he said, "We can compromise on TV or not TV, but this subject isn't open for negotiation.'' He paused thoughtfully. "Well, I suppose I ought to give you *some* say in the matter...."

She should have waited a tick in time to display her victorious smile.

"You have two choices—sleep upstairs or stay upstairs. It's entirely up to you."

His stern expression, his cross-armed stance, his no-nonsense voice made it clear she would not win this battle, and yet Ciara couldn't help thinking what a wonderful father he'd be if he disciplined their children with the same gentle-yet-firm attitude. She got so wrapped up in the concept that she didn't give a thought to the fact that if she gave in on this point, they'd be sleeping together every night, like any other married couple.

And they were nothing like other married couples....

Chester looked back and forth between them and whimpered, reminding her of how helpless and afraid she'd felt when her parents argued.

"You'd really leave me up there," she asked breathily, "all alone, all day?"

"I'd much rather have you down here, where you can keep me company, but we'll do it that way if we have to."

And so the deal was struck.

Ciara snuggled beneath the crisp top sheet, remembering the way he'd carried her up the stairs that first night. Her heart had drummed and her stomach had clenched. After all those nights alone, clutching her pillow...and pretending it was him...what would it be like, she'd wondered, lying beside the real thing?

Chester, who had become Mitch's four-legged, shaggy shadow, had tagged along and flopped in a graceless heap on Ciara's side of the bed. Almost immediately he'd rested his chin on his paws and fell asleep.

If only *I* could get comfortable that easily! she'd thought as Mitch tucked her in and turned out the light. It had been a dark night, without so much as a moon sliver to brighten the room, and for those first few seconds, Ciara blinked into the blackness, listening....

Silence.

Had he decided to sleep downstairs? Had he made up the guest bedroom for himself?

By then her eyes had adjusted to the darkness, and she'd seen his shadow pass in front of the window. Almost immediately, he'd been swallowed up by the blackness, and she'd strained her ears. First, the sound of heavy footfalls, padding across the carpeted floor, then a muffled *clunk* as his belted trousers had landed on the upholstered bedside chair. The mattress dipped under his weight, the sheet billowed upward, like a plaid parachute and settled slowly over them.

Then he'd rolled onto his side and slid his arms around her. "G'night," Mitch had whispered, kissing her temple. "Sweet dreams." He'd tucked a hand under his cheek, rested the other on her tummy. "G'night, li'l sweetie," he'd added.

More silence.

Then the unmistakable, comforting sound of his soft snores.

Ciara didn't know how long she'd lain there, snuggled against him, but listening to his steady, deep breaths had relaxed her, lulled her. Before she'd known it, the bright light of morning had beckoned her.

The morning after his return, Ciara had at first thought she'd been dreaming again, that he wouldn't be there when she opened her eyes, and then she'd seen him there, flat on his back, gentle breaths counting the seconds. One hand had rested on his slowly heaving chest, big fingers splayed like a pianist's. The other, he'd tucked under his neck. A lock of dark hair had fallen across his forehead, and the shadow of a night's growth of whiskers dusted his cheeks and chin. She had needed to use the bathroom, but he'd looked so peaceful—like an innocent boy, without a care in the world—that she hadn't wanted to wake him.

Instead, she'd tucked the misplaced curl into place. His thick black lashes had fluttered in response to her touch. He'd focused on the ceiling and frowned, as though trying to remember where he was. A tiny smile lifted the corners of his mouth, and he'd slowly turned to face her.

"G'mornin'," he'd said, the bass of his sleepy voice guttural and growly. He'd worked his arms around her. "Sleep well?"

Ciara had tucked her face into the crook of his neck. "Like a log," she'd answered. "And you?"

"Terrific." And as if to prove it, Mitch had yawned deeply. He climbed out of bed and thumped groggily around to her side, and carried her into the bathroom. "I'm going to go down and start the coffee," he'd explained. "I'll only be a minute, so don't you move from there, you hear?"

"I hear," she'd agreed as he closed the door.

Almost immediately, she'd noticed the milky white bottle in the wicker waste basket. "Homme Jusqu'au Dernier," she said, reading the label aloud. Mitch had never worn that brand before he'd left.... Ciara couldn't reach it without getting up, so she didn't know if she liked his new cologne. She would ask him about it when he came back for her.

The clatter of cabinet doors and canister lids, and the sound of running water had blotted the question from her mind. And true to his word, he was in their room in minutes, opening and closing drawers and doors, his big bare feet thudding as he crossed from closet to dresser and back again.

One sleeve of his white T-shirt had rolled up, and the legs of his boxers had wrinkled during the night; his dark waves were tousled, his cheeks sheet wrinkled when he burst into the bathroom. ''Finished?''

The little-boy, rumpled look had been so appealing that Ciara had been forced to look away to diminish the passion stirring deep inside her. She mumbled a polite ''Yes, thanks,'' and just like that, he'd lifted her into his arms and sat her on the edge of the bed.

On his knees, he'd gently gripped her wrists, held them above her head and slid her nightgown off. The nothing-but-business expression warmed as he focused on her naked stomach. Lifting his gaze to hers, he'd smiled tenderly, blinking and shaking his head slightly. He'd broken the intense eye contact, looked at her broadened waistline again and stroked its roundness.

The heat of his hands, pressing against her taut skin, sent eddies of desire coursing through her. ''You're beautiful,'' he'd rasped, kissing every inch of her stomach, ''so very beautiful.''

And then his eyes—dusky chocolaty eyes that blazed with need and yearning—had met hers. It seemed to Ciara that he hadn't wanted her to read his mind and discover the longing there; why else would he have slowly, slowly dropped the densely lashed lids?

No, she'd thought, almost sadly, don't shut me out. She'd placed a palm on each whiskered cheek, thumbs massaging the tight muscles of his jaw. She'd been stunned when he opened his eyes again, to see the thin sheen of tears glistening there. ''I'm so sorry, Ciara,'' he'd husked. ''I should have been here, right from the beginning.''

His arms had slid around her, his ear cleaving to her midsection. ''Can you ever forgive me?''

There had been moments, while he'd been gone, when Ciara had said she despised him. It would have been easier, accepting his absence, if only she could hate him. But try as she might, the words had never rung true. On the day they'd met, she'd fallen in love with his silly jokes and his opinionated politics and his bighearted nature. Standing at the altar of God, she'd vowed to love him for better or for worse, and no matter how many miles and months separated them, her last words on this earth would likely be "Oh, how I loved him!"

She had felt the dampness between his skin and hers that morning, as Mitch had nestled his face against their unborn child. Any anger she had felt for him was swallowed up by his heartfelt tears. Every maternal instinct inside her had risen up, and she'd held him near, fingers gently raking through his plush chestnut curls.

One day soon, she would ask him about the assignment that had put time and space between them. But for those few moments, it hadn't mattered where he'd gone, or why. He had come home, had come back to her.

He had sniffed, and shaken his head, then sat back on his heels to gather up the clothes he'd set out for her. He'd given the big white T-shirt—one of his own—two hearty flaps, and slipped it carefully over her head. She picked up the brush that had been hidden under the shirt. Mitch had held out his hand, and she'd handed it to him and, standing, he'd run the boar bristles through her hair, one hundred strokes; she'd counted them. "Shines like the sun," he'd said, then he'd lifted her in his arms and carried her downstairs.

Though he'd daubed a light kiss upon her cheek each time he brought a cup of coffee, a plate of cookies, Mitch had not repeated any part of that lovely scene since…despite the countless hours she'd spent wishing and hoping that he would. Was it something hormonal, induced by her condition, she'd wondered, that made her ache for the intimacy of his touch? And why had he stoically with-held it?

They'd been back together for four days now, and Ciara decided the best way to divert her attention was to focus on the burning questions—where he'd been, what he'd been doing—that had plagued her while he'd been gone. When the time was right—and she'd have to trust God to tell her when that moment arrived—she would ask Mitch about the assignment. Had he wanted to take it, or had it been foisted upon him? The answer would make all the difference in the world....

Now as Ciara watched him folding towels as he sat on the foot of the sofa bed, grinning as Chester wrestled with a Lambchops doll, she said, "Mitch, let me help. Folding clothes is hardly strenuous activity, and I feel so useless."

He looked at her and said, "Since I'm the one sitting here doing it, I know for a fact that the job requires the use of stomach muscles. You're not doing anything that puts any strain on that baby." Smoothing the washcloth he'd just doubled, he added it to the neat, colorful stack. "Got it?"

She flopped back against the pillows he'd stuffed behind her. "Got it," she droned.

He reached for the laundry basket. "When I'm finished putting this stuff away, I'll—"

Changing positions, Ciara winced slightly.

"What...?" He leaped up so fast, he nearly toppled his tower of towels. "What's wrong?" His big hands gripped her upper arms. "Are you in pain?"

"Goodness gracious sakes alive, Mitch," she said, frowning slightly, "my back is a little stiff from all this inactivity. It was a muscle cramp, that's all." Shaking her head, Ciara rolled her eyes and punched the mattress. "I *hate* being completely helpless. It makes me feel so...so."

He stood for a moment, pinching the bridge of his nose between thumb and forefinger, then heaved a deep sigh. "You scared me half to death." He stuffed the linens into a wicker laundry basket and grinned. "Mrs. Mahoney," Mitch said, rubbing his palms together, "get ready for the best back rub of your life."

She grinned. "I've never had a back rub, 'best' or otherwise."

Mitch's brows rose. "Never?"

Ciara shook her head. "Never."

"Never say never. Now, roll over, Beethoven."

She wouldn't have admitted it—not until she knew he loved her as much as she loved him—but having him near was like a dream come true. Ciara did as she was told. Hiding her face in the pillow, she closed her eyes and bit her bottom lip to gird herself. Those moments in their room, when he'd so lovingly held their unborn child, haunted her. He hadn't left her side, had taken such good care of her, all without a word of complaint. She had worried in the hospital that he might not want this child; what had motivated his loving ministrations...love for the baby, love for her, or both? Until she knew, Ciara could not admit how much his physical presence meant to her.

He lay down behind her, hiked up the oversize T-shirt and ran his palms over her skin, paying particular attention to the small of her back. His fingers slid up, kneaded her neck and shoulders, then moved down to rub her biceps.

Ciara relaxed her grip on the pillow, as unconscious sighs slipped from her lips. Her mind was wandering in a half awake, half asleep state, floating, soaring, surrounded by yards of satin under a sky full of puffy clouds when Mitch leaned forward and brushed her ear with his lips. "I love you," he whispered. And lowering his dark head to hers, he kissed her cheek, softly, then more urgently as moved down the side of her neck.

He pressed so close, that not even the barest wisp of a breeze could have passed between their bodies. She was his, and he was hers, and at the moment nothing mattered except her fierce love for him. She trembled as his fingers played in her hair, shivered as his palms skimmed the bared flesh of her back, tingled as his lips nibbled at her earlobe.

He climbed over her then, putting them face-to-face, and placed his palms upon her cheeks. Raw need glittered in his eyes as he held her gaze, analyzing her expression, studying her reaction. She blinked, feeling light-headed, and hoped he wouldn't read the passion smoldering inside her.

"I love you," he said again, a tinge of wonder in his voice.

She looked away, shifted restlessly, but the look of helpless uncertainty on his face wasn't that easily forgotten. He loved her. He loved *her!* Ciara ignored the voice inside her that warned her to be still, to be silent. It was surprisingly easy to admit the truth, once the words started tumbling out: "Oh, Mitch, I've missed you so." She wrapped her arms around his neck, drove her fingers through his thick curls. She kissed his cheeks, his chin, his eyelids, punctuated each with a heartfelt "I love you."

He cupped her chin in his large palm, his eyes scanning her face, as if to read her thoughts. "Do you?" he asked. "Do you really?"

She didn't understand the pensive darkness in his eyes. Ciara held his face in her hands. "You know I do."

"Just me? *Only* me?" he asked through clenched teeth.

He'd been so confident in her love before he'd gone away. What had he seen or heard or experienced to shake his trust in that love? Till now, she'd been struggling with her own emotions, trying to hold on to some semblance of pride. None of that mattered now. Ciara wanted nothing

but to comfort and assure him, to restore his faith in her.
She put everything she had into it, every happy memory,
every heartache, every nightmare, every dream she'd had
while he was gone. Would she have gone through all that
if she *hadn't* loved him? "I love *you*, Mitch Mahoney.
Only you, and no one *but* you."

He closed his eyes and heaved a great sigh. She hadn't
thought it possible for him to gather her closer, but he did.
The rhythmic thumping of his heart lulled her, soothed her
and quieted the child within her.

He was smiling slightly when she tilted her face up to
his. His dark eyes burned fervently into hers for a silent
moment. His kiss caused a small gasp of pleasure to escape
her lips. Her blood surged, her pulse pounded. "Mitch,"
she rasped. "Oh, Mitch…" She loved him hopelessly,
helplessly, blindly; the most powerful emotion she'd ever
experienced. Heart and mind and soul throbbed with devotion as she pressed her pregnant body against his. He
belonged to her and she to him, and this baby was theirs.
"Mitch," she sighed, "I wish…"

"Shhh," he said, a fabric softener-scented finger over
her lips. His fingers combed the hair back from her face,
and he looked deeply into her eyes. What *was* that expression on his beautiful face? Fear? Regret?

And then she knew: Guilt.

Mitch felt guilty for having left her alone. No doubt he
blamed himself for the complications of her pregnancy, as
well. Hadn't Dr. Peterson explained it to him? Hadn't he
told Mitch that her condition had been there, right from
the moment of conception?

Something told her this was a situation she must handle
carefully, delicately, or his ego could be forever damaged.
Ciara would not do to Mitch what her mother had done to
her father. She would not subject him to a lifetime of misery for not having done everything her way. Somehow she

had to find a way to let him know there were no hard feelings, nothing to forgive, everything to forget.

Ciara snuggled close, closer, until his lightly whiskered cheek bristled against her throat. They lay that way for a long time, Mitch stroking her back, Ciara running her fingers through his dark waves as his warm breaths fanned her. Finally she felt him relax. There's no time like the present to tell him he has nothing to feel guilty about, not now, not ever again. Ciara wriggled slightly, shifting her position so that she could meet his eyes.

She had to hold her breath in order to stifle the giggle…because she didn't want to wake him.

It wasn't until something cold and wet pressed against her cheek that she realized she'd fallen asleep, too…had been out quite a while, from the looks of things.

Chester's fur was still damp. "So you've had yourself a bath, have you?" she asked, rumpling his shining coat. *I must have done something mighty good in my childhood,* she thought, *to have earned a husband like this.*

Mitch bent over to pick a speck of lint from the carpet, noticed her staring. "What…? Do I have spinach on my teeth or something?"

"No. I'm just trying to decide if you're real, or a very pleasant mirage."

Grinning, he walked over to her, leaned down and kissed the tip of her nose. Her cheeks. Her lips. The kiss lasted a long, delirious moment. "Could a mirage do that?"

Sinking back into the pillows, she sighed, a dreamy smile playing on her freshly kissed mouth. "If it can, I don't know why folks are so all-fired disappointed when they discover they've seen one."

"I'm making your favorite for supper," he said, changing the subject.

Unconsciously she licked her lips. "Gnocchi?"

Mitch frowned slightly. "I thought breaded cubed steaks were your favorite."

"They're great," she replied with a wide smile. Maybe too wide, she quickly realized. *You are an insensitive boob, Ciara Mahoney. Now you've gone and hurt his feelings.* "Oh, *that* favorite," she quickly added.

"I don't even know what a naw…a no…what is it, anyway?"

"Nyaw-kee," she pronounced the Italian pasta. "And it's plural, because just one wouldn't be the least bit satisfying. They're fluffy little potato dumplings that melt in your mouth. They sell them, frozen, at the grocery store. They're not nearly as tasty as the ones they make at Chiaparelli's, down in Little Italy, but they'll do when a craving strikes."

He jammed the handle of his feather duster into a back pocket, leaned over to clean up her snack plates. "So, you're having cravings, are you?"

She shrugged, thinking of their massage session. "Maybe one or two…." Then, giggling, she added, "You look like a rooster, with that thing sticking out of your pocket."

He shook his bottom and cock-a-doodle-doo'd for all he was worth, sending Chester into a feather-chasing frenzy. Mitch and the dog rolled on the floor for a moment, playfully wrestling over the cleaning tool. "You two are going to make a terrible mess," she warned, laughing. "You'll be cleaning up feathers for a week."

"But," Mitch groaned, chuckling as he tugged on the plastic handle, "he won't let go."

"Chester," Ciara ordered, "sit."

Immediately the dog obeyed.

"And only one feather out of place," she boasted, buffing her nails against her chest.

He plucked the peacock blue feather from the carpet, tucked it behind her ear. "Did I ever tell you how beautiful you are while you're sleeping?"

"You're pretty cute with your eyes closed, yourself," she said.

Mitch smiled. "I've got to get back in there before the meat burns. Can I get you anything? Your wish is my command."

She couldn't think when he looked at her with that dark, smoldering gaze. "I can have any wish I want?"

"Any wish you want."

I wish we could make love, she thought, remembering their recent intimacies, the way we did before you left me. "Is it too late to whip up some of those fantastic home fries of yours to go with the steaks?" she asked instead.

Chapter Eight

~

"**D**on't pull the plug till I get back, 'cause we don't want you going down the drain...."

Ciara grinned with disbelief. "Six months ago, maybe, but now? Down the drain? I can barely fit in the tub, so you've got to be kidding." She adjusted her headset and snapped an Amy Grant tape into place, then waved him away. "Go on, read your morning paper and leave me to my bubbles."

"Back in ten," he said, smiling as he pulled the door shut behind him.

From the semicircular window in the landing, he could see all the way to the end of their driveway, where the mailbox stood. Earlier, Ciara had sent him outside to put a card in the box and flip the flag up. "Can't forget Ian's birthday," she'd said, grinning, "not this year. It's the big four-oh, y'know."

Mitch craned his neck; if the flag was down, it would mean the....

Instead of the red flag, Mitch spotted a sleek black Ferrari, parked behind Ciara's Miata. One of Pericolo's goons drove a car like that.... Every muscle in him tensed as he took off down the stairs. In the foyer he breathed a sigh of relief. All's secure here, he thought, jiggling the bolted knob. Now for the back door.... He headed for the kitchen by way of the family room and stopped dead in his tracks.

The man in Mitch's recliner wore a black suit, maroon tie, and peered over the pages of the newspaper he held in one hand. "Well, now," he said, assessing Mitch's summery attire, "aren't you the picture of suburban life...deck shoes, Bermuda shorts, madras shirt." With a jerk of his head, he indicated the side yard. "Don't tell me...there's a cabin cruiser out there with 'Mahoney's Bah-lo-nee' painted across its back end, right?"

Mitch's fingers balled into fists. "What're you doin' here?" he demanded, planting himself in front of the chair.

"Just paying my weekly visit to the little woman." He shrugged. "You don't expect us to go cold turkey, just 'cause you're home, do you?"

Mitch leaned both palms on the arms of the recliner. "I don't know what you're up to, Bradley, but it ain't gonna work. Now beat it." He straightened. "Way I'm feeling 'bout you, this is a dangerous place for you to be...."

Bradley shifted uneasily in the chair. "Hey," he said, grinning nervously, "is that any way to talk to your boss?"

"*Ex*-boss. I made a couple of phone calls, and—"

The grin became a scowl. "You tryin' to scare me, Mahoney? 'Cause if you are..."

Mitch's upper lip curled in contempt, his arm shot out as if it were spring loaded, and he grabbed a handful of Bradley's collar. "*If* I was tryin' to scare you," he snarled, twisting the shirt tight against Bradley's throat, "I wouldn't need a telephone."

Bradley shrank deeper into the chair cushions, eyes wide with fright as frothy spittle formed in the corners of his mouth. The hand that had been holding the newspaper went limp, and the sports section of the *Baltimore Sun* fluttered to the floor like a wounded gull.

Through the thin material of his T-shirt, Mitch felt something cold and hard pressing against his ribs. Looking down, he saw that Bradley's other hand, sheathed in a surgeon's glove, held a chrome-plated, pearl-handled .35 mm handgun.

The face-off lasted a terrifying moment, Mitch increasing the tension on Bradley's collar, Bradley stepping up the pressure of the gun. "Like I said," Bradley husked, his face reddening further from lack of oxygen, "just stopped by to see how the missus was doing."

In response to the unmistakable *tick-tick-tick* of the hammer being pulled back, Mitch unhanded Bradley's shirt and slowly straightened, held his hands in the air. The man had a loaded weapon trained on him, and he could see by the wild glint in his eyes that he was fully prepared to use it. "Nice piece," he spat. "New?"

"Yes and no." He smirked. "It shoulda been tagged as evidence, when our boys busted Pericolo last week." Shrugging, he added, "It got kind of, ah, misplaced."

Mitch's brow furrowed. "You stole it from the evidence room?"

"You're not as smart as everybody thinks, are ya, Mahoney? It never—"

"Never made it to the evidence room?"

Using the gun as a pointer, he answered, "Have a seat, Mr. High and Mighty, and keep your hands where I can see 'em."

Ciara was upstairs in the tub, alone, naked, vulnerable. Stress was as potentially deadly for her and the baby as that gun in Bradley's hand. *You've got to get that weapon,* Mitch commanded himself. *Somehow you've got to disarm this son of a—*

Still standing, he said, "They're on to you down at

headquarters. Anything happens to me, or to Ciara, they'll know exactly who to—"

"A bluff like that might be useful in poker…" A sinister smile cracked his face. "Speakin' of cards…" He slid a pack of Bicycles from his jacket pocket, slammed it onto the coffee table. "Pick a card, any card."

Mitch's lips formed a thin, stubborn line.

"Do it," Bradley demanded, leaning forward in the chair, tapping the deck with the .35 mm.

He wouldn't know about Pericolo's trick unless—

Stay calm, he warned himself. You lose your cool and you're a dead man. And Ciara… Mitch didn't want to think what Bradley might do to her in his present state of mind. He took a breath to steady his nerves, reached out and grabbed a card.

The ace of spades.

"You know what old Giovanni says about black cards…."

Mitch knew, only too well. He'd passed the sociopath's test that first night, but during his months in Philly, he'd seen two men fail it. Something told him he'd hear their screams of anguish and terror till he drew his last breath.

Bradley reached out, flipped the deck over. Skimming a hand over them, he spread the cards in a neat arc, displaying the ace of spades…times fifty-two.

Then he laughed, a sound that chilled Mitch's blood. "So where's your pretty little bride?" Bradley asked, interrupting Mitch's worrisome thoughts.

He stood taller, squared his shoulders, pretended not to have heard the question. He'd do whatever it took to keep Bradley's focus off Ciara, even if it meant stepping in front of a—

"Don't look so worried, Mahoney. I'd never do anything to hurt her." He snorted. "Won't have to. Once you're out of the way, she'll come with me willingly…she and that…baby she's carrying." He smirked. "Who do you think the little guy'll look like?"

His blood turned to ice, freezing in his veins. It isn't true, *can't* be true, Mitch told himself. Because if it was, everything he believed, everything he held dear about their relationship had been a lie.

And there sat the one man in the world who knew the ugliest fact about him. Mitch was filled with such fury that he wanted to teach him a lesson he wouldn't ever forget.

But Mitch had no proof of her sin. None…except the word of this…to call him a cur or a swine would be to insult all pigs and dogs! Mitch thought. He wanted to punish the smooth-talking, low-life predator. But having no weapon at the ready, he settled for a mild insult. "Come with *you?* Have you taken a good look at yourself lately? You're nothin' but a good-for-nothing hunk of garbage."

"Shut up," Bradley snarled.

"So when did you turn, Bradley? Or have you always been like this, even as a rookie?"

"Careful what you say," Bradley interrupted, waving the gun in the air, "or I'll…"

He was beyond reason now. Nothing scared him as much as the thought of this animal touching his wife. "Or you'll *what?* Take me out? How're you gonna explain *that?*"

Bradley licked his lips, wiped perspiration from his forehead with the back of his gun hand.

Mitch's fingers splayed, and he tensed, ready to grab it.

"I wouldn't if I were you," came Bradley's gravelly warning. His green eyes glittered, like a panther ready to pounce. Then he rested an ankle on a knee, balanced the gun there.

"I could always say I stopped over to see how you were doin'," he said, answering Mitch's question. He laughed softly. "Does this have post-traumatic shock written all over it, or what? I mean, think about it from the point of view of those knuckleheads down in Internal Affairs...guy like you, undercover all those months with a maniac like Pericolo...." He shrugged nonchalantly. Chuckling, he added, "Here's the cherry on the sundae—I could plug you, call it self-defense, and you'd still get a hero's burial. Wouldn't be *your* fault you went nuts."

The way Bradley was quivering, Mitch believed he could wrest the gun from his hand, if he could just get in closer....

"Naw, that's way too complicated. There'd be a hearing, I'd be on administrative leave while IA investigated. Truth is, you ain't worth all that bother."

He tilted the weapon left and right. "For your information, this little number here has Pericolo's prints all over it." He grinned proudly. "I've got this one all tied up with a pretty red bow, eh, Mahoney?" He stared hard, as if debating whether to answer his own question or pull the trigger.

"The weapon may have Pericolo's prints on it, but the guards on his cell block will give him an airtight alibi— or did you forget that small detail, Bradley?"

Bradley got to his feet. "Enough conversation, wise guy. Turn around."

Mitch lifted his chin defiantly and, crossing both arms over his chest, planted his feet shoulder width apart.

"You never did like taking the easy way, did you, Mahoney?" Bradley took a step closer, prepared to forcibly turn Mitch around.

It's now or never.... He grabbed the deck of cards. "Mind if I shuffle and draw again? Might improve my odds."

Bradley chortled. "What's the point? You know they're all—"

Mitch flicked the deck in Bradley's face, and as his

hands instinctively went up to protect his eyes, Mitch's left hand shot out, grabbed the gun barrel and pointed it at the ceiling. In a heartbeat, he elbowed Bradley in the Adam's apple, socked him in the stomach, stomped on his instep, rammed a hard shoulder into his nose.

Bradley doubled over, wheezing and moaning. Mitch had the gun now, and he knew it. Holding up the gloved hand, he choked out, "Don't...don't shoot...."

Mitch snorted with disgust. "You're not worth the mess," he ground out. "Now assume the position, while I—"

He heard a thump overhead, and Ciara's muffled voice: "Mitch...what's going on down there?" Mitch cut a quick glance toward the ceiling, and Bradley used that tick in time. Hot on his heels, Mitch ran for the back door and saw the lieutenant leap the fence and duck into the yard next door, where the neighbor's toddlers were splashing contentedly in their blue plastic wading pool.

Mitch drew a bead on Bradley's left shoulder, squeezed back on the trigger, slowly, slowly...

Just then, one of the twins jumped up, putting herself directly in the line of fire. "Mine!" she squealed, grabbing an inflatable horse from her towheaded brother.

Mitch eased up on the trigger as the little boy pulled her back into the water. "No," he insisted, "mine!"

Squinting one eye, he zeroed in on Bradley's shoulder once more, every muscle tense and taut as he held his breath. And then the kids were up again, right in his sights, hollering for their mommy.

From the other side of the forsythia hedge, Bradley saluted and disappeared.

The car...he's gonna circle 'round to get the Ferrari.

Slamming the back door, then bolting it, he blasted through the house. Cursing the knob lock and the dead bolt, he struggled to yank open the front door.

Somebody was out there, all right, standing behind the Ferrari's back bumper. "Good morning, Mitch," said Mrs. Thompson. "How's Ciara this morning?"

Heart hammering, Mitch ran a hand through his hair, jammed the gun into the belt at the small of his back. "Fine...you?"

"Oh, my arthritis is acting up, but in this humidity, what can a seventy-two-year-old expect?" She nodded at the Ferrari. "Fancy car...."

"Belongs to a—" He couldn't make himself say *friend*. "One of my co-workers left it here." The .35 mm wasn't Bradley's, and neither was the car. The lieutenant couldn't afford to come back for either. Mitch knew that now, like he knew his own name. "I think I hear my wife calling," he said, closing the door. "You have a nice day."

Mrs. Thompson smiled, waved. "Tell Ciara I said hi."

Mitch's shoulders slumped and he walked back to the kitchen. He hid the gun in the cookie jar on top of the fridge and grabbed the phone, dialed Parker's extension down at Headquarters. The guy didn't seem the least bit surprised when Mitch filled him in on what had just happened.

"He's never been wrapped too tight," Parker admitted, "but lately..." He whistled the "Twilight Zone" theme.

"You've gotta find him," Mitch interrupted. "My wife's—"

"I know, I know...Bradley told us all about her condition."

"Listen, Parker, he's still out there. I've got his weapon, but he won't have any trouble getting another."

"Okay, okay, Mahoney. Settle down."

"Don't tell me to settle down! If my guess is right, now that I know he's been on the 'take,' and his reputation is ruined, he's got nothin' to lose. I don't have time for your patronizing—"

"Sorry, Mitch. I didn't mean to." He paused. "Look, I know it won't be easy, but you have to settle down, for your wife's sake."

Mitch took a deep breath. "When you call in the APB, get a tow truck out here to pick up this Ferrari in my—"

"Ferrari?" Parker snickered lightly. "Did you get a raise for this last caper, buddy?"

"It's Bradley's...or else it belongs to whoever he's workin' for. You've got to get it out of here. If Ciara sees it, how am I gonna explain...?"

"I'm on it, Buddy."

"Keep me posted, will ya?"

"You bet."

"And send somebody to—"

"I'll get a surveillance guy out there, pronto."

"'A guy'? I put my neck on the chopping block to nab Pericolo. You'll send more than 'a guy'! Who knows what kind of backup Bradley's got...or where he got it. I'm a sittin' duck out here, and—"

"Sit tight, Mitch. I'll see what I can do."

He exhaled loudly, ran a trembling hand through his hair. "Keep me posted, will ya?"

"You bet," Parker said, and hung up.

Mitch glanced at the wall clock. When he came downstairs earlier, he had promised to get Ciara out of the tub in ten minutes. Amazingly, he had three whole minutes to spare. Three minutes to calm down and get up there and pretend everything was hunky-dory.

"Sweet Jesus," he prayed aloud, "give me strength."

Chet Bradley was a bald-faced liar. A turncoat, possibly a burglar—since he'd picked the back lock to get into the house—and a killer. The pampered little rich boy had never wanted for anything in his life—the fact that he was Mitch's boss without having had to pass the customary tests, was proof of that—so, was it any surprise that faced with temptation, he'd shown no self-control, snatching up bribe money with both hands? His whole life was a story of instant gratification...why should that change now?

In Mitch's mind, men like Bradley were worse than the Pericolos of the world; at least folks knew where they stood with a guy like Giovanni. Bradley was repugnant, foul, lower than a gutter rat. He'd come to the house for the express purpose of murdering Mitch, to keep him from testifying against him at an interdepartmental hearing...or in a courtroom. If he'd had to take Ciara down first to get to Mitch, he'd have done it in a whipstitch.

He raised the book he'd been pretending to read, glanced over its pages at Ciara, who absentmindedly twirled a length of flaxen hair around her forefinger as, word by word, she filled in the blocks of her crossword. Suddenly she exhaled a sigh of vexation, pencil eraser bouncing on the puzzle. The feminine arch of her left brow increased, the gentle bow of her lips smoothed, dark lashes dusted her lightly freckled cheeks as she slid a dainty fingertip down a column of definitions in the dictionary.

She was, in his opinion, the loveliest woman on two feet. Pregnancy had only enhanced her beauty, filling out the sharp angles and planes of her girlish face in a womanly, sensual way.

Sensual enough to reach out to Bradley for physical comfort in her husband's absence?

He remembered the things her mother had said, things that made it clear Bradley had spent countless hours in this house, alone with his wife. Mitch felt the heat of jealous fury rise in his cheeks, took a sip from the glass of the ice water, standing on a soapstone coaster beside him, hoping to cool his temper.

Is she the innocent young thing you married, or a passionate woman? She's both, he admitted, the edge of his uncertainty sharpening.

Mitch now pressed a thumb to one temple, his fingertips to the other, effectively blocking her from view, and remembered their wedding night, how she'd stared up at him, willing him to hold her close with nothing more than the silent draw of her long-lashed crystalline eyes.

The moment he'd slipped his arms around her, he knew...knew he'd be with her till the end of his life. Mitch knew it now, too, even if he discovered that every one of his ugly suspicions were true.

He'd lived a rough, rugged life, and his women had been a reflection of that, because he'd had neither the time nor the inclination for love. Life was mean, and so he lived it that way. Tenderness? Compassion? A lot of romantic nonsense, in his opinion. Besides, what did a man like him, who had committed himself to spending his days dogging bad guys and dodging bullets, need with love? He couldn't afford to fritter away even one precious moment, seeking something he believed he should not have.

And so he'd guarded his heart with extreme caution. Built a sturdy wall to protect himself. If he couldn't accept love, why bother to give it? But Ciara had burrowed under that wall. Yes, life was mean...past tense. She had changed all that. He'd built a wall around his heart, all right, but he hadn't built it nearly tall enough or strong enough, because he hadn't counted on meeting a woman like Ciara....

When she laughed, her whole body got involved. And if something saddened those close to her, it was apparent to anyone with eyes that she felt the pain, too, all the way down to her size-five feet.

That night on the cruise ship, when she'd looked into his eyes, he realized that she saw him as the man he'd always wanted to be. No need for a fancy suit or a Boston

education. No need for pretense or pretty words, not with
Ciara!

She could read his moods by something as insignificant
as a quirk of an eyebrow or the slant of his smile. Mitch
strongly suspected she could read his mind, too, for on
more than one occasion she'd spoken aloud the thoughts
pinging around in his head.

She seemed to sense how alone he felt, despite the fact
that he had three burly brothers and two sisters, parents,
grandparents, aunts and uncles and cousins. She had taken
one look at his college graduation picture, crinkled her face
with compassion and said, "Oh, Mitch, why do you look
so *sad?*"

When his mother had seen the photo, she'd said, "Such
a handsome boy, that youngest son of mine!" And his dad
had agreed. "He's got the Mahoney jaw, all right." Why
hadn't the people he'd known all his life been able to see
the quiet fear, the desperation burning in his eyes, yet
Ciara, who'd known him mere weeks the first time she'd
viewed the portrait, had spotted it right off?

Mitch had marveled at that, because until she'd pointed
it out and followed it up by dispensing her unique brand
of all-out love like warm soothing salve, *he* hadn't admitted it!

Starting on their wedding night, without regard for her
own needs and desires and fears, she gave what *he* needed.
And in her tender, feminine embrace, he felt at once shel-
tered and exposed, strong and weak, manly and boylike.

And more alive than he'd ever felt in his life.

Doggone if she isn't some kind of woman! he thought.
Li'l thing whose head barely reaches your shoulders, becoming the biggest thing in your life....

Mitch had never felt any regret about leaving places or
people when his cases ended, and it was time to move on.

But Mitch knew if he ever had to leave Ciara, he'd miss her more than he would miss water.

The breath caught in his throat as he recalled the sensation of her slender fingers, weaving through his hair on the night the preacher made them man and wife. Her whisper-soft sighs had floated into his ears as she responded to his touch, and her heart—the same heart that had beat hard and angry when faced with life's injustices—thumped wildly against his chest as he held her close.

The first time he'd said those three words on the cruise ship deck, he'd asked himself, Are you crazy? Shut up, man! Say whatever she wants to hear, but don't say that! And he'd shrugged, thinking that when a man thought a thing a thousand times or more, wasn't it just natural to say it out loud? He'd spent his whole adult life avoiding that phrase, words that, until Ciara, had been fearsome. Yet they'd linked together and rolled off his tongue so easily and naturally, all he could do was hope they'd spilled out quietly enough that she hadn't heard them.

"What did you say?" she'd asked, her voice husky.

He couldn't very well repeat it, now could he? It wouldn't have been fair to either of them, since he knew full well he wouldn't be seeing her once the trip ended, no matter how much he'd meant what he said.

Oh, how she'd *moved* him! She'd reached places in his heart and soul and mind that he would have bet his last dollar were impossible to reach...if they existed at all.

"What did you say?" was her quiet, honest question.

Mitch wouldn't have hurt her for all the world. He'd rather die than cause her a moment's pain. So he'd stood there, trying to conjure up a similar-sounding phrase that would answer her...painlessly. No matter what he said, *he'd* be hurt....

If she hadn't branded him with that loving, longing look as she traced his lips with her fingertips right then, Mitch might have summoned the strength to pull it off. But that intimate, yet innocent, gesture was the final hammer stroke to the already crumbling wall he'd built around his heart.

He'd watched her with his nieces and nephews, doling out instructions and admonitions and compliments with equal care. He'd seen her minister to her elderly aunt, and to her parents, with a compassion he'd once believed reserved only for God's angels.

He had never let anyone see him cry. Not even the threat of dying in the trunk of a car had pushed him that far. But gazing into her eyes, seeing the purity of her love looking back at him, woke emotions long asleep. And once awakened, those feelings bubbled up and boiled over like a too-hot stew pot. He'd never wanted anything in his life more than he wanted her and her pure, unconditional love.

So he'd gathered her close, closer, whether to hide his tears from her or hide her from his tears, Mitch didn't know, and rested his chin amid her mass of soft, pale curls. "I'd better get to my cabin," he'd said, his voice gruff and hard from biting back a sob. And he'd walked away, just like that, without a backward glance or a by-your-leave.

And the night stretched on endlessly.

He'd exposed his most vulnerable self to her. How could he face her again, knowing she'd seen his weakness? Mitch fretted about it all through the night. Yearning, he understood, was an emotion born of experiencing perfection, and he wished he'd never begun this dangerous game of flirtation-turned-fondness-turned-love. Because he didn't believe he deserved the devotion of one so fine, so pure, so innocent. Didn't believe he'd earned the loyalty of a woman that fine.

He'd been like an animal these past years, like a mole, always seeking shadows as he moved from place to place in search of safety, in search of peace. Survival of the fittest, he'd heard, was the law of the land. Well, he'd survived top-secret cases, but to what end? To find safety and peace in Ciara's arms, only to discover he didn't deserve it? Far better never to have tasted fine wine at all than to have it snatched away, forcing him to live forevermore without even the smallest sip.

He had learned to accept the fact that, because of his career choice, he'd never have a family. A home. The love of a good woman. But could he learn to live without Ciara's love, now that he'd tasted the sweetness of it?

A sob ached in his throat, and Mitch buried his face in the pages of his book. If she shared herself with *him,* he thought, gritting his teeth, even if it *was* because she was lonesome, and scared, I'll—

"Mitch? What's wrong?"

Like the angel she was, Ciara had read his heart. "Nothing," he said, holding the book high, to hide his teary eyes.

"I'm cold," she said, patting the mattress. "Would you hold me…get me warm?"

He put down his book, crossed the room in two strides and settled beside her. He buried his face in her neck and wrapped both arms around her, holding this fragile flower who had planted the seed of her love deep in his heart, as the wild rose vine plants its seed even in the craggiest outcropping of a snow-covered mountaintop. He would hold tight to perfection for as long as he could, so at least he'd have these moments to remember, in case she'd meant it when she told him to pack up and leave.

Placing a tiny hand on either side of his face, she brought him out of hiding. Tears shimmered in her eyes and glistened on her long, lush lashes when she said, "I love you, Mitch." She pressed her lips to his, softly at first as she combed delicate fingers through his hair, more urgently then, as those dainty fingers clutched at his shoulders, his back, his neck, with a strength that belied her size and condition.

Oh, how he wanted her! Wanted her with every echo of his soul, with every beat of his heart. But he dared not want....

He'd seen film footage of the floods in the midwest the summer before, when the rivers rose and threatened to devour every building and barn, every mortal man or mammal for miles. The surging water's awesome power humbled him as he watched it sluice through the streets, hissing like a giant turbid snake.

What emanated from Ciara, who felt so small and helpless in his arms, was far more powerful than the river's rage. And though she didn't know it—and certainly wouldn't have intended it—she stirred more fear and apprehension in him than the roiling waterway.

Mitch had survived numerous near fatal experiences, but with nothing to live for or look forward to, death had no authority over him. Even Bradley, brandishing his loaded gun, hadn't terrified him as much as this tiny woman in his arms. She loved him. He could see it in her eyes, in her smile. Could feel it in her touch, taste it in her kiss. And he loved her more than life itself. If she *had* succumbed to temptation, it had only been because he'd left her alone for so long....

He looked inside himself for the strength to turn away from the love so evident on her face, and rested his hands on her thickened waist.

They were strong hands. Hands that had not wavered, no matter how strenuous the task. And yet, when he put those work-hardened hands on this woman, they trembled, the way a crisp autumn leaf shivers at winter's first icy blast.

He looked into her eyes, read the love there. Hesitantly he ran a hand down her back, and when he did, a rough callus caught on the finely woven fabric of her nightgown. He stopped, pulling abruptly away, embarrassed that his big clumsy hand had damaged the pretty gown.

Yet again she read his heart. "It's all right," she whispered.

But it wasn't all right. Nothing would ever be all right, until he knew for certain whether she had betrayed her vows. Because he loved her like he'd never loved anyone, like he'd never known it was *possible* to love, and the moment he admitted it, Mitch was doomed.

She pressed his "offending" hand to her chest. "See? I'm nervous, too...."

He felt the wild thrumming of her heart, felt it vibrate through his palm, past his wrist and elbow, straight to the core of him. They were connected, for the moment, by hard-beating hearts, by desire that coursed from her into him.

In a move that stunned and surprised him, she boldly reached out and grabbed his shirt collar, drawing him near, her soft yet insistent kisses imprinting on his heart as surely as a cowboy's branding iron sears the rancher's brand to his cattle.

His mind whirled as a sweet, soft moan sang from deep within her, its music moving over him like wind ripples on a still pond, and he returned her kiss with equal ardor.

"Easy," she sighed. "Easy...."

Misunderstanding her intent, Mitch immediately withdrew. Ciara read the hurt and humiliation burning in his eyes. "I said *easy*," she smiled mischievously, "not *stop*."

His left brow quirked and his lips slanted in a grin. "You weren't really cold, were you?"

Ciara shrugged. "Would I have said I was if I wasn't?" He nodded. "I think you would."

Her fingertip traced his eyebrows, his cheekbones, his jaw. "Are you saying you think I'm dishonest?"

"Never intentionally," he said.

Frowning, she gave him a crooked grin. "What does *that* mean?"

You're a passionate woman, he told her mentally. You're not the kind who can be left alone, to wilt and die without—

"Mitch," she said, interrupting his reverie, "what's going on in that head of yours? You've been acting strange all day. Is there something you're not telling me?"

I could ask you the same question, he thought. And then Bradley, the gun, the knowledge that the fool was out there somewhere, carrying a heated vengeance around in that sick, twisted mind of his, blotted out Mitch's response.

She backed away to arm's length, gave him a stern look. "I'm not a child, Mitch. If there's something I should know…"

Mitch wasn't about to upset the apple cart. Her blood count, the readouts Peterson had been getting by way of the monitor, everything had been going fine, up till now, and he intended to keep it that way. "I'm just worried about you," he said truthfully, pulling her closer, resting his chin atop her head.

Worried that this baby is going to die, or kill you, and wouldn't that be ironic if it isn't even mine….

"Mitch?"

"Hmm?"

"I love you…."

He closed his eyes tight. *Dear God in Heaven, give me strength….* "I love you, too, sweetie. I love you, too."

Chapter Nine

The bright blue sky warmed the mourners who stood in a tight semicircle, heads bowed and hands folded, as sunlight glinted off the polished brass handles, pointing toward heaven like luminescent arrows. And Ciara, dry-eyed and tight-lipped, stared at the white enamel casket, trying to focus on the preacher's powerful voice.

"And our time comes to an end like a sigh...." He closed his eyes, smiled serenely and began reciting from the Book of Job: "'Thine hands have made me and fashioned me together roundabout; yet thou dost destroy me. Remember, I beseech thee, that thou hast made me as the clay; wilt thou bring me into dust again?'" Closing the Holy Book, he bent down, scooped up a handful of freshly-dug dirt and sprinkled it into the hole. "'You shall return to the ground,'" he quoted Genesis, "'for out of it you were taken; you are dust, and to dust you shall return.'"

Ciara wanted to shake a fist at the sky. *Why, God?* she wanted to shout. Don't You have enough cherubim and seraphim? Did You have to take *my* baby boy...?

She had not cried over the death of her child, had not

shed a single tear. Would tears bring him back to life? Would sobs revive him? Would the ache in her heart matter at all to the One Who had taken him?

Absentmindedly she kneaded her stomach, where so recently the infant had nestled in her nurturing womb, taking quiet comfort from her steadfast love. He had moved inside her, each strong jab and kick proof of his vitality and vigor.

In a flash, the bright blue sky turned blinding white, and Ciara was in the delivery room, perspiring and panting as the contractions contorted her face.

It's all right, *she told herself.* The pain is only temporary. When this is over, you'll have a beautiful baby boy....

She didn't know how she knew it was a boy, but she knew.

She knew....

Soon, the doctor would lay him on her chest, kicking, crying, arms akimbo. She'd smooth back his wet hair, count teensy fingers and toes, inspect every tiny joint, every minuscule crevice, each contour and curve and line of his warm little body. She'd soothe and comfort him, and his small, hungry lips would seek nourishment from her milk-laden breast.

"Just a few more minutes," the doctor said. "Just a few more minutes."

Pride and joy and thankfulness filled her eyes with tears, put a sob in her throat. Just a few more minutes, *she repeated, smiling.* In a few minutes, I'll be a mommy.

She made herself focus on the bustle of activity in the blindingly bright delivery room—shuffle of paper-shoed feet, the rustle of surgical gowns, banter of the staff, clank of tools against stainless steel trays—instead of the pain, the gripping, never-ending, powerful pain....

Then, for a half second, maybe less, silence—deep and still and falsely calm. No one moved or spoke or breathed, as if the world had stopped spinning and everything, every-one in it had ceased to exist.

In the next eyeblink, life!

Ciara knew—though she didn't understand how she knew—that during the instant of deadly quiet, her baby boy had died. She knew because the pain of childbirth had ceased, and in its place, heartache like none she'd experienced.

The doctor gave her knee an obligatory pat, pat, pat. "I'm so sorry, Mrs. Mahoney, but…"

Her heartbeat doubled, tripled.

"We did everything we could, but," he said softly, so very softly that Ciara thought perhaps she'd imagined it; perhaps it had been part of a pain-induced hallucination. "There's no easy way to say this, I'm afraid…but your baby is dead."

With every beat of her heart, every pound of her pulse, the word echoed in her head. Dead. Your baby is dead…dead…dead.

The eye-blinding white light warmed to a golden glow, and she found herself in the cemetery again, eyes locked on an ivory coffin hardly bigger than a breadbox. Any minute now it would be lowered into the rectangular hole carved into the earth by shovel and pickax. The hole was hardly bigger than the casket, yet it seemed to gape and yawn like a ravenous, savage beast, hungering to swallow up her newborn son, forever.

Ciara forced her gaze away from her boy's eternal bed, focused on the faces of the people who had gathered around: her mother, daubing her face with a lace-trimmed hanky; her father, staring stoically straight ahead; sniffling in-laws; sad-eyed neighbors and co-workers; a few of her students, looking bewildered by this thing called Death; and their parents, whose expressions said, I'm sorry, but better you than me.... Everyone had shed at least one tear for the infant whose birth caused his death.

So why not Ciara? People will think you didn't love him; people will think you don't care. And that was a lie, the biggest lie ever told.

Ciara had never held him to her breast. Had never looked into the miracle that was his face. Had never inhaled the sweet scent of his satiny skin. Would not hear his soft coos or his demanding cries. Could never feel the miraculous strength of his tiny fingers, wrapping around her own. But she loved him, and oh, how she missed him!

It began as nothing more than a solitary thought in her head:

No....

And became a soft whisper that no one, not even those right beside her could hear: "No...."

Then heads turned, and the monotonous din of voices, joined in prayer, quieted when she said more loudly, more firmly, "No."

"No!" she screamed, falling across the coffin. "No, no, no, no, no...."

A man's voice, deep, powerful—her father's?—floated into her ears. "Ciara, sweetie, don't—"

Don't what? Don't grieve for my baby? Don't make a scene? Don't make the rest of you uncomfortable?

She gripped the little casket tighter. "You can't have him, Lord!" she yelled. "You can't take him, because he's mine!"

Then, utter silence.

Ciara looked around her, surprised that the other mourners were gone, all of them.

Car doors slammed.

Engines revved.

The grounds crew stepped forward. Where had they come from? And a beer-bellied man in a grimy baseball cap stuck out one gloved finger, pressed the red button and started up the machine that would carry the casket down, down into the dark, damp dirt.

Rage roiled inside her. Don't! *she ordered.* Stop that, right now! *But the motor continued grinding.*

Ciara wanted to grab his fat wrist, crush every bone in the hand responsible for beginning her son's slow, steady descent into the cold, unwelcoming earth.

The mournful moan started softly at first, then escalated in pitch and volume, like the first piercing strains of a fire engine's wail. She couldn't pinpoint the source of the grief-stricken groan, and, frightened by it, Ciara clapped her hands over her ears. The keening call echoed all around her, bounced from marble headstones, granite angels, trellised tombstones and returned, like a self-willed boomerang to its genesis.

"No-o-o-o-o-o-o-o…"

Then, big hands, strong, sure hands gripped her shoulders.

"Ciara? Ciara…"

"Where's Mitch?" she sobbed. "Where is my husband? Why isn't he here? Why!"

"I'm here, Ciara, I'm here, right here, right—"

"That was some dream," Mitch said when her eyes fluttered open. He slipped an arm under her neck, pulled her near. "Aw, sweetie," he sighed, kissing her temple, "you're trembling." He tugged the sheet over her shoulder, tucked it under her chin. "How 'bout a cup of warm milk?" he asked, holding her closer. "Maybe that'll relax you, help you get back to sleep…"

"I hate milk," she mumbled, her voice sleep drowsy.

Something you should know after eight months of marriage, he scolded himself. Holding her at arm's length, Mitch cupped her chin in a palm. "You want to talk about it?"

Ciara shook her head, then buried her face in his shoulder. "You weren't there," she whispered brokenly. "You...weren't...*there*."

She sounded so forlorn, so frightened, like a child lost in the woods. His heart ached, because once again, he felt powerless to comfort her. "I wasn't *where*, sweetie?" he asked, brushing the bangs from her forehead.

Ciara shook her head. "Nothing...just, just a dream..."

Nearly every inch of her was pressed against him, yet Mitch felt as though someone had built a brick wall between them. Her taut muscles, her refusal to tell him about the nightmare, the way her voice trembled when she'd said, "You weren't there..."

He held her a long while, not talking, not asking her to. A shaft of moonlight had slipped under the window shade, cutting an inch-wide slice of light through the blackness. It lit the room just enough for him to see her sad, still-sleepy eyes.

"I know I wasn't here," he said at last, a tremor in his own voice. "I can't tell you anything that'll undo what's already done, but I can tell you this—I'll be here for you from now on. I promise."

He waited for a reaction of some kind: a nod, a sigh, *something*.

Either she's asleep, he told himself, or she doesn't believe you.

Tears stung his eyes, and he held his breath to keep them at bay. He had done this to her—he, and the Bureau—and if she *had* strayed during his absence...

He held her a little tighter, kissed the top of her head.

"What're we going to do, once this baby is born?" she'd asked earlier, worried he might spoil her, waiting on her constantly.

The question became a chant in his wide-awake mind: What're we going to do? What're we going to do?

Her health was precarious, at best.

The baby, if it survived, might not even be his.

And Bradley was out there somewhere, fully convinced that the only way to stay out of prison was to silence Mitch...permanently.

Mitch shivered involuntarily. He certainly didn't want to die, especially now that he and Ciara were so close to getting back what they'd once had. If something happened to him now, who would look after her?

Lord Jesus, he prayed, *what am I going to do?*

She couldn't get that dream out of her mind until the baby moved inside her. Even then, the eerie aftereffects flashed in her mind.

Ciara put her full attention on the cross-stitch she'd been working on. Better that than try and make small talk with Mitch, she thought. "I'm just tired, that's all," she'd fibbed, when he'd asked if she was feeling okay. "It's nothing," she'd answered, when he'd wanted to know if something was wrong. "Thanks, but I'm fine," she'd said, when he'd offered to bring her a snack. What else *could* she do...admit she was furious at him for something he'd done or hadn't done...in a *dream?*

Mitch made a few calls on the kitchen phone, pacing as far as the twelve-foot cord would allow, talking in low, steady tones, rousing her curiosity and more than just a little of her suspicion. Who was he talking to, and what topic demanded such privacy?

Had he met a woman while he'd been undercover? Someone who had made his lonely days more bearable; someone who hadn't been so easy to say goodbye to?

Or were there loose ends, still unraveled, ends that could choke him if he didn't tie them up?

This job of his is going to be the death of me, she fumed. The thought distracted her from the needlework, and she pricked her finger. "Ouch!" she said, popping it into her mouth.

Holding the phone against his chest, Mitch stuck his head into the doorway. "You okay in there?"

She held her finger up, as if testing the direction of the wind. "Stuck myself," she said, rolling her eyes. "No big deal."

Nodding, he smiled. "Whistle if you need me," he said, and popped out of sight again.

She could have picked up the portable, pretended she'd forgotten he was using the extension. Perhaps a snippet of conversation would answer her questions. Maybe a word, a phrase, overheard before he realized she'd joined him on the line, would ease her fears.

Or you could act like a grown-up, and ask him straight-out, she told herself. No...just because he's your husband doesn't mean you have a right to know *every* intimate detail of his life.

Intimate?

Could a man like that have sought comfort in the arms of another woman? Ciara shuddered, shook her head. Not Mitch. Anyone but Mitch. She had never met a more fiercely loyal man. He was devoted to his family. Dedicated to his job. Unwavering in his reasons for choosing a career in law enforcement.

"What are you making, there?" Mitch asked.

Gasping, Ciara lurched with fright.

He was beside her on the sofa bed in an instant. "Are you all right? Geez, I'm sorry, sweetie. I didn't mean to scare you."

"It's okay," she said, patting her chest, as if the action could slow the rapid beating of her heart. "It wasn't your fault." She had always liked working in complete silence, without radio or stereo or TV to interfere with her private thoughts. And at the moment when his voice had cracked the stillness of the afternoon, her thoughts had been very private, indeed.

He turned his head slightly, regarding her from the corner of his eyes. "You sure you're okay?"

She nodded.

"And you don't want anything? More tea? A cookie? Some—"

"I'm fine, honest," she interrupted.

Mitch continued to study her face for a moment more. "All right, if you say so."

The glint in his dark eyes told her he didn't believe a word of it. "You want the truth? Really?"

His brows rose in response to her terse tone. Blinking innocently he said, "Well, I asked, didn't I?"

Ciara narrowed her eyes, set her needlepoint aside, crossed both arms over her chest. "You asked for it...."

He lay on his side facing her, drove his elbow into the extra pillow, and propped his head on a palm. "Go on. Start talkin'. I'm all ears."

You weren't there for me in the dream, and you weren't there for me in real life, she thought, the stirrings of anger niggling at her. Ciara remembered the day she discovered she was going to have a baby. The first person she had wanted to tell, naturally, had been Mitch. And where were you? she demanded mentally. You were off somewhere making like James Bond.

And when the doctor had diagnosed her condition, warned her to stay off her feet. Where were you then? Where *were* you!

He had been so gentle and affectionate, so tender and loving when the nightmare had awakened her. He had been that way, practically from the moment they'd met, and those very qualities had made being without him all those months so much harder to bear. Ciara seemed to remember muttering and mumbling noncommittal responses to his quiet questions. But what would he have done if you'd told him the truth? she wondered. How affectionate would he have been then?

"What are you trying to do," he asked, grinning, "win the Alfred Hitchcock 'Keep 'Em in Suspense' award?"

Their gazes fused on an invisible thread of tension...his the result of confusion, hers caused by steadily mounting anger.

Mitch reached out slowly, gently laying a palm against her cheek. "You look so tired, sweetie," he said. "Let me hold you so you can take a little nap, right here on my shoulder."

She planted both palms on his chest, locked her elbows and managed to keep him at arm's length. "Do I smell beer on your breath?" she asked, narrowing one eye suspiciously.

He held up two fingers. "I had two. That's all. While I was cleaning up your lunch dishes." He snickered. "Just two...on an empty stomach."

Ciara looked into his eyes. He was right...he hadn't had a bite to eat all day. He looked so cute, so helpless; how could she lambaste him in this condition!

"So, what do you say? You want to take a little nap?"

"I'm not sleepy, Mitch. I'm...I'm bored, and I'm tired, and I'm achy from lying around like a hundred-year-old house cat all day. I'm sick of looking at these four walls, and I'm—"

"Tomorrow is the Fourth of July, you know."

She gave her head a little shake, drew her brows together in a frown. "What?"

"Oh, sweetie, I've got it all worked out! First, we'll have a big country breakfast...pancakes, home fries, eggs over easy. After your bath, we'll get you into some real clothes for a change, watch the parade on TV. This evening we'll have a cookout—steaks, potato salad, baked beans—the works! And after that, we'll lounge around in the deck chairs, watching the sky get dark...." Mitch wiggled his eyebrows. "Did you know that we can see the fireworks from the mall in Columbia from our backyard?"

Smiling, Ciara shook her head, so caught up in his excited recitation that she almost forgot why she'd been mad in the first place. "You're a grown man, Mitch Mahoney. How can you get so caught up in a light show?" she asked affectionately. "Besides, how do you know that?"

"I don't see anything wrong with looking forward to some stars and spangles," he said defensively. And just as quickly he added, "Old Mrs. Thompson told me the other morning. She's comin' over for the barbecue and bringing her grandson. He's four." Squinting one eye, he looked toward the ceiling. "His name is Nicky or Ricky or something like that. Your folks are coming, too, and so is the entire Mahoney clan."

Ciara's eyes lit up. "You're kidding. When did you plan—"

"This morning. I made about a dozen phone calls while you were working on..." He leaned forward. "What *is* that thing, anyway?"

She clutched the fabric to her chest. "I don't like people looking at my needlework until it's finished."

He went back to resting on his palm. "You've been working on it for days," he grumbled good-naturedly. "When is it going to be finished, anyway?"

He looked like a little boy, Ciara thought, when he pouted that way. Grinning maternally, she answered him as if he were one of her fourth-graders. "It'll be finished when it's finished, young man."

Mitch grabbed the finger she was shaking under his nose. "Didn't your mother teach you it isn't polite to point?" he asked, kissing it.

"She did. But I wasn't pointing. I was scolding. There's a difference."

"Not when you're on the receiving end, there isn't." He kissed her palm. "Besides, 'When you point a finger at me, you're pointing three more right back at you.'" Pressing his lips to her wrist, he added, "I learned that in the second grade, when I accused Carrie Butler of putting a valentine card in my tote tray."

"Carrie Butler, eh?" Ciara asked, one brow up in mock jealousy. "You sure pulled that name out of the air pretty quick, considering how long ago you were in second grade."

"Hey," he mumbled into the crook of her elbow, "watch it. It wasn't *that* long ago."

"I'd say a quarter of a century ago is a long time." She giggled. "Mitch. Stop that. It tickles."

"What…this?" he teased, kissing the spot again.

"Yes, that. Now cut it out," she insisted, laughing harder. "I mean it now…."

"Okay. Sorry. I was just trying to distract you, is all."

She looked into his handsome face. "Distract me? Distract me from what?"

"From asking any more questions about Carrie." He winked, then sent her a mischievous smirk. "I asked her to marry me, you know."

Grinning now, Ciara gasped, pressed a palm to her chest. "But…but you said *I* was the first woman you proposed to…."

"You were the first *woman.* Carrie was the first *girl.*" He rolled onto his back, tucked both hands under his neck and exhaled a dreamy sigh. "I met her in kindergarten, in the sand pit. She beaned me with a red plastic shovel. It was love at first strike."

Another gasp. "You said she was the *first* girl…there were others?"

He shrugged. "Oh," he said lightly, inspecting his fingernails, "one or two."

She grabbed a handful of his shirt. "How many others? I want names and addresses, mister, 'cause I aim to hunt them down, every last one of them, and—"

"Whoa," he interrupted, hands up in mock surrender. "I've never seen this side of you before."

"What side?"

"The jealous, vindictive side."

She blew a puff of air through her lips. "Jealous? I'm not jealous. I'll have you know I don't have a jealous bone in my body."

He looked almost wounded. "You don't?"

Shaking her head, she announced emphatically, "Not a one."

"So it doesn't bother you that Carrie was my first?"

She giggled. "Not in the least!" After a moment she added, "Your first what?"

"My first love, of course."

Grinning, Ciara rolled her eyes. "You weren't in love. You were *seven*."

"I wasn't seven."

"Everybody is seven in the second grade. Didn't you just say you asked her to marry you in the second...."

"Yes, but I asked her again when we were in high school."

This wasn't funny anymore. He'd known this Carrie person since kindergarten, had asked her to marry him in high school. "So what did she say?"

Mitch blinked. "What did who say?"

Ciara gave his shoulder a playful slap. "Carrie, silly. When you asked her to marry you...the second time...what did she say?"

"She told me to take a flying leap." He did a perfect Stan Laurel nod of his head.

"But...but you must have been sweet and handsome even then. *Why* did she say no?"

"Did I say she said no?"

"You said she told you to—"

"Take a flying leap. That's right."

Ciara exhaled a frustrated sigh. "If that isn't a rejection, I don't know what is."

"We were both on the gymnastics team. I was on the parallel bars. She kept pesterin' me to get off, give her a turn. And I said, 'Gosh, Carrie, you sound just like a wife. Maybe we should get married.' And she said, 'Mitch Mahoney, why don't you—'"

"'Take a flying leap?'" they finished together, laughing.

They lay there cuddling in silence for a moment before Ciara said, "What did this Carrie girl look like?"

"Mmmm," he growled, "she was hot stuff. Blonde, blue-eyed, with the cutest nose I ever—"

"Sounds like you're describing me!"

"Hmmm." He rubbed his chin thoughtfully. "I hadn't noticed...."

She quirked a brow. "Did you ever ask her to marry you again? After the uneven bars incident, I mean?"

"As a matter of fact, I didn't."

"Why not?"

"Hey, I wasn't the brightest bulb on the tree, but nobody coulda called me dim-watted, either."

"Dim-witted," she corrected with a twinkle in her eye.

Mitch sighed. Clapped a hand over his forehead. "*Carrie* always got my puns." He peeked between two fingers. "She thought they were funny, too."

Ciara sniffed indignantly. "Well, she must have had a very strange sense of what's funny." She paused. "Did you *want* her to say yes?"

"Maybe, but only a little."

She clucked her tongue, then said, "Say, our names are awfully similar...Carrie, Ciara...why you can barely tell them apart!"

"Hmmm." He went back to massaging his chin. "What do you suppose it means?"

"That you were searching for a Carrie replacement...for *years*...and you found it in *me!*"

He wrinkled his brow. "You think so?" He gave it a moment of consideration. "Naw. I don't think so."

"I wonder what Sigmund Freud would say about it?"

"He'd say, 'Mitch, if you have a lick of sense, you'll get your high school yearbook and show your pretty little wife what Carrie *really* looked like, before she boxes your ears.'"

"What are you talking about?" she asked, when he climbed off the sofa bed.

Mitch rummaged on the bookshelf, slid the black volume from between three other yearbooks. He flipped to the back, skimmed the glossary, chanting, "Butler, Butler, Butler...ah, there she is. Page two-sixteen."

He opened the book to the right page, handed it to Ciara.

She slid a finger over the glossy paper, stopping beside the postage-stamp-size black-and-white photo of Carrie Butler. The girl had short dark hair, a monobrow, and a slightly hairy upper lip. "'French Club president, Math Club, Chess Club,'" Ciara read. She eyed him warily. "You really asked her to marry you?"

"What can I say? The guys were always pickin' on her."

Her heart thumped with love for him. "You mean, you risked being teased by the other kids, because you felt sorry for her?"

He shook his head. "Shoulda let you go on thinking Carrie was your twin, 'cause this is embarrassing."

His reddened cheeks told her he hadn't been kidding.

''Mitch, I don't think I ever loved you more than I do at this minute.''

He tucked in his chin. ''Why?''

''Because,'' she said softly, ''you have a heart as big as your head, that's why.''

And a man with a heart like that, she told herself, smiling happily, couldn't cheat on his wife.

Chapter Ten

Ciara looked around her at friends and family who had gathered in response to Mitch's invitation. On blankets spread on the lawn, in deck chairs, at the umbrella-shaded patio table, they sat, sipping iced tea and munching hot dogs.

"How's my girl?" Joe Dorsey asked.

She held out her hand to the tall, gray-haired man who sat in the chaise lounge beside her. "Better than I've been in a long time, Dad."

He squeezed, then patted her hand affectionately, his blue eyes glittering. "I have to admit, you look good. You look happy."

"I am happy." Ciara turned slightly in the chair to face him more directly. "Am I crazy, Dad? Am I out of my ever-lovin' mind to feel this way?"

He frowned slightly. "Of course not. You're young and beautiful and a wonderful human being. You have every right to be happy."

Sighing, she glanced across the yard, where Mitch stood, tossing a softball back and forth with his nephew. The gentle July breeze riffled his dark curls, giving a boyish quality to the masculine angles and planes of his handsome face. Sunlight, dappling through the leafy trees overhead, sparkled in his dark eyes. His smile reminded her of the way she felt whenever, after days and days of gray skies and rain, the clouds lifted and the sun would come out. *Lord, how I love him,* she prayed silently.

But he'd left her, with no word or warning. Had put himself in harm's way to apprehend an unknown criminal who'd committed some heinous crime.... Would he ever tell her where he'd been? What he'd been doing? Why he'd left the way he had?

Ciara sighed. "I love him," she said softly, squeezing her father's hand. "Maybe I *am* crazy, because I don't know if I have what it takes—"

"To love him? Of course you have what it takes. Look at you," he said with a nod of his chin, "sitting there. You've been sitting around, doing nothing, for two solid weeks now." One graying brow rose as he added, "I know that must be tough, real tough, for a bundle of energy like you. But you're doing it, because..." He waved a hand, inviting her to complete his sentence.

Smiling, she said, "Because I love this baby, that's why."

"And no sacrifice is too great for one you truly love."

She gazed into his blue eyes. When she was a girl, they'd often played the "whose eyes are bluest" game. "Your eyes are so blue, the cornflowers will be jealous," she'd say. "And yours are so blue, the sky wants to duel at dawn." Shaking her head fiercely, Ciara would respond, "Mother robins could mistake your eyes for baby eggs." "And the miners in the sapphire mines come home depressed," he'd counter, "because they can't find any stones as blue as your eyes."

"Was it hard, Dad? Leaving the department, I mean."

He nodded so slowly it was scarcely noticeable. "I've done easier things, I suppose."

Ciara watched him glance around, saw that when he focused on his wife, his jaw automatically tensed and his lips tightened.

"She was miserable," he said in a barely audible voice. "You were too small to remember, I suppose, but there were times when I thought she might have a nervous breakdown." He met Ciara's eyes. "I couldn't let it go on. I had hurt her for so long already. I had to do something to stop her pain."

"You loved her a lot, didn't you?"

His eyes crinkled a bit when he smiled. "You say it in the past tense. What makes you think I don't love her still?"

"Oh," Ciara sighed, "I'm sure you love her...the way Mitch loves Ian, the way I love you." Slowly she shook her head. "But you don't love her in a romantic way."

For a moment—such a fleeting tick in time that Ciara would have missed it had she blinked—she read the gut-wrenching pain he'd buried in his heart for so many years. Her father tore his gaze from hers, stared at the dark green clover leaves between his sneakered feet. She had done more than strike a nerve with her observation. For the first time in her twenty-eight years, Ciara saw him not merely as her father, but as a flesh-and-bone man, with needs and dreams and yearnings like any other man had.

"You never did love her that way, did you, Dad?"

The corners of his mouth twitched as he struggled to retain his composure and control. "Ciara," came his raspy whisper, "she's your mother. You haven't the right to say things like that."

"I'm sorry, Dad. I just want to hear the truth...from you."

"Well, *I'm* sorry, because I will never say anything disrespectful about her. She did a spectacular job raising you, and—''

"And you're grateful for that. You even *love* her for that." Ciara paused. "It's all right, Dad. I'm not a little girl anymore. Lately," she said, looking over at Mitch again, "it's hard to believe I ever *was* a little girl."

She sighed, returned her attention to her father. "I saw more than you realized. I know you both tried to hide it from me, but I knew, I always knew, that whatever you had wasn't what some other kids' parents had."

He faced her, his eyes boring deep into hers. "What are you saying, Ciara?"

"That I love you both for what you did. You mentioned sacrifice a little bit ago. 'No sacrifice is too great for one you truly love.' You didn't leave the department because you were worried about Mom. You left because you loved *me,* and since Mom was mostly in charge of me..."

His broad shoulders slumped, and Ciara wanted to climb into his lap as she had when she was tiny, snuggle into the crook of his neck and hug him tight until everything was all right again. But she couldn't do that now, because she'd grown up and married, and soon she'd be a parent herself. If you didn't learn anything else in these seven months alone, she thought, eyes on Mitch again, it's that it takes a lot more than a hug to make everything all right again.

"If I'm even *half* the parent you've been," she said, patting her tummy, "this little tyke will be the luckiest baby ever born."

He swallowed. Blinked. Took a deep breath. "We were so young when we met, Ciara." Shrugging, he said, "I had no idea what love was at sixteen. Never had another girlfriend. Never had a chance to..." He cleared his throat. "And I was too stupid to get down on my knees, ask the Good Lord if she was the woman He intended for me."

He shook his head again. "I don't mind telling you, I did a lot of praying since you met Mitch."

"Praying? Whatever for?"

A mist of tears shimmered in his eyes when he looked at her. "I prayed that you weren't making the same mistake...handing your entire future over to someone who might have ulterior motives, to someone who saw what they could get and—"

He was angry now. Very angry. Ciara knew, because it was the only time he made that tiny pucker with his lips. Almost immediately he reined in his emotions. Taking a deep, cleansing breath, he cleared his throat.

"Ulterior motives? What ulterior motives would Mitch have had?"

"By taking all you had to give and giving nothing in return," her father continued. "By choosing their needs over yours, without another thought—" He clamped his jaws together suddenly. "I've said enough." He held one hand up as if to silence himself. "Said too much." He sandwiched her hands between his own. "I'm sorry, sweetie. I shouldn't have burdened you with—"

"You haven't told me anything I didn't already know."

His brows rose at that. "But how could— I worked so hard to hide it from you. And to give her her due, I think your mother did, too."

Ciara shook her head. "Don't get me wrong, because I love Mom, but contrary to the old cliché, love isn't blind."

The furrow between his brows deepened.

"I know what she is. I know what she's done. I know, because she told me, Dad. A long, long time ago."

"What are you saying, Ciara?"

He already looked so miserable, how could she tell him that she knew *why* he had so quickly agreed to leave the department. He'd been wounded in the line of duty, and the injury would have prevented him from front-line work, but it wouldn't have forced him into early retirement. He'd given it up because her mother had found out about his one marital misstep....

Ciara, still in elementary school at the time, had come home to find her mother crying at the kitchen table. Kathryn had wrapped her arms around her little girl and the words tumbled out in a puzzling, dizzying swirl. Words like *betrayal* and *affair,* and phrases like *stabbed in the back* and *best years of my life.* She'd been too young to understand fully...and just old enough to be afraid, more afraid than she'd been to date.

That night, through the wall that separated her room from her parents', she heard their muffled voices in heated debate. And heard more confusing, scary words, like *ultimatum* and *divorce,* and one phrase that would echo in Ciara's mind for a lifetime: "We'll disappear, and you'll *never* see her again."

A week later her father had handed in his badge and gun.

A week after that, he'd begun teaching at the university.

She remembered those months just prior to the confrontation. It was the only period in her memory when her father had seemed truly happy. Had the "other woman" put that joy into his eyes? Had she opened up the part of him that had been sealed off by loyalty and vows spoken, and shown him what a good and lovable man he was? Ciara knew she should hate this woman who had come between her mother and her father. But how could she hate the one person who had made him realize his self-worth, who had made him smile...*with his eyes?*

She had overheard him once, sitting at that same kitchen table with his brother. They'd tipped a few bottles of beer, loosening their lips, and her father had poured out his soul.

It didn't matter that Kathryn belittled and criticized him at every opportunity. Or that in place of the big family she'd promised, Kathryn coldly announced she would never have children. Years later, seeing the 'I'm leaving' handwriting on the wall, she appeased him by consenting to give him one child.

And it didn't matter that she'd always put her own needs ahead of his, spending money faster than he could earn it, stuffing their house full of ancient, ugly things despite the fact that he'd made it clear he preferred a simpler, sparser life.

What did any of it matter, her father had asked his brother. *Kathryn* had committed no "sin," and there was no getting around the fact that *he* had committed one of life's most grievous transgressions. Little-girl Ciara, still hiding behind the pantry door, had whispered to herself. But being mean is a sin, and pretending is the same as lying, and lying is a sin....

She had replayed that conversation in her mind, many times, and in Ciara's opinion, her mother's icy anger was also a sin, a sin all its own. For decades, Kathryn's acrimonious, acerbic feelings for her husband throbbed and seethed just beneath the surface, visible to friends, relatives, neighbors. Hadn't Kathryn gotten the meaning of Matthew, Chapter Seven, Verse One: "Judge not, that you not be judged"? Didn't she believe, as Ciara did, that God was all merciful, all-loving...no matter how great a man's sin? If a small child could understand this, and the Almighty could extend the hand of forgiveness, *why couldn't Kathryn?* Her father had admitted his sin, had atoned for it tenfold. The moment he acknowledged his wrongdoing, God had cleansed him of it, freeing him from further punishment. How long did his wife intend to penalize him!

"What are you saying?" her father repeated.

Ciara would not add to the burden that had bent him over, a little more each year, by telling him she knew what he had done as a younger man.

Ian stepped up just then. "You two must be discussing the stock market," he said. "I don't know any other subject that would put scowls on such handsome faces."

Admittedly, the conversation had forced Ciara to take stock....

"Are you staying to watch the fireworks with us?" she asked her brother-in-law.

"Wish we could, but I promised the kids we'd go down to the Inner Harbor this year." He rolled his eyes. "If it were up to me, we'd watch the fireworks in air-conditioned comfort on TV, but they've got their hearts set on it, and—"

"And as I've been telling him for years," his wife interrupted, wrapping her arms around him from behind, "our kids are nearly grown. This could be the last time we see the fireworks with them."

They're so much in love, she told herself, after all these years together, they're still crazy about each other, and it shows. Mitch had told her that Ian, the oldest of the Mahoney boys, had married at twenty; Gina had just turned nineteen. Theirs, too, had been a whirlwind courtship, speeding from a chance meeting to a date at the altar in less than a year. Isn't it ironic, Ciara thought, that Mom and Dad went steady for three years, were engaged for two more before they said I do. If anyone should have been sure of themselves, it should have been the two of them....

She remembered something her father had said earlier: he'd been too young to know, too foolish to ask for God's guidance. All the time in the world, she acknowledged, can't give us the peace and assurance that comes from a moment of heartfelt prayer.

Gina directed her attention to Ciara's father. "You're looking good, Joe. What have you been doing...taking vitamins or something?"

He shook his head. "I guess the prospect of becoming

a grandpa agrees with me. You know, seeing a part of me living on in a new generation.''

''Well,'' Gina huffed, ''you don't look old enough to be a grandpa, if you ask me.'' Playfully she elbowed Ian. ''I say that because Patrick has a steady girl now, and things seem to be heating up. *We* could be in your shoes in a year.''

Ian chuckled. ''Who, me? A grandpa?'' Smiling serenely, he added, ''Maybe I'd better reread *Grimm's Fairy Tales*. It's been a while since I told a good story.''

''Oh, give me a break,'' Gina teased. ''You tell a story every morning of your life, when you say I'm the loveliest thing you've ever seen.''

Opening his eyes wide, he tucked a finger under her chin. ''Sweetheart,'' he said, doing his best Jack Nicholson impression, ''you can't handle the truth.'' He punctuated his comment with a kiss to the tip of her nose.

''Ian, really,'' Gina scolded, smiling and blushing like a young girl, ''you know how I feel about—''

''*Public displays of affection*.' Yes, I do. And you know I don't give a whit who sees how I feel about you.'' As proof, he kissed her again, on the lips this time.

Giggling, she shoved him away. ''So tell me, Ciara,'' she said breathily, ''how're you feeling?''

Ciara grinned. Like I'm watching an X-rated movie, she thought. ''Well, let me put it this way,'' she said instead. ''If this baby doesn't get here soon, Mitch is going to have to hog-tie me, 'cause all this lying around is driving me nuts!''

''Hey,'' Gina advised, ''enjoy it while it lasts.'' She winked at Ian. ''Trust me, when that baby has you up every couple of hours, you'll be asking yourself why you were complaining!''

''Complaining?'' Mitch knelt beside Ciara's chair and slipped an arm around her shoulders. ''I'll have you know this girl hasn't uttered a word of complaint, not once in the two weeks I've been home." He kissed her cheek. "She's a real trouper," he boasted.

"Well, all I can say is you're lucky you didn't marry *me*," Gina admitted. "I'd be whimpering and whining every five minutes if I had to stay off my feet for four solid weeks." She wriggled into her husband's arms. "Isn't that right, honey?"

"Oh, I don't know. Hard as it is to get you out of bed on a Sunday morning…"

"Much as I hate to admit it," Gina said, bobbing her head, "he's right."

"Say, Joe," she put in, "tell your motorcycle story. I tried to tell it the other day, but I couldn't remember the punchline.…"

Ciara's father rubbed his palms together and grinned, blue eyes twinkling merrily. "Okay, you asked for it…" Standing, Joe held a finger aloft, and began:

"There were two Irishmen," he said with an exaggerated brogue, "travelin' the A-1 on a motorbike. 'Tis mighty cold, McAfferty,' said the one on the back. 'Well, no wonder, Casey, ye've got yer coat on backward.' McAfferty parked, turned Casey's jacket 'round, and zipped it up the back. 'There, now,' he said, tucking the fur collar under Casey's chin, 'that'll keep ye warm.' They took off again, and after a bit, McAfferty noticed Casey wasn't there, and headed back the way they'd come. He spied a couple of farmers, starin' at somethin' in the middle of the road. 'Why, it's me friend, Casey,' McAfferty said. 'Is he all right?' 'He were fine when we got here,' one farmer said, 'but since we turned his head 'round the right way,' said the other, 'he ain't said a word.…'"

Their laughter acted like a magnet, attracting Kathryn. "There you are, Joseph, I've been looking everywhere for you." The words, if printed on a page, might have convinced bystanders his wife felt something akin to affection for her husband. But Ciara had heard that "why do you torture me so?" tone in her mother's voice before, too many times to count. Had seen that look, too, hundreds of times...one brow up, lips pursed, shoulders slumped in long-suffering exhaustion. "Has he been telling that awful motorcycle story *again?*" she asked. Rolling her eyes, she sighed heavily. "Thank goodness I walked up when I did! If you only knew how many times I've heard that stale old story."

Gina, Ian and Mitch smiled stiffly in response to her obvious insult. Ciara had seen *those* looks before, too...looks that blended pity for Joe with disapproval for Kathryn. How long will she make him pay for his mistake? Ciara wondered.

She couldn't have known that her mother's contemptuous treatment of her father had started long before she'd learned of his affair, but evidence to support that fact was there, etched in the tired lines and weary smile on his sad-eyed face.

I won't live that way, she told herself. Better to let Mitch go...better to *send* him away than to condemn him to a life of arm's-length neglect and open disdain.

Mitch was looking at her when she tore her gaze from her mother's hostile expression, from her father's lethargic acceptance of it. He shook his head, a small smile lifting one corner of his mouth as he winked. "Don't worry," was the message emanating from his brown eyes, "we won't let that happen to us."

Her heart fluttered in answer to his promise. Ciara wanted to believe him, wanted to grasp it as truth.

Still...

So far, they had all but walked in her parents' marital footsteps. Dread and fear hammered in her heart. Is there any way to avoid other stumbling blocks along the way?

She loved him with every cell in her body, with every pulse of her heart. But like her father, she had not been wise enough to seek Divine Guidance in choosing a mate. What price would she pay for that foolishness? Was it too late to right that wrong, or could their marriage yet become what it might have been...if she'd had the foresight and the insight to ask the Lord what *He* intended for her future?

She looked at her parents, read the indifferent compliance that yoked them to each other, then looked at her in-laws, and saw the esteem, the friendship, the respect and admiration they felt for one another. *That* is what she wanted to see in Mitch's eyes, twenty, thirty, *fifty* years from now.

"What God has joined together, let no man put asunder," the preacher had said, sealing the vow that made Ciara and Mitch husband and wife. Surely, now that they were married in the eyes of God and man, He would show them how to make theirs a strong union, rooted in faith, nourished by steadfast devotion. If they could accomplish that, how could their love do anything but grow, like Ian and Gina's, as the years went by?

The words of a hymn hummed in her head: "Let there be peace on earth, and let it begin with me."

Mitch grasped her hand, gave it a hearty squeeze as Ian said, "Well, thanks for the eats, but we've got to make tracks."

"We ought to hit the road, too," her father said. "I have lesson plans to write."

She watched the two couples leave, walking side by side through the gate and out of the yard. How similar, yet how different, Ciara thought, biting her lower lip. Unconsciously, she gave Mitch's hand a little tweak. She thought she knew the secret that had given Ian and Gina years of happiness...and her parents decades of misery.

Teach us to love selflessly, Lord, she repeated, echoing the words of the song, *and let it begin with me....*

"What time is it?" she asked, her voice whisper soft.

"Don't know," Mitch answered. "Can't read my watch."

"Shouldn't the fireworks have started by now? It's been dark for an hour."

"You're a grown woman, Ciara Mahoney," he teased, quoting what she'd said the day before. "'How can you get so caught up in a light show'?"

There was just enough moonlight to allow him to see her playful sneer. He rolled onto his side, propped his head on a palm. "Yeeesh," he said, grimacing, "if looks could kill, I'd be worm food."

Ciara rolled over, as well. "Don't say things like that, not even as a joke," she scolded.

He drew her to him. "I'm sorry, sweetie. I keep forgetting…"

She laid a finger over his lips to silence him. "Shhh." She raised the same finger into the air. "Listen…I thought I heard one."

"Heard one what?"

"A firework, silly."

"'Firework?'" he quoted. "*Now* who sounds silly?"

"Well, if all of them are fireworks," she said, accenting the *s,* "doesn't it make sense that one is a—"

Chuckling, he nodded. "Okay. All right. 'Firework.' You're the teacher, after all."

"And don't you forget it," she said, smiling as her forefinger drew lazy circles in the chest hair poking from the vee of his shirt.

They lay on a makeshift bed he'd created from two thick quilts, a crisp bedsheet and three overstuffed pillows for each of their heads. Beside her, a foot-high table was laden with decaffeinated sodas, a bowl of strawberries, a plate of cheese and crackers. Beside him, nothing but a fly swatter. All the stars in the universe winked at them from the inky sky above. And all around them, crickets and tree frogs chirped.

"This is nice," Ciara told him. "I'm glad you thought of it."

He pulled her closer. "Me, too."

"I thought Mrs. Thompson was going to watch the show with us and bring Nicky."

Mitch shrugged. "Guess she changed her mind...or Nicky changed it for her."

"She's something, isn't she? Seventy-two and doesn't look a day over fifty. I hope I age that gracefully."

"Are you kiddin'? You'll be the envy of every old woman in the retirement home."

"Only because every old woman will be wishing they had *you*."

He grinned. "You think?"

She nodded. *"I know."* Ciara yawned, stretched. "If the fireworks don't start soon," she said, "I'm liable to sleep right through them."

"If you doze off, I'll set off a firecracker near your ear."

"You just try it, Mister Big Shot, and I'll...I'll...I'll fire *your* cracker!"

"What in the world does that mean?"

"I have no idea...."

Their laughter blended in sweet harmony, as Ciara snuggled closer, closed her eyes. "This is nice," she said again.

And he nodded. "Yep, nice." Two minutes, perhaps three, passed before her breathing slowed and shallowed, telling him she'd fallen asleep. He leaned back a bit, so he could see her face. The soft breeze combed through her hair, fluttered the ruffle at the collar of her blouse. Long lashes curved up from her pale cheeks, and soft breaths passed her slightly parted lips. He knew it might wake her, if he touched her, but Mitch couldn't help himself. Gently he pressed a palm to her cheek and marveled at the miracle in his arms.

Miracle, because she was lovely and sweet, and good to the marrow of her bones. The baby kicked, and he felt the powerful little jab against his own stomach...a subtle reminder that soon, he might be forced to call another man's child "son."

Mitch held his breath, ground his molars together. Why, he asked himself, when you've been praying like crazy for weeks, can't you get that thought out of your head?

Because of what Bradley had said, that's why: "She'll go with me willingly." And "Who do you think the baby will look like?"

Headlights panned the yard, distracting him, and Mitch squinted into the brightness. They'd considered themselves fortunate to have found a corner lot...the appearance of twice the land, with only one neighbor to contend with, but it had its negative aspects, as evidenced by the beams of every passing car.

Hey...that's the same car that went by not ten minutes ago, he told himself, staring harder at the four-doored black sedan. It's just someone looking for an address, he told himself, someone lost in the maze of streets that comprised the neighborhood.

Ciara sighed quietly as the car slipped out of sight. He rested his chin upon her head and relaxed a bit—but only a bit. A quiet *pop,* followed by several more, told him the fireworks had begun. "Sweetie," he whispered, kissing her cheek, "they're starting...."

Wriggling, she blinked. "Hmmm?"

"The fireworks," he repeated, gently shaking her shoulder, "hear 'em?"

She rolled onto her back, smiling as the sky brightened

with starbursts of red and blue and white. "It's beautiful," she said. "Isn't it just beautiful?"

He hadn't noticed. He was too busy watching her face, painted in shades of pink and gold and green by the reflected light. "It's beautiful, all right," he agreed. "Most beautiful thing I've ever seen."

If not for the darkness, he'd have seen a blush, Mitch knew, for her big eyes fluttered in response to his scrutiny. "Pay attention," she scolded sweetly, "you're missing all the good stuff."

"That's a matter of opin—" The black car crept by, choking off the rest of his words.

"What's wrong?" she asked, eyes on the sky.

"Nothing," he lied, levering himself up on one elbow as the car inched past. "I'm having the time of my life. How 'bout you?" He could almost feel the intense gaze of a back-seat passenger boring into him through the blackened windows. Had Bradley rounded up the troops? What better night to pull a stunt than the Fourth of July, when explosions in the sky competed with Roman Candles and other assorted firecrackers on the ground? Who'd notice a gunshot amid all the rest of the noise?

"This is the most fun I've had in—" She gasped. "Mitch, what is it?"

He was torn between keeping his eyes on that car and looking into Ciara's face to reassure her. The hammering of her heart against his rib cage decided it. "Just a little headache," he fibbed, wanting to calm her, soothe her, because a rise in blood pressure could be deadly.

"Are you sure? Because you look like you've just seen a ghost."

He kissed her cheek, gently turned her face toward the sky show. "It's no big deal. I'll get an aspirin when the fireworks are over."

He felt her relax in his arms. "Well, if you're sure...."

"I'm sure." And with the tip of his forefinger, he gently pushed her chin, until she was looking up into the sky again. "Wow," he said, "I felt that one all the way to my toes!"

Ciara giggled. "The rib-rackers are my favorites. Those, and the ones with the squeaky little squiggles...."

The night had swallowed up the car again; either its driver had found the address he'd been looking for...or had found a place to park, where he could watch the Mahoney house, undetected.

Except for the half-dozen or so strange phone calls he'd intercepted, Mitch had no reason to believe he was in any danger. The U.S. Attorney had pretty much assured him Pericolo's men, relieved to have gotten rid of the boss with the hair-trigger temper, had lined up behind Chambro. And it wouldn't be very smart for Bradley to show his hand, not with everybody from the dog catcher to the CIA looking for him.

Mitch remembered that old saying: "Just because you're paranoid, doesn't mean they're not out to get you."

But who was *they,* and what would they get him *for?*

Ciara had been right; his job was dangerous. In the past he'd been the only one in harm's way. Now, simply because she'd chosen to stand beside him through life, she stood in the line of fire with him.

If anything happens to her because of my job...

Mitch clutched her a little tighter to him, pressed a kiss to her temple as she oooh'd and ahhh'd at the skylights. *Lord Jesus,* Mitch prayed, *thanks for protecting her from reading my fears. I'm counting on you to keep her safe and sound.*

Clenching and unclenching his fists, David Pericolo sat in the blackness, counting to ten, taking deep breaths. It was natural to be a little nervous, even though he'd taken

every precaution. He recalled his last visit with his father
at the penitentiary, how his father had laughed at his plan.
Well, he'd prove himself worthy of respect yet. He'd make
his father proud. For weeks, he'd been watching Mahoney
from his hiding place across the street.

It was time to make his move. And this time, there
would be no slip-ups, as there had been a week ago...

You got too sure of yourself, and it made you lazy, he
told himself. You overlooked something, all wrapped up
in memories the way you were....

He'd been thinking of his grandfather, who'd been a
demolitions expert during World War II. If the old man
could see you now, he'd thought.

What was the expression his grandfather had used? "A
rude awakening," that's it! He'd lifted the black lid of the
boot box on the dresser, wiggled a red wire, jiggled a black
one. Agent Mitch Mahoney, he thought, smirking, is in for
a rude awakening.

He had waited until the letter carrier filled Mahoney's
box with a handful of mail, slipped the bomb inside, carefully attaching the wires to the hinged door. Then he'd
climbed back into the car, wondering as he waited if, like
himself, Mahoney had ever wanted to be an astronaut. The
minute you open that door, kaboom! you're gonna experience space flight, first hand.

Then some kid in baggy jeans shorts and a backward
baseball cap had sauntered up, and slipping the top flyer
off the pile of bright blue papers tucked under his arm, and
opened the Mahoney mailbox. It had taken every bit
of control he could muster to keep from hollering "Get
away from there, you little jerk!" He rolled the window
down an inch, intending to distract the boy, offer him a
couple bucks for his bundle, and send him safely on his
way.

But he hadn't been quick enough. "Cool," he'd heard

the boy say, grabbing the bomb. "Hey, Gordie," he called to his buddy, who was delivering flyers on the other side of the street, "check this out." The boys stood, cap brim to cap brim, muttering under their breaths for a minute before the taller one said, "It ain't nothin' but a hunk of junk." The first kid shrugged, then tossed the bomb into a nearby trash can.

Junk!

He had rolled the car window back up. It took me three hours to build that "hunk of junk"!

Now, in the steamy darkness of this July night, he stared at the Mahoney house and grinned. This bomb was no hunk of junk.

He had never missed the fireworks before…but then, if everything worked as he expected it would, he wouldn't miss them this year, either.

Any day now, Mahoney would open his front door, reach for his morning paper, and get the worst news of his life.

Chapter Eleven

Ciara looked up from her needlework when the doorbell rang. "Who could that be? It's nearly supper time."

Mitch shrugged. "I didn't feel much like cooking tonight, so I ordered us a little something special."

"Pizza?" she asked expectantly. "I haven't had pizza in weeks. I hope you got two large ones, with the works, 'cause I'm famished."

Grinning, he fished his wallet out of his pocket and headed for the door. After a moment of front-porch small-talk, she heard the door close, bolts click into place, Mitch's bare feet padding up the hall and into the kitchen. The clatter of dishes and the clank of silverware inspired her to call out, "No need to get fancy, Mitch. Paper plates will be—"

He was back before she could complete the suggestion, positioning a tray table over her lap, putting a neatly folded napkin on the left side of her plate, arranging a knife and fork on the right. "I made lemonade and decaffeinated iced tea. Which would you prefer?" he asked, bowing low at the waist.

"Lemonade, with—"

"Lots of ice," he finished. "I know."

When he returned this time, he balanced a crockery bowl and a basket of bread on the tray carrying the drinks. "This," he said, removing the towel that hid the bowl's contents, "is to calm a craving."

Her eyes widened with surprise and delight. "Mitch! Where did you—"

And then she read the label on the napkin that lined the bread basket. "Chiaparelli's? You ordered gnocchi from Chiaparelli's?"

"None other," he said, spooning a huge portion onto her plate.

She waved a hand over the steaming dumplings to coax the tempting aroma into her nostrils. Closing her eyes, she sighed. "How did you know?" she asked, looking at him. "Surely not from that little slip of the tongue the other day...."

"That," he admitted, "plus you talk in your sleep."

"I do not." She speared a gnocchi.

Nodding, Mitch sat in his recliner and balanced his plate on his knees. "Oh, yes you do. It's just a good thing we have air-conditioning, because I don't know what Mrs. Thompson would think if she heard you moaning through the open windows, 'gnocchi, gnocchi, *gnocchi!*'" he said, pronouncing each louder than the first.

"She'd think you have a very strange appetite," Ciara explained, wiggling her brows suggestively. Then she popped a pasta into her mouth, and uttered a satisfied "Mmmmmm."

"Is it good?" he asked, taking a stab at one.

"Better than good," she breathed. The fingers of her left hand formed a small tulip. *"Delicioso!"*

He bit into one, chewed for a moment, nodded thoughtfully. "Not bad," he affirmed, eating the other half. "Not bad at all."

She gobbled up a dozen more dumplings before saying, "I have a feeling when Donna comes to weigh me tomorrow, I'm going to tip the scales!"

"Gimme a break. If you come in at a hundred and twenty, even in your condition, I'll be surprised."

"I was a hundred and thirty-five day before yesterday, I'll have you know."

"A hundred and thirty-five? You don't say!" He chuckled. "There's probably not a woman within a one-hundred-mile radius of this house who'd say a thing like that with such pride in her voice." He smirked, patted her tummy. "Come to think of it, *you're* almost a hundred-mile radius...."

"Stop it," she said, giggling, "and let me enjoy this. It's the most I've weighed, ever."

"Well, since you seem to like it so well," he said, pinching her big toe, "maybe I oughta just keep you barefoot and pregnant *all* the time."

Her smile waned, her eyes filled with tears, and she hid behind her hands.

He leaped out of the chair, nearly overturning his plate when he deposited it on the cushion. "Sweetie, what's wrong? Did I say something? I'm sorry if..."

"Stop it," she sniffled. "It isn't your fault my hormones are raging out of control."

"But you were fine till I..."

She blotted her eyes with a corner of the napkin. "You didn't do anything wrong, I'm telling you! It's me. All me." Ciara thumped a fist onto the mattress. "It's because I've been cooped up inside so long, getting no exercise. I'm trying to stay current...reading the paper, watching the news...but my mind is turning to mush. I'm becoming the kind of woman I've always despised, Mitch, weak and wimpy and whiny and—''

''Aw, sweetie,'' he said, taking her in his arms. ''You're the strongest woman I know, and the proof is the way you're handling this situation. You're a hundred months pregnant, for goodness sake. Cut yourself a little slack, why don't you?''

She mulled that over for a moment, then started to giggle. ''A hundred months?'' she repeated, her voice muffled by his shirt. ''Even elephants have babies in less time than that.'' She shook her head. ''Sometimes I think I'm doomed to stay this way for the rest of my life.''

Ciara leaned back slightly to meet his eyes. ''Oh, Mitch,'' she whimpered, ''do you think your baby will *ever* be born?''

His eyes widened slightly. *My baby?* Would she have said it that way if she suspected Bradley might be the father? Mitch didn't think so. She'd blurted it out without even thinking, so it must be true. *My baby,* he repeated, kissing her tears away, struggling to hold back tears of his own. *My baby!*

''Shhh,'' he soothed. ''Your gnocchi is getting cold.''

''Do you really want to have more children with me?'' she asked, her voice small and timid, like a child's. ''What if I'm like this every time I get—''

''Ciara, listen to me now,'' he said, tapping a finger against her nose. ''I mean, think about it...a lifetime with whoever that is in there,'' he added, patting her tummy, ''for a few weeks of inconvenience.''

''Easy for you to say,'' she teased, ''I have to lie here like a lump while you get to empty the trash and do the dishes and—''

''I'll be more than happy to turn all the fun stuff over to you after the blessed event,'' he said, laughing. ''Promise.''

''So you really wouldn't mind going through this all over again?''

''Peterson assured me the chances of this happening a second time are practically nil, but no, even if the whole thing repeated itself exactly, I wouldn't mind. Not a bit.'' He pushed a pink satin nightgown strap aside to kiss her shoulder. ''Look at it from my point of view—how many other husbands get to see their wives in gorgeous lingerie all day, every day, for weeks on end?''

Another soft giggle, then, ''How many times?''

''How many times would I do this?''

She nodded.

He kissed her shoulder again. ''Until my lips wear out.''

''No, silly, I mean…''

''Six,'' he said without hesitation, ''just like we discussed before we got married.''

''Half a dozen,'' she sighed. ''We'll have to add a whole wing onto the house.''

''Or buy a bigger one.''

''In the country, maybe,'' she said dreamily, ''where we can have cats and dogs and—'' Ciara looked around. ''Speaking of dogs, I haven't seen Chester all afternoon. Is he out back?''

Mitch nodded. ''He treed a cat out there, and I couldn't get him to come in, not even for a rawhide bone.''

Ciara frowned a bit. ''I wonder what he'll think of the baby.''

Snickering, he said, ''Are you kiddin' me? He's gonna make that big-hearted old nanny mutt in Peter Pan look like Cujo. Now eat your gnocchi, before I do.''

Ciara stuck her fork into a dumpling. ''I don't suppose there's dessert.…''

''As a matter of fact,'' he said, picking up his plate, ''there is.''

''Cheesecake?''

He sat in the recliner. "With cherries on top."

"How big a piece?"

"I went for broke. We've got a whole cake to ourselves."

She licked her lips. "If I break the visiting nurse's scale," she asked, grinning mischievously, "will our insurance pay for a new one?"

"Blood presh-ah and pulse rate are fine," Donna said, her Boston accent making the details of the routine exam sound far more interesting than it was. "Your blood count is a little low, but nothin' to worry about." She strapped the monitor into place. "Now, let's see how the little one is doing...."

The machine clicked and beeped quietly for a few minutes as the nurse squinted at the screen. A thin green line of phosphorescent light blipped, counting the baby's heartbeats. "Lookin' good. Lookin' real good...." The diminutive woman had small, deceptively powerful hands. With firm gentleness, she palpated Ciara's stomach. "Hmmm. He's dropped some since I was here day before yesta-day. If I had to guess, I'd say you have a week till you join the ranks of mothahood. Maybe less." Propping a fist on a hip, she narrowed one blue eye. "You experiencin' any cramping?"

Rolling her eyes, Ciara shook her head. "Not unless you count the ones in my rear end, from sitting on it hour after endless hour."

"Well, don't you fret. It won't be much longah now."

"You're not sugarcoating things to keep me calm, are you?"

"Oh, right...I've stayed in this line of work all these years 'cause I enjoy fibbin' to my patients." Then she got serious. "Stretchin' the truth makes everything seem scarier, no mattah how good or bad the situation really is."

The perky blonde winked at Mitch. "I'll leave the shugah-coatin' to your hubby, here. He looks like a man who knows how to lay it on thick...."

"Now, wait just a minute here," he said, grinning in mock self-defense. "I believe in telling it like it is." Then, in a more serious tone, "You'd tell us if something wasn't quite right...even slightly?"

"I would indeed. You two have got to stop all this fussin', now, 'cause everything is fine. And do you know why?"

Like obedient students, husband and wife shook their heads simultaneously.

"Because *you,* Mistah Mahoney, have been doin' a bang-up job takin' care of the missus. There oughta be a medal for husbands like you. I've seen plenty of men go through this, but not one of 'em handled things like you have." She gave an approving nod. "No mattah what time of day I drop by, this house is squeaky clean from top to bottom, Ciara's sheets are always fresh and crisp, and by the looks of those roses in her cheeks, you must be a dandy cook, too."

"It'll probably take me two years to get my girlish figure back!" Ciara agreed.

"Well, don't let this one out of your sight, missy," was Donna's advice. "He's a prize, and I know a dozen gals who'd snap him up in a heartbeat!"

"They might *think* they want to snap me up," he said, slipping an arm around his wife, "but none of 'em would have the *stomach* for me." He patted her tummy. "Would they, sweetie?"

"Yeah, well, if they try, they'll have to go through me first!"

"Might be a bit difficult, in your condition," Donna pointed out. "Aren't you glad he's the trustworthy sort?"

She nodded, met his eyes. "Yes. I'm glad," she said in

all seriousness. "And thankful, too. He hasn't left my side for a minute, not once in sixteen days."

"Cut it out, you two," Mitch said, smiling sheepishly, "or I'm going to have to make all the doorways keyhole shaped, so I can fit my swelled head through 'em."

"Joke if you want to," Donna said matter-of-factly, "but men like you are one in a million. I've seen my share...personally and professionally...I know what I'm talkin' about." Hefting her nurse's bag, she headed for the door, waving to Ciara. "See you day after tomorrow." As she passed him, she whispered to Mitch from the corner of her mouth, "Stick close by from here on out. She could blow any day now!"

Blinking, he stood gap-jawed in her wake. Any day now? he repeated. Yup, any day now, you'll know for sure who that baby's daddy is....

He had tossed and turned so much through the night that Ciara didn't think either of them could have slept more than two hours. What had he been dreaming about as he'd writhed so fitfully, moaning and groaning under his breath? Was he reenacting scenes from his undercover days? Reliving the day he brought the bad guy in? Experiencing a near-death experience, like the time he'd been locked in the trunk of a car?

Today is the day, she decided, that you'll ask him to tell you about the case. Good or bad, his answers would be a blessed relief, because anything was better than not knowing at all!

Mitch was sleeping peacefully now, and she turned on her side to get a better look at him. Once, before he'd left her, she told him he had the most amazing profile she'd ever seen. Totally masculine, it was Michaelangelo's *David* and Rodin's *The Thinker* all rolled into one. She had traced it with a fingertip, saying, "I wish I were an artist, so I could sculpt it from clay, or carve it from wood. That way, I'd have it to look at, even when you were at work...."

She looked at his profile now, the strong forehead, the patrician nose, the powerful jaw that was boldly, wholly *man*. Long, thick lashes fringed his eyes, giving him a boyish quality that softened the look, kept him from appearing too severe, too stern. And his lips, those full, well-rounded lips, only added to his very male appeal. Lightly, lovingly, she skimmed the backs of her fingers over his whiskered cheek. "I hope our baby looks exactly like you," she said in a voice so soft, even she barely heard it.

Ciara rested her hand on his chest and, assured by the steady *thump, thump, thump* of his heart, drifted into peaceful slumber and dreamed of a chubby-cheeked infant with dark curly hair and enormous brown eyes, and a smile that could charm the birds from the trees....

He'd been dreaming he was walking through their house, pointing out things of interest to the baby boy in his arms. "Now son, this is your mom's favorite afghan," he said. "Her grandma brought it over from Italy, so whatever you do, don't spit up on it. And this," he added, plucking the strings of his guitar, "is your dad's git-fiddle. Maybe when you're older, I'll teach you to play...."

He hadn't known know what woke him...Ciara's feathery touch, tickling over his stubbled cheek or her rustling sigh: "I hope our baby looks exactly like you." All he knew was that her touch, her words washed over him like warm Caribbean waves.

I love her, and I love that kid because it's part of her. If she'd transgressed—and it was beginning to look less and less like she had—it had only been for want of him; could he begrudge her a stolen moment of comfort? Would it have mattered, really, whether he or Bradley had fathered her child? In truth, it would have mattered a great deal. But he thought he knew the truth now. "And the truth shall set you free."

Smiling, he pressed a palm to her roundness, hoping to feel forceful little feet or the powerful punch of a tiny elbow. After a moment of absolute stillness, Mitch admitted, regretfully, that the child, like its mother, was at complete rest.

When he was a little boy, his mother would listen to his prayers, tuck the covers under his chin and sing a verse from a song she'd learned as a child: "May the Good Lord grant you beautiful dreams and send a legion of angels to watch over you," she'd croon, brushing back his wild, wayward curls. He sent the same prayer heavenward on Ciara's behalf, then succumbed to drowsiness himself.

But not before this soughed from his lips:

"I love you, Ciara Mahoney, and I always will."

They woke slowly, gently, to the distant trilling of the phone. "Who can be calling at this hour?" he grumbled, reaching for it.

"Mitch, it's after ten o'clock! How could we have slept so late?"

Stretching, he said around a yawn, "Must have needed it, that's all I can say." And then, into the telephone's mouthpiece, he muttered a groggy "Hullo?"

Silence.

He cleared his voice and said more firmly, "Hello."

Nothing.

"Who is it?" Ciara asked.

He banged the receiver into the cradle. "Wrong number, I guess."

But he knew better. This hadn't been the first such call they'd received; it was the eleventh or twelfth, by his count. At first, he'd dismissed it. Could be some kind of computer error down at the phone company, he'd told himself, or maybe one of Ciara's students has a crush on his pretty teacher and he's calling just to hear the sound of her voice.

He had learned to trust his gut instinct, and his gut was telling him not to blame coincidence or accident or happenstance.

But who had been calling…and why?

Could be Bradley.

One of Pericolo's men.

Some other felon he'd arrested….

Truth was, he could think of a hundred possible explanations for the silence on the other end of the phone; *trouble* was, the more explanations he came up with, the more nervous Mitch became.

A week or so ago, while Ciara was napping, he'd tiptoed upstairs, taken his trusty Rossi completely apart and thoroughly oiled every piece. After he'd reassembled it and loaded six rounds into it, he'd listened to the reassuring *whirr-tick-tick* of the spinning chamber, then snapped it shut with a flick of his wrist. Paranoid? he'd asked, sliding the revolver onto a high shelf. Probably, he'd answered, but better safe than sorry….

Hopefully, he'd never have to use it. But just in case, every now and then he rehearsed his trip upstairs to fetch it. He was in the kitchen now, fixing breakfast, when he went over it again. If he took the stairs two at a time, he believed he could get into the closet and back downstairs again in thirty seconds flat. If he could figure out a way to explain it to Ciara, he'd practice physically as well as mentally.

She had asked for a bowl of corn flakes this morning, and he topped them off with a sliced banana and cold milk. He'd put strawberry slices in her orange juice, to surprise her when she finished it off. He'd plucked a rose from the shrub beside the back fence, too, broke off the thorns and tucked its stem into her napkin.

"When I'm on my feet again," she said when she saw the tray, "I'm going to spoil you so rotten, you're going to stink!"

"My mom used to call me a little stinker. Maybe she's clairvoyant?"

"She's a mother, and mothers know things."

"Is that right?" He settled in his recliner and waited for Ciara to tell him what she knew about their baby. *Their* baby. *His* baby. She'd said so in the middle of the night, when she thought he was asleep.

"I know, for instance, that this baby is going to be brilliant and musically gifted and kind and..."

"How do you know all that?" he asked, chuckling good-naturedly. "Did the Baby Fairy tell you?"

"Make light of it if you must," she sniffed, "but it's all very scientific, actually."

"Scientific?"

Ciara began counting on her fingers. "You're very intelligent, and I'm not exactly a dull bulb, so the baby *has* to be smart." She held up a second digit. "I play a pretty mean piano, and you play just about every other instrument God ever created." The ring finger popped up. "And the way you've been taking care of me, well, if I didn't already know you were a kind, big-hearted man before I was quarantined, I know it now. Isn't it natural to assume our baby will have a blend of our finer qualities?"

He merely sat there a moment, nodding as he assessed what she'd said. Ciara hadn't mentioned one trait that even closely resembled Chet Bradley. And why would she? It's your kid....

"You know, when you put it that way, why wouldn't

our kid be terrific?" He smiled. "But I hope he looks like you."

"And I hope he'll have your *character*."

Chuckling, he nodded at the plaques and awards hanging on the fireplace wall. "Don't you mean my reputation? I've won—"

"'Reputation is what men think you are,'" she quoted. "'Character is what God and the angels know about you.'"

She had fixed him with that no-nonsense, all-loving stare of hers, so he couldn't very well argue with her, now could he? And so he said, "Well, this *character* is gonna go down to the end of the driveway and see which shrub our paperboy has hidden the newspaper under this morning. And then he's gonna refill his coffee cup, and put up his feet, and make like a man of leisure till he's read every last page."

Ciara patted the mattress. "I'd like to ask you a question first...."

She'd been behaving strangely all morning. Till now, he'd chalked it up to her condition, to cabin fever, to being forced to stay off her feet. Mitch perched on the edge of the sofa bed. "Ask away, li'l lady," he drawled.

"When are you going to tell me where you were, when we're both old and gray?"

He frowned. "Where I was?"

"You know perfectly well what I'm talking about."

She wasn't teasing. He could tell by the lift of her left brow, by the slight narrowing of her wide eyes. Their hands, flat on the sunflowery sheets, were nearly touching. He inchworm-walked his forward until his forefinger rested atop hers. "The case, you mean...."

"Where were you? Why didn't you write, or call?"

"I tried, remember?"

She rolled her eyes. "So you've said. Didn't you wonder why, if you wrote so many letters, I never answered them? Didn't you think it was strange, that after one little fight, I'd completely write you off?"

"Didn't seem so little to me."

Ciara sighed. "It was the first time we'd ever disagreed about anything." She crooked her finger around his. "You didn't expect us to spend our whole marriage in a state of harmony, did you?"

Mitch shrugged. "My folks never fought."

"Maybe you never heard them fight, but they disagreed, I'm sure. Every married couple does. It's normal. It's natural. It's...unavoidable."

He met her eyes. "I guess...I guess I just hadn't gotten used to the idea."

"We did sort of rush things, didn't we?"

Their eyes locked on a thread of understanding. "Do you still think it was a mistake?"

The pain in her voice was matched only by the agony shining in her eyes. Mitch pulled her to him. "Sweetie, I've *never* thought it was a mistake. From the moment I first saw you, I knew...."

She pressed a palm to each of his cheeks, her eyes searching his with fierce intensity. "Then why did you let them send you away? Why would you go undercover, and leave me here to wonder where you were...how you were?"

"Because I'm a proud, thick-headed, know-it-all."

Her brow crinkled with confusion. "A know-it-all?"

"I'd been hearing about Pericolo for ages. I knew it was going to take some fancy footwork to get him. The agency wasn't about to send some rookie in there to nab a guy like that. I guess I felt sort of proud they'd picked me."

"I see," she said softly, nodding.

"Well," he shrugged, "that, and Bradley made it pretty clear that if I didn't go *in*, I was on my way *out* at the Bureau."

"You could have found another job...what made you so sure I'd still be here when you came home...*if* you came home?"

"I wasn't." He exhaled a heavy breath. "Till recently, that is."

She leaned against the pillows and hid behind her hands. "I must need a nap already, because I'm not following you."

"I thought...." Mitch licked his lips. He wished she hadn't pulled away, because nothing felt so reassuring, so comforting as having her in his arms. He looked at his empty hands, filled them with hers. "I thought maybe you found a way to replace me."

A tiny, nervous giggle popped from between the tightly-clenched fingers that hid her face. A second passed in utter silence. She folded her hands in her lap. "Replace you? How?"

"Bradley." The word ground out of him like a mono-syllabic growl.

"Bradley?"

And then the light of understanding gleamed in her eyes. Ciara gasped, touched her fingertips to her lips, shook her head. "Mitch...you don't mean...." Her brows lifted and her eyes filled with tears. "You thought...." She bit her lower lip. "You thought I had...."

"Just look at you, trembling and tense. Forget I ever said anything. I'm a total idiot." He tried to gather her in his arms.

"Stop it," she said, one hand up like a traffic cop. "Just give me a minute to wrap my mind around this thing." Ciara took a deep breath. After a moment, she rested crossed arms on her ample belly. "What had I ever done to make you think such a thing?"

"Nothing. And I didn't think it. Not once in the whole time I was gone." He held up both hands in a gesture of defensiveness. "I knew I'd have a price to pay for leaving the way I did, for staying gone so long, but I figured we could work it out. I figured eventually, we'd...."

She lifted her chin. "What changed your mind?"

He took a deep breath. "Aftershave."

Ciara rubbed her eyes. "You're not making any sense...."

"Bradley's brand. In the medicine cabinet in the master bathroom.

She inclined her head. "Bradley's brand," she repeated, more to herself than to Mitch. And then she began nodding, tapping a finger against her chin. "So *that's* why he insisted on going upstairs that day...."

Mitch rested a hand on her thigh, and listened.

"He came over one day to see if I needed anything...and to tell me you hadn't been in touch, as usual...and acted as if he'd heard a noise upstairs. Drew his weapon and everything!" Lips narrowing with suspicion, she added, "Now I understand why he spent more time in our room than...."

"When?" Mitch demanded. "How long ago?"

"Right before you came home." A note of alarm sounded in her voice, and panic brightened her eyes. "Why?"

"Because it had been part of his plan all along. We were both pawns in his little game of 'kill two birds with one stone.'"

"What?"

"He used me to get rid of Pericolo, so Chambro could take over and Bradley's pay-offs would continue. He never figured I'd survive being underground with a maniac like that, and when I did...." He emitted a low groan of frustration. "And he used you to drive me over the edge."

"By planting the aftershave."

Mitch nodded.

"What I don't understand is why you believed I could have done such a thing."

He met her eyes, still damp from her bout with tears. "You're a beautiful woman, Ciara. Beautiful and warm and loving...." He shrugged helplessly. "You saw my mom's prized roses. She spent hours tending them every week."

"They're spectacular, but what do they have to do with...."

"She says the lovelier a creature of nature, the more time and attention it needs."

"I don't know whether to be flattered at being compared to a rose, or insulted that you think I'm so high maintenance."

"Not high maintenance, Sweetie, just deserving of some tender loving care."

"I suppose I can't fault you for doing the very same thing I did, can I?"

"Me? When would I...."

"I didn't know where you were, what you were doing. For all I knew, you'd been sent undercover to guard a beautiful singer, like in the movie that came out a couple years ago, where the bodyguard fell in love with his charge...."

"I never so much as looked at another woman," he said, hand forming the Boy Scout salute. "I swear."

"And I never looked at another man," she responded, mimicking the gesture. "So tell me, what changed your mind?"

"How do I know that baby's mine, you mean?"

She gasped again, and hugged her tummy. "You thought our baby...? You thought...*Bradley?*" Ciara shuddered. "Now I *am* insulted. How could you think so little of me, Mitch? Was it because I fell for you so quickly? Was it because I let you talk me into getting married after only a three-month courtship? Was it because...?"

"I already told you why," he said, grasping her hands. "I'm an idiot."

When she blinked, a silvery tear broke free of her long lashes, landed on the back of her hand. Mitch kissed it away. Kissed away the tears remaining on her cheeks, in her eyes. "I'm sorry, Ciara. About everything. If I could go back in time and do it all over, I'd...."

"Would you still take the assignment?"

"Not if I knew then what I know now."

"What do you know now?"

He cupped her cheeks in his palms. "That—cliché as it sounds—I love you more than life itself, and nothing, no one, is more important than you." He wrapped her in his arms. "I can't live without you, Ciara. I'm so sorry for everything I put you through. It's all my fault you're in the shape you're in."

"Is that what you think?" she asked, pulling away.

"How else do you explain it?"

"Didn't Dr. Peterson tell you there's no known cause for this condition?"

"Well, yeah, but...."

"And didn't he tell you there's no predicting who it'll affect and who it won't?"

"Yes, but..."

"But nothing. It just happened, and you know what?"

"What?"

"I think it was a blessing."

"A blessing! To be practically flat on your back for over a month, worrying every minute whether...."

"It brought you closer to me than anything could have. And Mitch," she said, voice softened and warmed by tears, "it taught me so much about you."

"About *me?*"

"That's right, Daddy." She smiled. "It taught me that, despite the fact that you wear a big gun to work, and despite the fact that you talk tough, you're as gentle as Mary's little lamb. I couldn't have chosen a better husband and father if I'd ordered him from a catalog. I love you, you big idiot!" she teased, and kissed him soundly.

"I love you, Ciara."

"Now why don't you get the morning paper, and I'll 'scissors-paper-rock' you for the sports section."

Grinning, he headed for the door. He was on the porch when he said, "Do we have a new paper boy?"

"Not that I know of. Why?"

"Because the regular kid likes to chuck it into a shrub or halfway up the crabapple tree, and today it's lying smack in the middle of the driveway."

"Stop complaining," Ciara called from the living room, "get that newspaper so we can see how the Orioles did in last night's game...."

"Good morning, Mitch," sang Mrs. Thompson. "And how are you on this beautiful morning?"

"Couldn't be better," he said, stooping to pet her toy poodle. "How're ya doin', fella?" Mitch ruffled the dog's curly ears. "Tell me, how is it that you're always so cheerful?"

The old woman smiled brightly. "I'm seventy-two years old, lived through five wars, the birth of three kids, eight grandchildren and two great-grandchildren. I buried two husbands and a business enterprise or two. After surviving all that, the world seems like a happy, peaceful place. Why wouldn't I be cheerful?"

"I like your outlook," Mitch admitted. "And I like your pup, here, too." Standing, he added, "I'll bet he could last a year on one bag of Chester's dog food."

"You'd be surprised how many Kibbles my little Bruno

packs away.'' She clapped her hands, and the poodle leaped into her arms. ''Isn't that right, sweetums? You eat Mummy right out of house and home, don't you?'' Mrs. Thompson unclipped Bruno's rhinestone leash and draped it around her neck, then put the dog back onto the ground. ''He hates to be tethered,'' she explained, heading for the porch. ''How's that pretty little wife of yours today?'' she asked, one foot on the bottom step. ''I must say, she looked lovely yesterday. And you take such good care of her!'' She patted her stomach. ''By the way, the cookout was splendid. That potato salad of yours was scrumptious. Maybe you'll share your recipe....''

''There's a huge bowl of the stuff in the fridge. You'd be doing me a favor if you took some of it off my hands.''

She grinned. ''Oh, that would be lovely!''

He started for the house. ''I have a memory like a colander. If I don't do it now—''

''Bruno, you leave Mr. Mahoney's paper alone now, you hear, before I—''

Mitch had no time to react. He looked back in time to see bits of smoking, flaming debris raining down from the sky.

In a heartbeat, he was beside the old woman. ''Mrs. Thompson, are you all right?''

''I'm fine,'' she said, as he helped her sit on the top step of her porch, ''but where's Bruno?''

He'd been on his way back inside when the explosion had cracked the peaceful July morning—hadn't seen what happened. But the last thing he'd heard was Mrs. Thompson, scolding the dog. If that was the case—

Act fast, he told himself. Ciara is inside alone....

''You sure you're okay?'' he said.

Nodding, Mrs. Thompson clung to the wrought iron railing.

Mitch breathed a sigh of relief as he spied the dog, shivering under an azalea bush. "Found him," he called, pointing.

"Bruno," Mrs. Thompson cried, clapping her hands. "Bruno, you come here this instant!"

The dog was on her heels in an instant.

The old woman gripped the wrought-iron rail so tightly that her knuckles turned white. Mitch helped her to her feet and guided her through her front door.

"Just sit tight, Mrs. Thompson," he said. "As soon as I check on Ciara, I'll come back to see how you're doing."

"Yes, that would be best. You must go to Ciara. I'm perfectly fine," she said.

"Now then," she said, as he dashed out the door. "Lighten up! You don't want to frighten Ciara with that sour expression, do you?"

Frightening Ciara was the least of his worries right now. *Saving her*—from whomever was trying to even a score—*that's* what he was worried about....

Chapter Twelve

No one had made an outgoing call since the telephone woke them earlier that morning. Mitch dialed "star sixty-nine" and waited for the operator to identify the caller. "The last number to call your line was 410, 555-1272," said the smoothed-voiced recording. He scribbled the digits on a sheet of scrap paper and handed it to Bob Knight, the lead investigator from the Howard County Police Department.

Knight was tall and wiry, with coal black eyes and a shock of thick, nappy hair. "Maybe you oughta tell me about this case you were workin' on, Agent Mahoney."

Mitch snuck a peek at Ciara, who had been listening intently. "I'm cool as a cucumber," she said, crossing both arms over her chest. "And I agree with Officer Knight. It's high time we heard about this case you were working on...."

Mitch studied her calm face, her relaxed demeanor. He had to give it to her; she'd kept a tight rein on her emotions after the blast, and he knew that couldn't have been easy.

Not for a woman whose feet left the floor if someone walked into a room and surprised her....

Ah, what a mother won't do to protect her young, he thought wryly.

"Really, Mitch," she added, trying to sound more convincing, "I'm fine. In fact, I think it'll be good for me to hear it...finally."

"The night I left here," he began, sitting beside her on the sofa bed, "I went straight to headquarters."

Knight made himself comfortable in Mitch's chair. "Go on...."

"Bradley was at my desk when I got there. He had Giovanni Pericolo's file and my undercover identity with him." Shrugging, he cut to the chase. "He told me the Bureau locked Pericolo up, but they couldn't stop Pericolo from doing business."

"It's sad but true," the cop agreed. "Guys run drug rings from prison every day."

Ciara sighed heavily. "And this is the man you were 'up close and personal' with for seven months."

Mitch nodded. "I posed as an accountant. Kept his books."

"How'd you get inside?" Knight wanted to know. He'd stopped taking notes. His interest was personal now.

"We busted one of Pericolo's right-hand men for trafficking, cut a deal with him. He'd get me into Pericolo's organization, we'd let him stay outside the federal pen."

"It's a miracle you're still with us," Ciara said, her voice trembling slightly. "You see why I was so afraid? Do you understand what—"

He squeezed her hand. "Yes. I admit it. I'm in a dangerous business."

"That's putting it mildly," Knight said. "You've got your neck in a noose every time you go under. Why don't you come to work for us? I happen to know we need a few educated, well-trained guys, right here in Howard County.''

''Do you send men undercover?'' Ciara asked.

''Uh-huh, but it's rare, and even then, only the narcs and homicide guys do stuff like that. What your husband, here, would be doin' would be relatively safe, all things considered.''

'' 'Relatively safe'?'' Ciara's brow furrowed with confusion. '' 'All things considered'?''

''Nothing comes with a guarantee these days, little lady, least of all a cop's safety. Every time you pull a guy over for speeding, you wonder if—''

Mitch saw her frown with resignation and roll her eyes, as if to say Where have I heard that before? and decided it was time to change the subject. ''So what's your take on this, Knight? Based on what you've already got, that is.''

''Well, whoever set the bomb wasn't an expert, that's for sure.''

''How can you tell?''

''For one thing, amateurs always want to use too much explosive. It's like they think if a gram will go ''Pow,'' then an ounce is sure to go 'Boom!' But they don't take that into consideration when they're putting the rest of the thing together. It was sheer luck it went off at all.''

Knight took a deep breath and got to his feet. ''Well, I've done all I can do here for the time being.'' He handed Mitch a business card. ''Give me a call if you can add anything that'll help. And give some thought to ditchin' the agency and comin' to work for us.''

Mitch tucked the card into his shirt pocket, shook the officer's hand. ''I'll do that. Thanks, Knight.''

''I'm putting round-the-clock protection on you guys.'' He chuckled. ''Till the Feds bully their way in and take over, anyway. I hear they like to take care of their own.''

"You hear right."

"Yeah, well, that ain't nothin' to be proud of, way I see it. Doesn't make much difference what the emblem on your badge says, we all took the same oath."

He looked at Ciara. "So when's that baby of yours due?"

"A week, maybe two...*never,*" she said, rolling her eyes.

"I have three young'uns myself, five, six and seven. My wife just takes it in stride. Except for the big tummy, you'd hardly know she was havin' a baby at all!"

"I hope next time I'll be that way, too."

Mitch walked Knight to the door. "Can she hear us from here?" the cop mouthed when they reached the foyer.

Mitch nodded.

He grabbed Mitch's forearm and leaned in close. "Stay away from the windows," he growled softly, "you hear?"

"No way. When did they find the body?"

At the mention of the word *body,* he saw Ciara's needle hover over the cream-colored linen square she held.

"I'm not surprised," Mitch said, "considering. Still, it seems a shame. He was a good agent...once."

He watched as she tried to pretend she wasn't listening. What was it his Italian grandma used to say when he pouted? "You face, she gonna freeze-a that way!" The old wives' tale seemed to fit Ciara's present condition....

"He did what?" he asked Parker. "You've gotta be kidding." Shaking his head, he said, "Ironic, isn't it?" Then, "Yeah, I'll kick in ten bucks, but who's gonna see it? Yeah. Okay. Thanks for calling."

"Who was *that?*" she asked the moment he hung up.

He slumped onto the edge of the sofa bed, flopped back on the pillow beside hers and linked his fingers behind his neck. "Parker. Down at headquarters. They found Chet Bradley...."

"Found him? I didn't even know he was missing. Did the Bureau send him undercover, too?"

"Hardly," Mitch groused. "He's been workin' both sides of the street for years now. That's why I got sent to Philadelphia."

She put her needlework aside, snuggled against him. "I don't get it."

He'd never told her about his set-to with Bradley, right there in their living room. If she had known the guy had broken into their house, planning to murder him... Mitch didn't want to think about what might have happened.

"He worked a case, couple years back," he explained, "busted Pericolo for possession of cocaine, distribution, the whole nine yards. But the slimeball got off, thanks to our sophisticated immigration system. Anyway, it seems Bradley decided he could make a few quick bucks if he didn't turn in all the evidence. If he sold what he held aside on the street." Mitch took a deep breath. "The fool taste tested his own merchandise, got himself hooked but good and ended up having to make a deal with Pericolo."

"Chet Bradley?" She seemed surprised, then shook her head. "Well, he's a liar, why not a coke-head, too?"

Mitch turned slightly to read her face. If the news had secretly upset her, she was doing one fine job of masking it. He stared at the ceiling again. "He started doing odd jobs for Pericolo—muffing up investigations, losing evidence, running errands...."

"And Pericolo provided him with the cocaine."

"Uh-huh. Had himself a four-hundred-dollar-a-day habit at the end. You know how many favors a guy has to do to satisfy an addiction like that?"

"But why did he send you to Philadelphia? Were you

involved in that drug bust all those years ago? Did you know something that would—''

He shook his head. ''He had a falling out with Pericolo, and the boss man cut him off, cold turkey. Bradley was desperate to ensure his supply, so he cut a new deal…with Eduardo Chambro, Pericolo's next in command.''

''How do you know all this?''

''Seems his upbringing got the better of him, and he made what you might call a deathbed confession.'' Mitch shook his head. ''Nobody thought much of Pericolo, it seems. Chambro would have taken over years ago if he hadn't been scared witless of the guy.''

''But…if Chambro was on Pericolo's side, what did he have to fear from him?''

''Plenty, believe me. I saw Pericolo waste a guy for interrupting a phone call. Heard that he'd done the same thing to men who dared to question his judgment or entered his office without knocking. The man had no heart, no soul, I tell you. Life meant nothing to him…except his own.''

''So the lieutenant made a deal with Chambro,'' she said, bringing him back to the point. ''How did you fit in?''

''He called me the best man on his team. Said I was perfect for the job. Not to sound arrogant, but he was right, and he knew it. The deal he cut with Chambro was to get me inside so I could take Pericolo out of the picture. And when Chambro took over…''

''He'd continue to supply Bradley with bribes,'' she said, thinking out loud. ''A lot of things make sense suddenly.''

He rolled onto his side. ''Things like what?''

She met his eyes. ''I had no reason to believe his lies. I'm ashamed to say I wanted to. It was easier to hate you that way, for leaving me here alone, for not getting in touch, for not being with me when—''

He pulled her to him. ''Sweetie, I'm sorry you had to go through all that alone. Hindsight is twenty-twenty—I guess it got to be a cliché for good reason...every word of it is true—but if I had known then what I know now—''

''You would have come home that night? You wouldn't have accepted the assignment?''

''Exactly,'' he said firmly and without hesitation. ''How could I have left my beautiful wife, pregnant or not? No amount of glory is worth a sacrifice like that.''

''My dad said something like that the other day,'' she told him. ''He said no sacrifice is too great when it's made for love.''

''Smart guy, your dad.'' He kissed her cheek.

''Were you ever in any danger in Philadelphia? From Pericolo, I mean?''

He thought of that first night, when Giovanni had asked him to choose a card. ''If you had picked a black card, you'd be a dead man now.''

''Not really,'' he fibbed. ''I was acting as a numbers man. A pencil pusher. A four-eyed geek. I suppose I didn't look like much of a threat, so—''

''Didn't look like a threat!'' she stopped him. ''As big and muscular as you are? As handsome and intelligent and—''

''I'd better get to work on those door frames,'' he said, laughing. ''Any more of this flattery and my ego won't fit through the door.''

''Mitch...''

''Hmm?''

''That explosion was intended for you, wasn't it?''

Every muscle in him tensed. Tell her the truth, and risk sending her blood pressure sky high. Tell her a lie and risk the trust she's beginning to put in you again. "It's possible," he said carefully.

"Who do you think was responsible...if you were the intended victim, I mean?"

"Truthfully?"

Ciara nodded.

"I have no idea.

"I suppose Pericolo might have had *one* loyal follower, but I don't think so. And it can't be Bradley, unless he's operating from the grave." Eyes and lips narrowed, she exhaled a sigh of frustration. "It could be anyone you ever arrested, or a family member of someone you locked up, or..."

"Sweetie, it's not good for you to get worked up over this. We're safe."

"For now. How long can that last? The cops won't hang around here forever. Whoever planted that bomb will wait until they leave, come back and finish what he started."

She voiced the fears that had been on his mind every moment since the explosion.

"Ciara, let's not talk about this now. It's not good for you to get upset, honey."

"You can't sweep it under the rug, Mitch. It's bigger than both of us. You can't deny it anymore. Like it or not, you have responsibilities now, to me, to this baby of ours. You can't just keep running off, playing cops and robbers. Not when it can backfire, blow up your family!"

He sat up. "Ciara," he said, his voice stern and scolding, "this isn't doing you any good. Let's—"

"Hiding from it isn't doing me any good, either," she said, sitting beside him. "Have you given any thought to what Officer Knight said?"

"Quitting the Bureau, you mean, to become a Howard County cop?"

She nodded, the barest hint of a hopeful smile playing at the corners of her mouth.

"Yeah. I've thought about it," he said dully. "I've thought about how I'd like to stop arresting nationally renowned criminals and start writin' speeding tickets. I've thought how nice it would be to give up apprehending drug lords and murderers, and spend my time shooing teenagers off the street corners after 11:00 p.m. instead." On his feet now, he added, "I'd be about as happy as your dad has been all these years, pretending that what I'm doing is what I *want* to be doing."

"But, Mitch," she said, her eyes welling with tears, "what about the baby and me? What will we do, if something happens to you?"

The smiling, the laughing, the playfulness...it had all been an act, and he'd known it all along. Worse, he'd *let* her put on the act, because it had made it easier for him to deal with his own guilt.

She was a tough little thing, and he knew if it weren't for everything that had happened—this illness, being confined to bed, the explosion—she wouldn't be crying right now. And he felt like a heel for being the one to put tears in her beautiful blue eyes. But she had asked him a straight question, and after all those months of silence, deserved to hear a straight answer. But did you have to make it *that* honest? he asked himself. He could blame the very same occurrences for his thoughtlessness, but the truth was he had no excuse for behaving like a self-centered lout.

And she deserved better than that.

He climbed back onto the sofa bed, took her in his arms. "Aw, sweetie. Seems all I ever do is apologize for hurting you. Sometimes I wonder why you married me. I'm sure as heck not very good for you." And the awful thing was, he believed it was true.

Ciara gripped his forearms, gave him a little shake.

"You *are* good for me!" she insisted, her eyes blazing with unbridled affection. "You're the best thing in my life, if you want to know the truth. *That's* why I married you. That and the fact that I love you like crazy."

She felt so good, so right in his arms. She was the most beautiful woman he'd ever seen, the most affectionate and loving. Why wasn't it enough? Why did he feel he must have her *and* the Bureau to be happy?

"I did some thinking last night," she said softly, "about something Dad said at the cookout yesterday."

"You're all flushed, sweetie," he said, all but ignoring her. "Lie down, will you, before something—"

She did as she was told, but continued talking. "I know how unhappy he's been all these years, sacrificing the job he loved for his family. But he seemed to have derived some sort of satisfaction for having done the right thing. That's why he said no sacrifice is too great, if—"

"If your love is strong enough?"

Ciara nodded. Then she grabbed his wrists, forced him to place his hands on her stomach. "*This* is what's important, Mitch. *This* is your future. I know you're a good agent, one of the best. Of course the Bureau recognizes that and appreciates who you are and what you do...."

She placed a hand alongside his cheek. "But, Mitch, the FBI doesn't *love* you! If you die, they'll add your name to the already-too-long list of agents killed in the line of duty. They'll give me some sort of medal to lay on your grave, another plaque to hang on the wall. And by week's end, another agent will take your place." Her voice trembled, and fresh tears filled her eyes when she said, "*I* won't be able to replace you, Mitch, not if I live to be a hundred."

What *was* so all-fired important about his precious agency? he asked himself. *Why* couldn't he just give it up, walk away from it, without looking back?

She was right about one thing—he had a lot of thinking to do.

His big hands bracketed her face, his thumbs wiping the tears from her cheeks. "I don't deserve you," he said after a while.

"You deserve the best that life has to offer, which is why I intend to try and be the best wife who ever lived." She managed a tremulous smile, her voice whispery. "I love you, you big lug! Can't you get that through your thick, Irish skull? I love you, and I don't want to live a day of my life without you."

"I'm half Italian, don't forget," he said in a feeble attempt to lighten the mood, change the subject....

"And so am I."

He was aware of her scrutiny, aware that she wanted— no, needed—to hear him say he'd leave the agency. In truth, Mitch wished he *could* say it, because he wanted and needed to comfort and reassure her. Guilt ached in his chest like a huge painful knot. He looked away, feeling restless and uncomfortable with the fact that he couldn't tell her what she wanted to hear.

Ciara's small hand cupped his chin, turned his face and forced him to meet her eyes. Her tears were gone now, and she spoke slowly, with careful dignity. "You don't have to make up your mind right now. You have two weeks of R and R left. Please say you'll use that time to think about it, at least."

Mitch set his jaw. He could give her that much, couldn't he?

It was quietly disturbing to even consider leaving the Bureau, and his stomach knotted with tension. His voice began as a hushed whisper, then he spoke in neutral tones. "I'll give it some thought," he promised, his mouth tight and grim.

"And some prayer?"

"And some prayer."

"Thank you," she said, gently, serenely. "Thank you."

When she snuggled close, he felt the rhythmic pounding of her heart against his chest, and the strong, sharp kicks of the baby against his stomach. "*This* is what's important," she had said.

And it was.

For the first time in days Ciara put aside her secret needlework project and spent every moment, it seemed, making lists.

She had spent hours fixing up every room of the house, and it showed. But for a reason she couldn't—or wouldn't—explain, she hadn't done a single thing in the nursery. And now, it seemed, she was in a frenzy to get it all done before the baby came.

She insisted that Mitch sit beside her and help her pick out the furniture for the baby's room. Everything had to be neutral, yet stimulating, a concept which thoroughly confused him. "Nothing frilly or girlie, but nothing too strong or masculine, either," Ciara explained. "Colors capture babies' attention and help them learn faster."

They decided on a pale oak crib and ordered a dresser, changing table and toy box to match. He suggested the teddy bear wallpaper border. "Lots of color, without being masculine or feminine." Rather than repeating the print in the baby's bedding, Ciara ordered bright red sheets, a deep blue quilt, fluorescent yellow curtains and an emerald green bumper pad.

Portable phone in one hand, department store catalog in the other and list in her lap, she placed the order. "For an extra twenty-five dollars," she told him, "they'll deliver it tomorrow. Should I tell them to go ahead?"

It was by far the happiest he'd seen her since returning

from Philly—small price to pay, in his opinion, for her pink-cheeked complexion and wide smile.

The next day when everything arrived, Mitch had the deliverymen put the boxes into the white-walled room across from the one he shared with Ciara. When they were gone, he took one of the chaise longues from the deck and dragged it upstairs, outfitting it with a downy quilt and pillow. And once he had her settled comfortably in it, he hung the wallpaper border and continued to focus on it as he hung brackets and rammed rods through the pockets of a pair of tailored curtains.

Then it was on to a more interesting—and difficult— project: assembling the crib.

"This manufacturer must be from Timbuktu or something!" Mitch growled. "I can't make heads or tails of these instructions. And what're all these nuts and bolts for? There aren't half as many holes to stick 'em into!"

"Sweetie," she said, repeating what he'd told her a day earlier, "it isn't good for you to get so worked up."

He shot her a narrow-eyed smirk. "Careful, lady," came his mock threat, "'cause I'm the guy in control of the cheesecake...."

Amazingly, she seemed to know what fit where without ever having so much as glanced at the directions. And once he got over the humiliation of being bested in a construction project...by a woman...the crib went together in no time flat.

She had him rolling the thing to every conceivable spot in the ten-by-twelve-foot space, and finally settled for putting the crib against the only blank wall in the room. The changing table, she decided, looked best under the window, and the dresser simply *had* to stand on the short wall, just inside the door, with the toy box right beside it.

Ciara clasped her hands under her chin when it was

finished. "We'll have to get another catalog," she gushed, "and fill that toy box to the brim!"

"That's what Christmas and birthdays are for," he muttered, hanging the last picture on the wall.

"Oh, don't be such a Grinch," she scolded playfully. "Besides, his *birth* day isn't very far off, you know...."

Mitch tried to read her face, but couldn't tell if the silly expression was part of her excitement at having completed the nursery, or some strange way of masking pain. "Are you okay?" he asked, kneeling beside her chair.

"This has been driving me crazy for weeks. Now that it's done, I feel so much better!"

The doorbell rang, and Mitch grinned. He couldn't have timed it better if he'd tried.

"You didn't order in from Chiaparelli's, did you?" Ciara asked, narrowing one eye.

"Nope. Now you stay put, while I see who it is."

How the women for the baby shower had all managed to arrive at the same time boggled his mind. Leave it to Gina to get a bunch of women organized, he thought, grinning.

Gina had her back to him when he opened the door, and Mitch would have bet his last nickel that folks clear on the other side of the street had heard her severe "Shh-hhh-hhh-hhh!"

Silently he waved the ladies inside, nodding and smiling as they passed, each carrying a brightly wrapped package. "Get back upstairs," Gina whispered, "and turn on a radio or something so she won't hear us putting up the decorations."

"How will I know when to bring her down?"

"I'll send Chester up to fetch you," she whispered, smacking his bottom. "Now git! Before I take a broom to the seat of your pants!"

He ducked into their bedroom and turned the clock radio

on full blast before returning to the nursery. "Who was it?"

"Wrong house number," he fibbed.

"Wrong—"

"Somebody looking for the Smiths. I think they were on the wrong street. I hope I didn't get them lost...." And without another word he scooped her up and carried her into their room.

"Goodness, Mitch," she said, hands over her ears, "aren't you a little young to be experiencing your second childhood? What's with the loud—"

"Didn't you ever get an itch to dance?" he asked, spinning in a dizzying circle, still carrying her. "Listen to that," he added, swaying to and fro in time to the music. "Ain't it a shame? They just don't write 'em like that anymore."

"I think you must have clunked your head on something while you were putting the furniture together," she observed, giggling. "You're acting very—"

She cocked an ear toward the doorway. "What was that? Did I hear voices downstairs?"

"Maybe...I left the TV on in the family room." He danced her farther from the door, danced her back again and kicked it shut.

"Put me down, you big nut," she scolded, "you're starting to perspire. I'm not exactly a featherweight these days. All we need is for you to develop a hernia right—"

"I'm fine," he interrupted. "Now stop being a spoilsport. Who knows when we'll get another opportunity to go dancing?"

"What's that noise?" she asked, a finger aloft.

Mitch plunked her gently on the bed and turned off the radio. "Scratching?" He opened the door. "Hey, Chester. What're you doin' up here, old boy?" He ruffled the dog's thick coat, then hoisted Ciara in his arms once more and hurried down the stairs.

"Mitch, I wish I knew why you're acting so—"

Her eyes widened as both hands flew to her mouth. "Balloons, streamers, cake," she said, taking it all in, then seeing the women. "When did all of you— How did—"

Giggling, she buried her face in the crook of his neck and whispered, "How's my hair?"

"Can you believe all these wonderful presents?" she asked, holding up a tiny terry cloth jumpsuit. "We'll have enough diapers to last for months, and all these T-shirts and booties and…"

He'd been stuffing wrapping paper and bows into a gigantic lawn and leaf bag when he noticed she'd stopped talking. Mitch peered over his shoulder, surprised to find her crying. Dropping the trash, he wrapped his arms around her.

"I'm so lucky," she sobbed into his shoulder. "I have such good friends and so many wonderful relatives, and you…you're the best husband any woman could ever hope for!"

"But those are good things, sweetie. Why are you crying?"

She settled down a bit to say, "Because…because… because I'm so happy, that's why."

"I sure will be glad when this baby gets here," he teased, handing her a tissue, "'cause you're costing me a small fortune in blotting materials!"

Giggling, she blew her nose. "You could always buy stock in the company…."

He popped a kiss onto her forehead. "That's what I like, a woman with business sense who isn't afraid to cry."

"I hate crying," she admitted, sniffling. Then, eyes wide with panic, Ciara added, "What if I never go back to the woman I was before I got pregnant? What if I've turned into a big fat crybaby forever? What if—''

"What if I start hauling some of this loot up to the baby's room while you take a nap. You're looking a mite pooped, if you don't mind my saying so.''

"You know, I think I'll take you up on your offer,'' she said, snuggling under the covers. "Two parties and a bomb blast in three days can be exhausting!''

He plucked a trash bag from the box and chucked a load of stuffed animals into it, filled another with miniature shorts and hats and shoes, and dragged both up the stairs behind him. It isn't like her to give in so easily to a suggestion to take a nap, he told himself. And she did look paler than usual....

Should he call Donna? Peterson? His mother? What could they do that you're not already doing? And the answer was, Nothing.

He continued making trips upstairs until every gift had a new place to call its own. She'll be happy to know the baby's toy box is filled to the brim, he thought, smiling as he left the last of it. Mitch stood in the doorway, arms crossed over his chest, and looked at the nursery. Soon, a baby boy or girl would call it home. Soon tiny cries would wake them from a sound sleep, demanding food or a fresh diaper or a dose of affection.

The telephone interrupted his reverie, and he crossed the hall to answer it in the master bedroom.

"Hey, Parker,'' he said, "what's up?''

"Well, I have the answer to your question, for starters.''

"Yeah?''

"Bradley's blood type is AB Negative.''

The news made him weak in the knees, and he sat on the edge of the bed. The card in his wallet said he was O Positive. And according to Donna's chart, Ciara was O Positive, too. Peterson had "typed'' the baby weeks earlier, so they'd have a plentiful supply on hand in case of an emergency...and the baby's blood matched his mommy's and his daddy's.

His mommy's...and his daddy's!

How could he have ever doubted her? He felt terrible about it now.

The heat in his cheeks and the buzzing in his ears had usually accompanied bad news. Not this time. *Thank you, Lord,* he prayed. *Thank you!*

"What did you need that information for?" Parker wanted to know.

"Uh—confidential at this point," Mitch replied curtly. He wasn't lying. He'd no interest in sharing his suspicions about Ciara with anyone.

"Gotcha," Parker said.

"You said the info was 'for starters'?"

"Well, it'd be nice if you'd fill us in once in a while, Mahoney. How's that gorgeous wife of yours?"

"Tired, but holding her own. I think it's going to be soon. Very soon."

"Want some friendly advice?"

"Sure..."

"Get all the shut-eye you can, while you can, 'cause once that little one gets here, you're gonna need a dictionary to remember what *sleep* means."

Sleep? Mitch thought. I don't know what that is *now,* what with all that's been going on around here. Chuckling, Mitch thanked him and hung up. Then he headed down the stairs to climb into bed beside his sleepy wife and try to take Parker's advice.

"Mitch," Ciara whispered, shaking his shoulder. "Mitch!"

He draped an arm over her middle. "Mmmm?"

"I think I heard something...."

"Where's Chester?"

"Right here at the foot of the bed. There it is again…in the kitchen…."

"Can't be," he muttered, opening one eye, "there are half a dozen cops outside. Houdini couldn't get past 'em undetected." He yawned. "But I gotta admit," he said, wiggling his hips against hers, "I like the benefits of comforting a frightened—"

"Did you hear that?"

He laid a finger over her lips and nodded, then held the finger in the air, as if commanding her to listen.

"What do you—"

One sharp look from his worried eyes silenced her. "Don't say another word," he instructed, his whisper hoarse and stern. Mitch handed her the phone, where he'd taped Bob Knight's cell phone number. "You hear anything funny in there, call him. Okay?"

Wide-eyed, Ciara nodded. She grabbed his hand. "Please," she said, a hitch in her voice, "be careful…."

Trying to appear cavalier, he sent her a wink.

"Mitch," she added as he got to his feet. "I love you."

"Love you, too," he whispered, and headed for the stairs.

He took them two at a time, as he'd planned, then ducked into the closet and grabbed the Rossi. *Lord,* he prayed, switching off the safety, *I think we both know I'll use it if I have to. Don't let me have to….*

Mitch crept back down the stairs and peered around the double-wide doorway leading from the foyer to the family room. Hiding the gun behind his back, he caught Ciara's eye. "He still in there?" he mouthed.

Ciara nodded.

Thumb to his chin and forefinger to his ear, he pantomimed, "Did you call Knight?"

Another nod.

He blew her a kiss and headed up the hall. It seemed to take hours, rather than seconds, to reach the kitchen. Since he could see the reflection of a dark-haired man in the black glass oven door, the man could see him, too. Mitch flattened himself against the wall, heart hammering as he tried to plan his course of action.

Where are those confounded County boys? he wondered. They must have been asleep on the job. How else had this guy penetrated their line of defense? It happened so quickly, he never saw it coming…the karate chop that sent his service revolver clattering to the hardwood floor. He gave it a solid kick, sent it careering to the end of the hall. If I can't reach it, neither can—

A fist crashed into his jaw, killing the thought.

In the next seconds, amid the flurry of fists and arms, Mitch managed to grab hold of the man's T-shirt.

Pericolo's men never went out in public without a shirt and tie. But who was he to complain; the soft, cottony fabric of the T-shirt was a whole lot easier to grasp than a starched white collar. In a heartbeat, Mitch wrestled the intruder to the floor, straddled him and attempted to disable him with a wrestler's hold.

The high-pitched whimper made him stop just long enough to look at the face he'd been beating.

A boy's face.

David Pericolo's face.

Mitch pinned the kids' wrists to the floor. "What are you doin' here?" he demanded.

"You put my father in jail," he said haltingly, his lips swollen and bloodied. "'Eye for an eye,'" the boy added. "'Eye for an eye.'"

Bob Knight burst through the back door just then, and three uniformed officers came in on his heels. "Cuff him," Knight ordered, "wrists *and* ankles."

Shaking, Mitch got to his feet and leaned both palms on

the kitchen table to steady himself. "Meet David Peri-colo," he said to Knight.

"You'll pay," David whimpered, as Knight's fellow po-licemen secured the handcuffs.

"Get him out of here and keep him quiet," Knight barked, shaking a big fist in the air.

Once they'd dragged David off, kicking and screaming, Knight closed the kitchen door. "You okay, buddy?" he asked, patting Mitch's back.

"I'm fine." His gaze shot daggers into the cop. "How'd he get in here, anyway? Your boys oughta be ashamed of themselves."

Knight shook his head. "That number you gave me...the one you star sixty-nined?"

Mitch nodded.

"Pericolo's...car phone."

"I see."

"Heads are gonna roll for this one," Knight said, "trust me."

"You're just lucky nothing happened to my wife."

At the mere thought of her, Mitch tensed. "Ciara—" He ran into the family room and gathered her in his arms. *Thank God she's all right.* "You okay, sweetie? How are you feelin'?"

"Not so hot," she said in a small, shaky voice. "I've already called the hospital. They're expecting us." She buried her face in his shoulder. "Oh, Mitch, I was so scared. I thought...I thought...."

"Shhh," he soothed, stroking her back. "Nothing hap-pened, and—"

"*This* time." She sat back, eyes bright with tears, and faced him down. "You're not a cat, Mitch. You don't have nine lives." Her lower lip quivered when she added, "If you were, I imagine you'd have used up at least six of them by now. How much longer do you expect your luck to hold out? How much—''

Gripping her stomach, she winced with pain.

''Ciara, sweetie, what is it?''

She met his eyes. ''It's time, that's what it is....''

She was right. It was *time*. Time to stand up and act like a man. Not a gung-ho, macho, hot-doggin' FBI agent, but a man, who took his responsibilities seriously. He only hoped it wasn't too late....

Ciara took a deep breath and said on the exhale, ''Could we...could we continue this later, do you think?'' she said, smiling past clenched teeth. ''Because if it's all the same to you, I think I'd rather have a baby right now.''

Epilogue

Ciara snuggled deep into the pillows on her hospital bed, smiled contentedly into her newborn's face. "Your daddy went to get me a cup of soda," she cooed, kissing the tiny fingers that had wrapped around her thumb. "He'll be back any minute now."

And when he comes back, she thought, I'm going to tell him that it doesn't matter to me *what* he does for a living or where he does it; all I care about is that he's happy, and healthy, until the Lord calls him home.

She closed her eyes, hoping to blink away the horrible scene that had taken place hours ago. Until the sounds of the life-and-death struggle penetrated her brain—when she knew and understood that she could lose him, right there in her very own kitchen—Ciara had not realized just how much she loved having him in her life. *Whether you have a week or a year or a lifetime more with him,* she told herself, *you'll enjoy every moment, and thank God for it!*

How could she say that she loved him, really loved him, and demand that he give up the Bureau? He had worked too long, too hard, to leave it all behind now.

No doubt she would keep a careful eye on the clock until he arrived home from work safe and sound, but she would lose no sleep over his absences, because faith would see her through. "When I'm afraid, I will look to the Lord," she paraphrased Micah, Chapter Seven, Verse Eight. "I will wait for the God of my salvation, and He will hear me."

The coins dropped into the machine with a metallic *chink-chink-chink,* and Mitch pressed the button that said All Natural Orange Juice. That oughta hold her over till they bring her supper, he thought, nodding when the can hit the tray with a hollow *thud.*

Those hours in the delivery room, when it was touch and go for a while, he knew what he had to do. You could have lost her, he reminded himself, but you didn't, and you'd better thank God for that!

Ciara had asked him to think about changing jobs. He could tell by the way she'd phrased the question that she fully intended to stand by him, regardless of his answer. He also knew that, even if he decided to stay with the Bureau, she would never do to him what her mother had done to her father. And you haven't earned devotion like that...yet....

While the nurses were getting Ciara and the baby cleaned up, he pretended to need a breath of fresh air. Instead, he placed a phone call, straight to the director's office. The director took the call, not so surprisingly, considering what Mitch had just accomplished on behalf of the agency. He would put in his resignation, here and now.

"What can I do for you, Mitch?"

"Well, I have a big favor to ask, sir."

"If it's within my power, it's yours. We owe you that much, son...."

Wait till Ciara hears the news, Mitch thought later, grinning. Merely imagining her reaction caused him to quicken his pace down the corridor. That and the fact that he couldn't wait to hold his firstborn in his arms....

"I'm so proud of you. You're the bravest woman I've ever known."

Ciara giggled. "You act like I'm the first woman on earth to have given birth."

"You're the first woman to give birth to *my* child." How good it felt to say that, and know for certain that it was true. Mitch knew that he would spend the rest of his life making it up to her for so much as *thinking* that she could have betrayed him.

"She's so beautiful," Ciara sighed. "Just look at her, Mitch."

"She's beautiful 'cause she takes after her mommy."

She met his eyes. "What are we going to call her? I didn't think up many 'girl' names—everybody kept saying 'he' and 'him' and 'his,' and I guess I got caught up in it myself."

"How 'bout Carrie, for old-time's sake?"

She branded him with a playfully hot glare. "You think I want a reminder, right under your nose, of your first love? No way, José."

He kissed the baby's round little head. "She smells so sweet. We could name her after a flower...Rose or Tulip or Daisy...."

"I'm glad you're having fun with this. At least *one* of us should be, I suppose."

"I want her to have a strong name. Something memorable. Like Hannah or Eden or Shana."

Ciara nodded. "Now that's more like it. Let's look them up in my baby book...."

Mitch dug around in her overnight bag. "It opened to

the *M*s," he said, narrowing one eye suspiciously, "all by itself."

"Well, I have a confession to make," she said, flushing. "I *did* sneak a peek at a *few* girls' names...just in case...."

"Is that so?" He placed the book on the edge of the bed. "Let's see if I can figure out which name you chose." His thick finger ran down the pulpy paper page. "'Mildred' means 'gentle strength,' but I don't think so. 'Misty, Mitzi, Molly,'" he recited.

Suddenly, he thumped the book. "I know which name you picked."

"Which?" she asked, eyes twinkling with mirth.

"'Worthy of admiration,'" he quoted, then said with meaning. "Miranda."

"Do you like it?"

"I love it." He took the baby from her arms, held the tiny bundle tight against him and kissed her soft pink cheek. "Now," he said, drawing his big face close to his daughter's tiny nose. "I'm going to read you your Miranda rights. Number one—you have the right to have a healthy, happy daddy all the days of your childhood—number two—you have the right to the bravest, most loving mommy in the world—number three—you have the right to—"

"Mitch, what are you talking about?"

"I'm talking about my new job. I've been thinking," he announced, "and you're right. I've built up a lot of seniority at the Bureau. I can retire earlier if I hang in there...."

She lifted her chin and smiled.

Lord, I love her grit and determination, he said to himself. She thinks she's in for a lifetime of same-ole, same-ole, but wait till she gets a load of this:

"I talked to the director, not half an hour ago."

"The director? *Of the FBI?*"

"Hey," he said, looking wounded, "don't act so surprised. He takes calls from agents who bring in the big tuna...."

Ciara stroked the baby's head. "Did you hear that, Miranda? Your daddy has the big boss's ear." She wiggled her eyebrows and bobbed her head coquettishly. "Ooh-la-*la*.... So why did you call him?"

"To quit."

Her eyes widened.

"But he begged me to stay. He's putting me in charge of assignments, Miss Smarty Pants...or should I say *Mrs.* Smarty Pants."

She wasn't smiling when she said, "Sounds dangerous."

"Yeah. I guess it does," he said, squinting one eye. "But it isn't. It's the best of both worlds. I don't have to take a boring desk job, but I won't be on the front lines anymore."

Her eyes brightened. "You won't?"

"I'll have to do some minor investigating, so I'll know which agents should work on what cases, but I won't have to go undercover ever again."

She gasped. "Never?"

"Never. Probably won't ever fire my weapon again, except on the gun range."

"Never?"

"Never." Balancing Miranda in the crook of one arm, he slid the other across Ciara's shoulders. "So what do you think of that, pretty Mommy?"

"I think God works in mysterious ways."

"How do you mean?"

"Well, you know the story 'Gift of the Magi' don't you?"

Mitch nodded. "The one where the guy sells his watch to buy combs for his wife's long hair, and she sells her hair to buy a chain for his watch?"

"That's the one. It's a direct parallel to us, don't you see?"

He gave it a moment's thought, then said, "Ahh, because you were willing to live the rest of your life in fear, so I could be happy, and I was willing to give up the job that made me happy, so you wouldn't worry."

"Exactly! Neither of us has to make a sacrifice. God has seen to it we *both* have our heart's desire. It's a miracle, Mitch. He has given us a bona fide *miracle.*"

"I can't very well deny that, now can I?" He slid the tray table aside, and laid Miranda in her mother's arms. "But let's make that miracles, *plural,* because I'm lookin' at two more, right this minute."

Ciara smiled sweetly. "There's a present for you...in my bag."

"Another present, you mean," he said, one hand on his daughter's head. He dug in her suitcase, pulled out the needlework project she'd been working on for weeks. "Except for your nightie, this is the only thing in here."

"That's it."

Mitch handed it to her.

"I'm going to have it framed and hang it over our bed."

"Lemme see this thing," he said. To Miranda he added, "It's been a big secret, for weeks." He turned it around, read aloud: "I am my beloved, and my beloved is mine."

"From the 'Song of Songs,'" she explained.

"From the bottom of my heart," he said, and kissed her.

She saw a wistful look and then a radiant smile come across his face. "Mitch, what is it?"

He met her eyes. "It suddenly struck me," he said, grinning happily, "I'm a daddy!"

* * * * * *

Dear Reader,

When people ask where I got the idea for the SUDDENLY! series, I tell them, "It came to me—suddenly!" Seriously... I was perched outside the yogurt shop, eating a chocolate swirl cone drenched in rainbow sprinkles when a handsome man sat down beside me. Totally captivated by the beauty in his arms, he was oblivious to everything around him.

"First baby?" I asked. Without looking away from his baby girl's face, he nodded. His loving, awestruck smile reminded me of the way my uncle looked as he recalled the day he found out *he* was going to be a daddy....

One of many soldiers aboard an aircraft carrier, Sam was on his way home from World War II. "I was standing at the rail, looking out to sea," he said, "thinking of my sweet Margie." Except for a weekend pass, Sam had barely seen Margie during the past two years. "The last time I'd seen her," he said, "she was slim as a dime." Imagine Sam's surprise when he stepped off that boat to find that Margie "looked like she'd swallowed a watermelon!"

What must it have been like, I wondered, to find out in such a sudden and surprising way that you're going to be a father?

The answer conceived the idea that gave birth to the SUDDENLY! series. If you enjoyed *Suddenly Daddy,* please drop me a note at c/o Steeple Hill Books, 300 East 42nd Street, New York NY 10017. I love hearing from my readers, and try to answer every letter personally.

All my best,

Loree Lough

P.S. Be sure to look for my next Love Inspired novel (second in the SUDDENLY! series), *Suddenly Mommy,* which will be available in August 1998.

Continuing in July from
Love Inspired™...

FAITH, HOPE
& CHARITY

a series by
LOIS RICHER

**Faith, Hope & Charity: Three close friends
who find joy in doing the Lord's work...and
playing matchmaker to members of this
close-knit North Dakota town.**

You enjoyed the romantic surprises in:
FAITHFULLY YOURS
January '98

A HOPEFUL HEART
April '98

And the matchmaking fun continues in:
SWEET CHARITY
July '98

Can a small town's dedicated nurse learn to let go of
her past hurts and accept a future with the new
doctor—a man who must soon return to his life
in the big city?

Available at your favorite retail outlet.

ISW

Love Inspired™

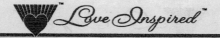

Welcome to *Love Inspired*™

A brand-new series of contemporary inspirational love stories.

Join men and women as they learn valuable lessons about facing the challenges of today's world and about life, love and faith.

**Look for the following July 1998
Love Inspired™ titles:**

SHELTER OF HIS ARMS
by Sara Mitchell

SWEET CHARITY
by Lois Richer

EVER FAITHFUL
by Carolyne Aarsen

Available in retail outlets in June 1998.

LIFT YOUR SPIRITS AND GLADDEN YOUR HEART
with *Love Inspired!*™

Steeple
Hill™

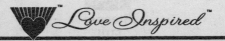